SHOULD HAVE KNOWN BETTER

A J MCDINE

Cherry Tree
Publishing

FOREWORD

I began writing this book in November 2019, a month before my father was diagnosed with terminal cancer.

David McDine was a journalist, press officer and author and I was proud to follow in his footsteps in all three careers.

While my go-to genre was psychological fiction, he wrote a series of swashbuckling historical naval adventures, the Lieutenant Oliver Anson thrillers.

When we were together we liked nothing more than talking about writing and books.

In fact, he was one of the first people to hear my initial plot ideas for *Should Have Known Better*.

As his illness worsened, this book became a refuge for me, a welcome distraction from the grief and heartache.

Sadly, he never had the chance to see the book in print - he passed away at the end of February 2020, three months before its publication.

I hope he would have enjoyed it.

DMcD, this one's for you.

CHAPTER ONE

KATE

Kate Kennedy drained the dregs of her coffee, grabbed her car keys, and shot a desperate look at her watch.

'Come *on*, Chloe!' she yelled up the stairs. 'We're going to be late.'

Overhead a floorboard creaked and a door slammed. Footsteps pounded down the wooden staircase. Kate picked up her handbag and slipped her mobile into the back pocket of her jeans.

Chloe appeared in the doorway. Kate stared at her daughter in disbelief.

'Go and get changed. You can't go out looking like that.'

'Like what?'

Chloe, wearing frayed denim hot pants, a pink crop top that showed a generous expanse of golden-brown midriff, and a pair of navy Converse, lounged against the doorframe.

'Like a...' Kate bit back the words. 'Like you're off to

the beach. Today's important. Wear that dress I bought you.'

Chloe rolled her eyes. 'The one that looks like a curtain? Why on earth would I wear that? It's hideous.'

'It's not hideous. It's pretty. It suits you,' Kate said. 'And you want to make a good impression, don't you?'

'It's a university open day, Mum. No-one's going to notice what I'm wearing. I'm going to see if I like the look of them, not the other way around.'

'But -'

'Anyway, you said it yourself; we're going to be late. There's no time to get changed.' Chloe selected an apple from the fruit bowl and smiled at her mother. 'So are we going or what?'

Kate sighed inwardly and followed her daughter along the hallway and out of the front door. She'd learnt long ago that it wasn't worth arguing with Chloe, who had an answer for everything. That's why she'd make a brilliant lawyer.

But she was wrong about one thing. Someone did notice.

If Kate had been hoping the two-hour drive to Kingsgate University would give them a chance to catch up, she was disappointed. Chloe plugged in her earphones before she'd even fixed her seatbelt.

'What are you listening to?' Kate said, as she rammed the gearstick into first and pulled away from the house.

Chloe hit pause on her phone and took one earphone out. 'What?'

'I said, what are you listening to?'

'A podcast.'

'What's it about?'

'It's one of those true crime ones.'

'Like *Serial*?'

'*Serial*'s ancient. This is a new one. It investigates cold cases.'

Kate stepped on the accelerator as they headed out of the village. 'Old murders? You can plug it into the Bluetooth if you like. We can listen to it together.'

'What, change the habit of a lifetime and turn off Radio 2?'

'I don't mind.'

'Nah, you're all right thanks. Anyway, you'd hate it.'

'What makes you say that?'

'Because it's about a college student who gets murdered on her way home from a night out.' Chloe looked sidelong at Kate. 'Parts of her dismembered body were found scattered all over the campus.'

A kiss of cold air touched the back of Kate's neck, making the hairs stand on end, and she grimaced. 'Why on earth would you want to listen to something so gruesome?'

Chloe shrugged. 'Because it's interesting. It's relevant. It's *real*. They talk to her friends and family, the detectives and the police psychologist and they use new DNA technology to see if they can crack the case.'

'And do they?'

'I don't know yet, do I?'

Kate's grip on the steering wheel loosened. 'Sorry,' she said. 'You go ahead and listen to your podcast. I'll stick with Radio 2, the creature of habit that I am.'

Chloe tucked her hair behind her ear and popped the earphone back in.

Kate turned the radio up and let the inane chatter wash over her as the Mini ate up the miles. Why did every conversation with her seventeen-year-old daughter sound like an interrogation by the Gestapo? No matter how hard she tried to keep the chat light and friendly, she always felt as though she was cross-examining her. And Chloe always clammed up.

What happened to the ten-year-old girl who would chatter non-stop all the way home from school? For years Kate knew the minutiae of Chloe's life, from the moment she woke up to the minute she fell asleep. What she'd had for lunch, what spellings she had to learn, what song they'd practised in recorder club, who had fallen out with who.

When Chloe had first started secondary school, she'd still told Kate about her day over a companionable hot chocolate at the kitchen table. When had it stopped? Probably at the beginning of Year Nine. Instead of joining her in the kitchen after school, Chloe would take her hot chocolate upstairs, muttering about homework. If Kate did ask about her day, Chloe gave her a conversation-stopping 'fine'. It was easier not to ask. These days Kate had little idea how Chloe spent her time, let alone what went on in her head. And Chloe had no interest in Kate's life beyond what she was cooking for dinner. Once so close, they were virtual strangers, and it made Kate's heart bleed.

Traffic was light on the motorway, and they reached the junction for the university as the nine o'clock pips sounded.

Chloe took her earphones out, stretched and looked around with interest as they negotiated a series of round-abouts, heading towards the campus.

'Are we nearly there?' she asked, shades of her ten-year-old self just visible beneath the teenage veneer.

Kate resisted the urge to smile. Instead, she checked the dashboard. 'Almost. Satnav says we're about ten minutes away. How was the podcast? Did they find out whodunnit?'

'Not yet, although my money's on her boyfriend. Everyone knows you're more likely to be killed by someone you know than by a random stranger.'

'How reassuring.' Kate paused. 'You will be careful, won't you? At uni, I mean.'

'Seriously?' Chloe shot her an incredulous look. 'You're worried I'm going to get murdered? I'm more likely to be run over by a bus. Or die in a plane crash. Or… I dunno… be electrocuted by a dodgy toaster. Come on, Mum, keep a sense of perspective. I'll be fine, honest. Things like that don't happen to people like me.'

CHAPTER TWO

KATE

K ate followed the long line of cars heading towards the university's sports centre. As they pulled into the entrance, a marshal wearing a high-vis jacket gestured them to stop.

'Here for the open day?' he asked.

Kate nodded.

'Once you've parked up, make your way over to the main building. A shuttle bus is operating between here and the campus. Have a great day.'

'He was cute,' Chloe said, as Kate reversed into a space and unclipped her seatbelt. 'If all the boys here are that hot it's definitely going to be my first choice. Sod Nottingham.'

'Don't you think you should be basing your opinions on the course and the law school's reputation rather than whether the undergraduates are hot or not? You're here to study, remember.' Kate hated the prim tone to her voice. She was hardly in a position to criticise. But Chloe didn't take offence. She tutted good-naturedly, muttered something about only being young once, and loped across the car park, leaving Kate scurrying in her wake.

An uncomfortable mix of middle-aged parents and their scowling teenage offspring were loitering outside the sports centre, waiting for the shuttle bus. A set of older parents in matching Berghaus waterproof jackets with identical twin boys; a blonde woman with an expensive-looking haircut and a Mulberry handbag who was trying to talk her monosyllabic daughter into signing up for the university's hockey team; and two dark-haired men who at first glance looked so similar they could have been brothers but on closer inspection must have been father and son.

Kate turned to Chloe. 'It's a pain that the sports centre's a bus ride away.'

'Is it?' Chloe said, not looking up from her phone.

'Fares'll be expensive. And you'll have to factor in the extra time if you go to the gym or join a club.'

'I'll have a student bus pass. And when I pass my driving test and buy a car I won't need to bother with the bus.'

'You haven't even had your first lesson yet. And how exactly are you going to afford a car?'

'I'll get a job, won't I?'

'Where?'

'I don't know, Mother. In the student union bar or something. There's bound to be plenty of work.' Chloe finally looked up and narrowed her eyes. 'What's that look for?'

'What look?'

'Like you think I'm totally naive or something.'

'Jobs don't grow on trees and cars cost a fortune to run. You need to tax and MOT them, put petrol in them. Never mind the insurance, which will be astronomical for a new driver.' Kate caught the eye of the dark-haired man, and they shared a wry smile at the artlessness of teenagers.

'Why do you always have to be so negative about everything?' Chloe said, forcing Kate's attention back.

'All I'm saying is that it would be better if the sports centre was on the main campus,' she said.

'Well, it isn't,' Chloe glowered. 'So get over it.'

They sat behind the blonde woman and her daughter on the bus and Kate attempted to make amends.

'Where d'you want to go first?' she said brightly.

Luckily, Chloe wasn't one to hold a grudge. 'The law school, obviously,' she said, reaching in her bag for the open day programme. 'I want to check out the accommodation. And the library and student union. Oh, and the theatre, which is next to the library,' she said, her fingers tracing a route on the campus map. 'But the first thing I need to do is sign in, so they know I came.'

'Sounds good to me,' Kate said, leaning back against the headrest and watching the streets change as they headed from the leafy outskirts of the city to the grittier centre.

Before long they passed an enormous sign welcoming them to Kingsgate University's main campus. Chloe hitched her bag onto her shoulder and jumped to her feet as the bus came to a halt. Kate followed her off, and they trailed behind the other parents and kids towards a large round tent decorated with helium-filled balloons which danced and bobbed in the breeze.

Chloe gave her name to the woman at the desk, and was handed a prospectus, a free pen and a sherbet lolly on a stick in return.

'Have you come far?' the woman asked.

'Kent,' Chloe said. 'Not too far, but far enough, if you know what I mean.' She grinned, peeled the wrapper off the lolly and popped it in her mouth.

'What a coincidence. We're from Kent, too,' said a voice. The dark-haired man and his son were two paces behind them. 'Tunbridge Wells,' he added.

'We're near Maidstone,' Kate said. 'Small world.'

'It is indeed.'

She fished around for a pithy reply. 'The M25 was lovely and quiet this morning.'

'Wasn't it? I said the exact same thing to Ben, didn't I, Ben?' He turned to his son who grunted a reply.

'Next, please,' said the woman behind the desk.

'Come on, Mum,' Chloe mumbled through a mouthful of lolly. 'There's a tour of the library in fifteen minutes.' She grabbed her mother's arm and began dragging her towards the entrance.

'I'd better go,' Kate said.

'You'd better had,' the dark-haired man agreed. 'Have a good day.'

'We will.' Kate smiled. 'You too.'

After the library tour, they trailed through the student union building and peered into the vast catered dining hall.

'This is cool,' Chloe said, taking in the floor-to-ceiling windows and the two vast television screens on the walls.

'Where's the actual accommodation?' Kate said, looking around.

Chloe waved the map under her nose. 'It's a fifteen-minute walk from the main campus. Don't pull a face. I bet it only takes ten if you walk quickly.'

They marched through a scruffy housing estate following signs for the university's halls of residence. Kate tried to ignore the graffiti on the walls and the black sacks sprouting like cancerous tumours on the rubbish bins at the front of every neglected garden.

'I don't like the idea of you walking through here on your own,' she said, as a scrawny kid on a BMX bike careered out of an alleyway and almost knocked them flying.

'You worry too much,' Chloe said. 'It's no worse than walking through Maidstone on a Saturday night.'

Kate sidestepped a pile of dog mess. 'If you say so. Funny that man and his son are from Tunbridge Wells, isn't it?'

'What man?'

'You know, the man at the... oh, it doesn't matter. Is this us?'

An undergraduate with a clipboard greeted them at a Kingsgate University sign and handed them a map listing the different types of accommodation.

'Which is the one you liked the sound of?' Kate asked.

'Springett Court,' Chloe said. 'It's one of the older blocks, but it has the biggest rooms. And views of the woods.'

Kate glanced at the estate. 'Woods?'

'They're on the other side. But I'd like to see one of the newer blocks, too, so I can compare.'

The newer accommodation blocks were bright and functional, but the rooms were small, and the ensuite bathrooms barely larger than a cupboard.

'How much are these?' Kate asked. If she held her arms wide she could almost touch both walls.

Chloe consulted her map. 'Thirty quid.'

'A week?'

Chloe squawked with laughter. 'Are you mad? Thirty quid a *night*. More than two hundred a week. Eight-and-a-half thousand for the year.'

Kate blanched. 'Bloody hell.'

'Springett Court's eighty quid a week cheaper. It's less than five grand a year.'

'It still sounds ridiculously expensive. And you'd better see if you like it before you make up your mind.'

But the moment Chloe walked into Springett Court, she declared, 'This is the one.'

'You'd have to share a bathroom,' Kate pointed out.

'I don't care. Look how big the rooms are.' Chloe wandered over to the window. 'And they were right about the view.'

Springett Court backed onto a dense area of oak, sweet chestnut and birch. The dark green canopy of leaves was yet to be tinged with russet even though it was mid-September. Once autumn took a proper hold, it would be stunning. The only blot on the otherwise beautiful landscape was a dilapidated building with boarded-up windows and a desolate air a couple of hundred metres away. Bright blue wooden hoardings surrounded the perimeter.

'I wonder what that building is,' Kate said.

'Does it matter? It looks like it's about to be demolished.' Chloe trailed her hand along the built-in desk. 'There's so much space.'

'It is quite nice,' Kate conceded. She paused. 'You think you'd feel at home here?'

Chloe's eyes shone. 'I love it, Mum.'

Suddenly the trees blurred as tears glazed Kate's eyes. She gave her head a little shake. 'You haven't seen the law school yet. You might hate it.'

'I doubt it. It has a great rep. Anyway, we'll find out soon, won't we? The law talk starts in half an hour.'

Kate sucked in a lungful of air and breathed out slowly. She had to be strong. 'Come on, then,' she said. 'I suppose we'd better check it out.'

CHAPTER THREE

KATE

The law school was an impressive structure of glass and steel that, according to the brass plaque outside, had only been completed the previous summer. The windows gleamed in the September sunshine. There was an arrogant look-at-me vibe about the place. Beside it, neighbouring faculty buildings looked down at heel.

'Now this is really cool,' Chloe said, striding through the open doors into an airy atrium with a wide staircase in the middle and a café at the far end.

Regretting the second cup of coffee she'd downed at breakfast after yet another restless night, Kate saw a sign for the ladies and touched Chloe's arm. 'I'm nipping to the loo. Won't be a sec.'

Glad the toilets were empty, Kate closed the cubicle door behind her and sat on the toilet seat with her head in her hands. Chloe had been looking forward to the open day for months. She couldn't wait to finish her A-levels and leave home. From the moment the first prospectus dropped onto the doormat with an ominous thud, she'd been single-minded in her search for the perfect university, compiling spreadsheets listing the pros and cons of each. Kate had to admire her dedication, even if night-life did appear to figure higher on her score sheets than the courses themselves.

But Kate was dreading her leaving with every cell in her body. The mere thought of an empty nest filled her with sadness.

At least Kingsgate was only two hours' drive from home, she thought, as she attempted to dry her hands on a square of blue towel that promptly disintegrated into a pulpy mess. Imagine if she'd set her heart on Newcastle. Or, even worse, Edinburgh. Rubbing her hands on her jeans and reminding herself to be grateful for small mercies, Kate marched back into the atrium and scanned the crowds for her daughter's familiar blonde curls.

Chloe was standing on the periphery of a group of parents and kids milling about as they waited for the talk. She was nodding and smiling and waving a hand in that expressive way she had. At first, Kate assumed she was on her phone, but then realised she was talking to someone out of Kate's line of vision. Typical of Chloe to strike up a conversation with a complete stranger.

Later, Kate would think back to that moment. What if they'd gone to the afternoon talk instead? What if she'd slept better, hadn't needed a double dose of caffeine and a subsequent visit to the loo? Would that have changed anything? Would he have chosen someone else? Maybe. Maybe not. But it was pointless obsessing about it.

Because by the time Kate had weaved her way through the throng to join her daughter it was already too late.

'Mum, there you are,' Chloe said. 'Come and meet my new friends.'

Kate barely had time to paste a smile on her face before Chloe stopped in front of the dark-haired man from Tunbridge Wells and his sulky-looking son.

'Mum, this is Ben and his dad. Ben's studying law, too. Isn't that a coincidence?'

'Lots of coincidences today. Hello, I'm Kate.' She held out a hand.

'Adam.' His handshake was warm and firm.

Chloe frowned. 'Have you two met already?'

'Only briefly.' Adam laughed. 'You were too busy with your lolly to notice.'

Chloe's cheeks turned pink.

Adam finally let go of Kate's hand. 'Chloe's been telling us all about the social life here.' He sounded amused. 'She's pretty clued up.'

'That's Chloe for you,' Kate said. 'Did she tell you about her spreadsheet, too?'

'Mum! Don't embarrass me.'

Adam laughed again. 'Isn't that our main role in life, to embarrass our kids?'

Kate found herself smiling. 'Absolutely. It's payback for all those sleepless nights and nappy changes.'

'The tantrums and the sick bugs.'

'The nits and the chickenpox,' she countered.

'The endless hours in the pool watching swimming lessons.'

'The constant ferrying back and forth. After school

clubs, drama classes, dancing and riding. I needed a sign on my car, Mum's Taxi.'

'Agreed. Or in our case, Dad's Taxi,' Adam said.

A woman in a fitted trouser suit with a university lanyard around her neck cleared her throat. 'If you're here for the law school talk, please make your way to the Edmund Plowden Lecture Theatre. The talk is due to start in five minutes.'

They shuffled up the stairs and into the lecture hall. Adam stopped by an empty row and gave a little bow. 'After you.'

Kate stopped at a seat halfway along the row, and shrugged off her jacket. Chloe sat beside her and motioned Ben to join her. Adam was still in the aisle, deep in conversation with the woman in the trouser suit.

'Who's your dad talking to?' Chloe whispered to Ben.

Before he could answer, the lights dimmed and Adam took his seat next to his son. The woman strode to the front and stepped onto the stage. Introducing herself as Professor Jan Steel, head of the law school, she welcomed them to the faculty.

Kate's mind drifted as the professor launched into a polished pitch about compulsory and elective modules, league tables and employability records. It all sounded so terribly dry. A profession for pedants. Or was that being unfair? Chloe had her heart set on advocacy, the drama of the criminal courtroom, defending people who couldn't defend themselves. Ethical and sincere, she saw herself as a crusader, fighting against injustice.

As Professor Steel blathered on, Kate turned her attention to Adam and Ben. They shared the same brown eyes and thick, dark hair the colour of wet peat. Ben wore his longer than his father and it curled over the nape of his neck. Their ears were identical, too. Small and neat with hardly any lobe. But Adam's shoulders were much broader than his son's. Ben still had the almost effeminate narrowness of an adolescent boy who had yet to fill out.

Adam was wearing a grey crew-neck jumper over a white teeshirt. It looked expensive, a cashmere mix. Ben's teeshirt was a faded red. The neck was stretched loose, and Kate soon realised why. Ben was pulling it away from his neck as if he was trying to loosen a chokehold. Adam had noticed too. He bent his head towards his son and murmured something Kate couldn't catch. Ben's hand fell to his lap, and he was still.

Finally, Professor Steel thanked them for coming, and the lights went up.

Kate stood and stretched her back. 'Where next?'

'I was thinking we could grab a coffee.' Chloe turned to Ben and Adam. 'Fancy joining us?'

Adam's eyebrows creased in a question mark. 'What d'you think?' he asked Kate.

Her usual rule was no more than two cups of coffee a day. Too much caffeine made her anxious. 'A coffee sounds perfect,' she said.

CHAPTER FOUR

KATE

Adam commandeered a table in the small café in the foyer of the law school. 'My treat,' he said when Kate offered to pay. 'Sit down. I'll bring them over.'

Chloe was prattling away while Ben worried at the hem of his teeshirt. Every so often, his eyes would dart to her face, lingering for a beat before he lowered his gaze again.

'It's crazy. You can do law and languages, law and criminology, law and philosophy, law and social anthropology, law and economics. You can even do law and English literature. I just want to do plain old law,' Chloe was saying.

One of the spaghetti-thin straps of her pink top had slipped off her shoulder. Kate reached over and hoicked it back up.

'Mum! Your hands are freezing,' she screeched.

'Cold hands, warm heart,' Adam said, setting a tray of drinks on the table. 'What did you think about the talk, son?'

'Good, yeah.'

Adam raised an eyebrow. 'Just good?'

Ben took a sip of his hot chocolate, leaving a line of froth on his upper lip. He wiped it off with the back of his hand. 'To be honest, I preferred Bristol.'

Kate realised it was the first time she'd heard him speak. His voice was growly, deeper than she'd expected, and at odds with his slight frame.

'Bristol? Tell him Kingsgate ranks much higher, Chloe,' Adam said. 'And look at this place.' As he gazed up at the glass and steel roof, the sun appeared from behind a cloud and bathed him in a golden light that turned his eyes hazel. 'You kids don't know how lucky you are.'

'Yeah, totally,' Chloe said. 'Apart from the fact that we'll be paying over nine grand a year for tuition fees, never mind the thousands in maintenance loans we'll have to take out just to live. Whereas your generation had full grants, you lucky buggers.'

Kate shook her head, but Adam laughed. 'Touché. But it was all a lot more run-down when I was a student here.'

'You came here?' Kate asked.

'A lifetime ago.'

'You never did!' Chloe cried. 'Why didn't you say?'

'Probably because you never gave the poor man a chance,' Kate said, smiling at Adam. It occurred to her that she hadn't smiled so much in years and a flush crept up her neck. She hoped he didn't think she was flirting with him. Because she really wasn't.

'That's why I want Ben to come here, isn't it, Benjy?' Adam biffed his son gently on the shoulder. 'I want him to follow in the old man's footsteps.'

'Did you do law, too?' Chloe asked.

Adam nodded. ''Fraid so. I'm a solicitor. Family law.'

'I want to be a barrister like my uncle and grandad, although Grandpa was a judge when he retired. What about you, Ben?'

'A f-finance lawyer,' Ben stammered.

Adam looked at Kate. 'Are you a lawyer, too?'

She opened her mouth to recite the 'why I didn't go to university' spiel she'd perfected, but Chloe beat her to it. 'Mum had a place at Durham to read law, but she had me instead.'

Adam looked sidelong at Kate, who remained silent.

'And now she works at a wedding venue in the village and looks after Grandpa.'

'The retired judge?'

Chloe nodded.

'I'm sure Adam and Ben don't want to hear our life story, Chloe.' Kate's voice was sharper than she'd intended and her daughter blinked.

Adam didn't seem to notice. He'd turned his attention to Ben. 'I want you to put Kingsgate as your first choice.'

'You should, Ben.' Chloe's face was earnest. 'If we volunteered with the law clinic here, we could help with real cases. The replica courtroom's amazing. And if we both came, we could hang out together.'

'I guess,' Ben said, the tips of his ears turning pink.

He may have inherited his father's height and hazel eyes, but he had none of Adam's easy charm, Kate thought, as she sipped her coffee. He was so awkward she wondered if he was on the spectrum, before chastising herself for being so narrow-minded.

'This is going to be your first choice?' Adam asked Chloe.

'There are still a few things I want to see, but I think so, yeah.'

'Speaking of which, we'd better make a move,' Kate said. 'Thank you so much for the coffee. It was lovely to meet you both.'

Adam jumped to his feet. 'The pleasure was all ours. I'm sure our paths will cross again.'

'I'll see you around,' Chloe said to Ben.

'Cool,' he said, smiling back, his face transformed.

After Chloe dragged Kate around the students' union, they bought sandwiches and ate them on a bench outside the library. Kate found herself scanning the crowds for Adam and Ben. When she saw a dark-haired man waiting in a queue by a hotdog stand, her heart beat a little faster.

'Is that Adam?' she said squinting, wishing she hadn't left her glasses in the car.

'No.' Chloe frowned. 'Why? Oh my God, you fancy him, don't you?'

'Don't be ridiculous.'

'I wouldn't blame you if you did. I wouldn't say no,' Chloe said. 'If I was into older guys. Which I'm not,' she added hastily.

'I thought it would be polite to return the compliment, that's all.'

Chloe raised an eyebrow.

'Buy him and Ben a coffee,' Kate clarified, ignoring the smirk on Chloe's face.

The man she'd thought was Adam walked towards them, ramming a hotdog in his mouth as if he hadn't eaten for weeks. Her nostrils filled with the cloying smell of fried onions.

'Ben's not hot, but he's kinda cute,' Chloe continued.

'He doesn't say much, does he?'

'You know me. I like the strong, silent type.'

'You're not coming to university to meet boys,' Kate reminded her. Don't make the same mistakes I did, she nearly added. And then felt a stab of guilt. She may have screwed up her chances of university and a meaningful career and wrecked her relationship with her father, but there wasn't a single day she regretted having Chloe. She was the glimmer of golden perfection in her otherwise grey and mundane existence.

'Anyway, Ben messaged me to say they've gone. They'd seen everything they needed to,' Chloe said.

'You gave him your number?'

'Messaged, Mum. Snapchat.'

'Oh, right.' Kate supposed it was fine. It was how kids operated these days, wasn't it?

'You could have given Adam your number,' Chloe said. 'He was definitely into you.'

Kate held up a hand. 'Enough. Can we please change the subject?'

'You're thirty-seven, Mum, not sixty-seven. You are allowed to have a life.'

'You're my life.'

Chloe groaned. 'I knew you'd say that. But I'll be gone

soon. You don't want to be on your own forever, do you? Like a bitter Miss Havisham, sitting in your decaying mansion in your dusty wedding dress?'

Not for the first time, Kate wished Chloe wasn't studying *Great Expectations* for her English Literature A-level.

'I'm fine. I've got work and Grandpa to keep me busy.'

'You should think about getting a boyfriend, though.'

'You don't just "get" a boyfriend, Chloe. It either happens, or it doesn't.'

'You could be proactive and use a dating app. Not Tinder though, you'd meet all sorts of weirdos. But one of the upmarket ones for professionals.'

'And tell them what - I'm a professional waitress?'

'Or try speed dating. Or an evening class in car mechanics.'

'And meet a load of other sad, single women on the hunt for a man? I don't think so. Anyway, I don't know why we're even having this conversation. I'm perfectly happy as I am. I'm not one of those women who needs to be one half of a couple to feel validated.'

'Whatever you say. But I'm right, you know. Adam definitely has the hots for you. And I think you like him, too.'

CHAPTER FIVE

KATE

By four o'clock, Kate and Chloe had both had enough, and caught the shuttle bus back to the sports centre to find the car. While Kate set the satnav for home, Chloe rolled up the picnic blanket they kept on the back seat and positioned it between her head and the window. She was asleep in seconds, her left hand under her chin and her right hand curled protectively around her phone.

Kate wondered yet again how she would cope with Chloe away at university.

'What d'you mean you'll be lonely? You've got Pa to keep you company,' her brother Rory had said when she'd voiced her fears after one too many glasses of Chablis at Christmas.

Kate had snorted, the crisp white wine making her nose fizz and her eyes water. 'You've got to be kidding.'

They'd glanced at their father, who was playing a rowdy game of Scrabble with Chloe by the fire.

'Look at him,' Rory had said. 'Nearly ninety and still as strong as an ox.'

'He's not an ox. He's a cranky old goat who finds fault with everything I do. He's hardly company.' Kate had taken another slug of wine and glared at her brother. 'It's all right for you, buggering back to your beautiful beachside apartment in Sydney while I'm left in this draughty old wreck of a house with a curmudgeon for company. I know where I'd rather be, but I don't have a choice, do I?'

'It's a grade two listed Queen Anne house that's the envy of the village. Poor me, poor me. Pour me another,' Rory said, topping up her glass and winking. She batted him on the arm. It was hard to stay cross with him for long. Like Chloe, he had inherited their late mother's amenable nature. The sun was always shining in Rory's world.

'Seriously though, sis, why don't you look at Chloe leaving home as an opportunity, not a death sentence? You've always wanted to teach. What's stopping you from signing up for a teacher training course while she's away?'

'Duh, what about Pa?' Kate said, waving a hand in the old man's direction. 'Who would look after him?'

'You could do a part-time degree close to home. Or one with the Open University. You can't seriously want to spend the rest of your life waitressing.'

Kate bristled. 'Don't be such a snob. There's nothing wrong with waitressing. I like my job.'

Rory held up a hand. 'I didn't say there was. But you had a place at Durham. Your A-level grades were way better than mine. Just because you missed out when you were eighteen, doesn't mean you have to miss out again.'

By the fire, Chloe was high-fiving her grandfather after scoring fifty-seven points with *maximise* on a triple word score.

'It could have been eighty-four, and I'd have been in the lead if you'd let me have US spellings,' she was grumbling.

'One needs standards, m'dear,' the old man told her. 'Else, where would we be?'

Chloe pouted. 'Winning?'

Kate had turned back to her brother. 'I know I never made it to Durham,' she had said softly. 'But I didn't miss out.'

Chloe was still asleep when Kate pulled into the drive. As she turned off the engine, Chloe's phone bleeped softly. Surprised it didn't wake her, Kate couldn't resist taking a peek. Chloe's grip on the phone had loosened as she slept, allowing Kate to see a Snapchat message from Ben.

Hey Chloe, it was great to meet you today. I hope we can stay in touch. xxx

Kate raised an eyebrow. Three kisses. And more in one text than she'd heard him say all day. She stroked her daughter's cheek.

'Chlo, we're home.'

Chloe opened her eyes and yawned.

'What time is it?'

'Just gone five. Come on, I expect Grandpa's waiting to hear all about your day.'

Chloe checked her phone before she unclipped her seatbelt, as Kate knew she would. She was surgically attached to the bloody thing.

'It bleeped while you were asleep. Anyone interesting?'

'Only Ben.'

'He must be keen.'

'Mum!'

'Sorry. I know. None of my business. But can I say one thing?'

'What does it matter what I think? I expect you will, anyway.'

'This is such an important year for you. Your mocks are only a few months away, and you'll be sitting your A-levels before you know it. You are so nearly where you want to be. Don't get distracted by a boy now. You've got the rest of your life to meet someone.'

'I'm not going to get distracted by Ben. He's a mate. I probably won't see him again before uni. If he even goes to Kingsgate. There's nothing to worry about, OK?' Chloe bit her lip. 'I know why you're saying this, but I'm not you. I would never let a boy wreck my dreams.'

Ouch. It was no more than she deserved, but still. She was only trying to help. To stop Chloe making the same mistakes she did.

Because Ben clearly wanted to be more than a mate.

Take care, he'd said.

Three kisses.

CHAPTER SIX

KATE

Although Kate had always planned on going to university, she'd never been interested in the law. She'd always wanted to teach. She'd backtracked to appease her father in the dark days following her mother's death. He'd been a husk of a man, wrung dry with grief, but when she'd told him she had chosen law after all it had lit a spark of interest, given him a glimmer of hope.

As they'd traipsed around half a dozen university campuses, her father had shared stories of his student days and recounted big cases he'd won. He'd fired questions at the lecturers and pored over the course structures. Kate had felt like a fraud, terrified she was about to make the biggest mistake of her life.

As the deadline for applications crept closer, she'd had a major wobble. Not about getting the grades - she knew straight As were achievable if she did the work - but about the degree itself.

Rory, two years her junior and about to sit his GCSEs,

had found her in her bedroom, tears streaming down her face as she stared at her UCAS form.

'I can't do it,' she'd hiccuped.

'It's three years of your life, sis. You can do a year's teacher training afterwards. You don't have to become a lawyer. But it's the only thing stopping the old man from taking his shotgun, walking into the woods and blowing his brains out. Please don't change your mind now.'

Kate had wept. Great heaving sobs that wracked her whole body. Tears of self-pity for a motherless daughter who felt pressured into a career she'd never wanted. Rory had put a clumsy arm around her shoulder and given her a squeeze.

'What if you told him you wanted to defer for a year?'

Kate wiped her nose on the back of her hand. 'Like a gap year?'

'Exactly! Tell him you need to find yourself and go travelling. You've always wanted to visit Asia. Do it. Come back, do law for three years and then train to be a teacher.'

'He'd never agree.'

'How do you know if you don't ask?'

So Kate had asked, and to her astonishment, her father had agreed. One last hurrah, he'd called it. He was from a generation who'd left home at eighteen for National Service and had spent almost a year in the sticky heat of the Malayan jungle defeating a communist revolt. As far as he was concerned, National Service had made him a man and the country wouldn't be going to hell in a hand-cart if they brought it back.

There were two conditions. The first that Kate self-funded the trip. The second, that she applied to Durham, her father's alma mater, and that she'd be back in plenty of time for the start of her first year.

Kate had no problem meeting the first condition. She found herself a job as a waitress at The Willows, a Georgian manor house on the outskirts of their village that had recently launched as an upmarket wedding venue. Working every hour she could for the next eight months, she saved enough to see her through a year in South East Asia.

It was the second condition that was the problem. Because by the time Kate was due to fly home, three weeks before the start of Freshers' Week, she was already four months pregnant.

Kate's father was sitting in the kitchen in his Barbour and a tweed bucket hat, threading a live maggot onto a fishing hook. More maggots writhed in an open Tupperware sandwich box on the table. At his feet, their chocolate brown Labrador, Max, gazed at him adoringly.

'Do you have to do that in here?' Kate said, slamming her handbag on the kitchen counter with more force than was necessary.

Max thumped his tail on the floor and woofed a greeting. Her father ignored her.

'How was it?' he asked his granddaughter.

'Oh, Grandpa, it was amazing.'

'Remind me, what are they asking for?'

'Three As, same as all the Russell Group unis.'

He smiled. 'That shouldn't be a problem for my favourite granddaughter.'

Chloe tutted. 'Your only granddaughter.'

'Fair point well made.' He held the hook to the light to inspect it. The impaled maggot twisted and jerked like an obscene marionette. Kate dragged her eyes away and flicked on the kettle.

'Tea, anyone?'

'Not for me, Katherine. I'm off to catch a couple of trout for supper.'

'But there's a casserole in the slow cooker. I made it before we left.'

'We can have that tomorrow.' Her father pushed his chair back and pulled himself to his feet. He had always been big: tall and broad-shouldered, an imposing man, both physically and intellectually. As a circuit judge, he had commanded courtrooms, reducing even the most experienced barristers to quivering wrecks and earning the respect of defendants and juries alike. Now in his late eighties, his physical presence was waning, but his mind was as sharp as ever.

'What if you don't catch anything?' Kate asked, snapping the lid on the Tupperware box and shoving it to the back of the fridge.

His gaze was unwavering. 'I will.'

He returned less than an hour later with two good-sized rainbow trout, their silver-brown flanks peppered with dark spots. He handed them to Kate and washed his hands under the kitchen tap.

'Sun's over the yardarm. G and T?'

Her father may drive her mad ninety-nine per cent of the time, but he made a mean gin and tonic. While he fixed their drinks, Kate reached in the cutlery drawer for her favourite paring knife and began gutting the first fish. Holding it firmly, she sliced off its head with one swift motion before expertly running the knife along its underbelly, deep enough to pierce the skin, but not so deep as to cut into the guts.

She reached into the body cavity and pulled out the intestines, running her thumb along the trout's spine to make sure everything was out. She rinsed it until the water ran clear before reaching for the second fish.

Once both fish had been gutted, she rubbed their skin with olive oil and filled them with slices of lemon and sprigs of parsley. She seasoned them, wrapped them in foil and popped them into the oven next to three baked potatoes.

Her father settled himself at the kitchen table with the Telegraph crossword while Kate sipped her drink as she topped and tailed green beans.

Chloe appeared in the doorway. 'Mum, I've been thinking about what you said.'

Kate raised an eyebrow. 'There's a first time for everything.'

'Very funny. Can I have a few shifts at The Willows over Christmas? I want to start saving for uni.'

'Are you sure? It's a tough gig. Long hours on your feet

for the minimum wage. At least if you worked at the pub, you'd get tips.'

Frown lines furrowed Chloe's brow. 'Don't you want me to work with you?'

Kate plunged the beans into a pan of boiling water. 'Of course I do. I'm working tomorrow. I'll have a word with Patrick. I'm sure it will be fine. He never says no to a pretty face.'

CHAPTER SEVEN

CHLOE

Chloe tried to ignore the flutter of nerves in the pit of her stomach as she followed her mum up the gravelled driveway. Ahead, The Willows, in all its haughty Georgian splendour, gazed down at them. People at school thought her house was posh, and she supposed it was, although they didn't know it was also draughty, leaky and threadbare and basically falling down. But The Willows was proper posh: a five-star wedding and events venue with a spa, beautiful boutique bedrooms and immaculately manicured gardens.

Chloe's squeaky-new black loafers were already pinching her feet. Her mum said she needed sensible shoes for the ten-hour shifts. Chloe thought they were the ugliest things she'd ever seen. But her mum had insisted on buying them, along with a terrible pair of black, tailored trousers and black pop socks, the kind of thing grannies wore. Not that Chloe had a grannie, but, anyway, they were beyond gross. Not even a glimpse of bare feet was allowed, her mum said. Patrick would provide an apron, tie and white gloves. White gloves! It was like Downtown flippin' Abbey. And for the first time in her privileged seventeen years, she was the wrong side of the green baize door.

'I remember my first shift,' her mum said as they took a path around the side of the house to the back. Staff weren't allowed in the main doors, apparently. Go figure. 'I was your age. But I was saving up for my gap year, not uni.'

'What was it like?'

'A bit weird. Everyone else knew exactly what they were doing and were like this well-oiled machine, and I was completely clueless. It's like the first day at school. You don't know where anything is, or what you're supposed to be doing. I breezed in through the front door and was offered a glass of champagne.' She laughed. 'When I said I was here for my first waitressing shift, I was sent round the back with a flea in my ear.'

'By Patrick?'

'No, by his mum, Shirley. She was a miserable old cow. Nothing was ever good enough. Patrick's dad, Henry, was much nicer, even if he was completely under the thumb. But I was glad when they retired.'

'Who does Patrick take after, his mum or his dad?'

Her mum laughed again. 'Good question. Well, you never know with Patrick. Some days he takes after Henry, and some days Shirley. Which keeps you on your toes.'

'What will I be doing today?'

'A bit of everything. Laying tables, serving canapés, and clearing glasses. The wedding breakfast is due to start at four.'

'That's when I have to do the hand thing?'

Her mum had explained how they would start serving the top table and work their way around the room a table at a time. Each member of the waiting staff would be given hand numbers, so they picked up the correct dish for each guest. It sounded fiendishly complicated.

'Don't worry,' her mum said as if reading her thoughts. 'You'll soon get the hang of it. And we always have a practice run. Look, there's Pete, the chef. Come and say hello.'

Pete was unloading a delivery of meat from the back of a van. He set down a tray of chicken breasts and walked over to meet them.

He grinned at Chloe. 'Ready for your first day at the madhouse?'

'I guess,' Chloe said. She didn't know Pete well - her mum liked to keep work and home separate - but he seemed nice, and wasn't afraid to take the piss out of her mum, which awarded him automatic brownie points in her eyes. Her mum was always so uptight.

'Patrick's on the warpath. The bride's announced that four of the guests are gluten-free,' Pete said.

'Why's he getting his knickers in a twist? That impacts on you, not him.' Her mum's voice was indignant.

'You know me. I go with the flow.' Pete turned to Chloe. 'Fancy giving me a hand?'

'Sure.'

Once Chloe had finished helping Pete, she joined her mum in the Great Hall, the enormous vaulted room where wedding receptions at The Willows took place. Strings of fairy lights decorated the beams and on each table was a floral centrepiece of holly, ivy and velvety roses the colour of cherries.

'I love a Christmas wedding,' her mum said, depositing a pile of white napkins on the nearest table. 'I'll show you how these are folded and then we'll lay the tables.'

Chloe quickly mastered napkin-folding - it was hardly rocket science - and soon she was following her mum around the room, laying cutlery, napkins and side plates with clinical precision.

'It all seems a bit pointless. The minute they sit down, they're going to mess it all up,' Chloe grumbled.

'Don't let Patrick hear you say that,' her mum said.

'Don't let Patrick hear you say what?' said a smooth voice behind her. Chloe spun around to see a short, stocky man with perfectly-coiffed hair and piercing blue eyes looking her up and down.

'Chloe, I presume?' he said.

Chloe nodded and held out a hand. It seemed the right thing to do. He took it, his eyes never leaving her face.

'As beautiful as your mother.' He dropped her hand. 'Welcome to The Willows.'

Chloe's phone buzzed in her back pocket. A flicker of displeasure crossed Patrick's features.

'Chloe, I thought I told you to turn that damn thing off,' her mum said.

'Sorry.' Chloe pulled the phone from her pocket. Her eyes slid over the message on the screen as she switched the mobile to silent. She felt a tiny spark of elation but kept her expression neutral, aware her mum and Patrick were both watching.

'Don't let it happen again,' Patrick said, walking away.

Chloe turned to her mum and mouthed, 'Is he actually joking?'

When he was safely out of earshot, her mum shook her head and said, 'No, he isn't. Today's a Shirley day.'

———

While her mum was checking the place settings one last time, Chloe headed across the small staff car park to the low-slung building that housed the storeroom and staff toilets. She locked herself in one of the cubicles, flipped the lid of the loo seat down and unlocked her phone.

Hey, Chlo, how's your first shift? Been thinking about you all morning and hoping it's going OK. Xxx

Ben. Smiling to herself, Chloe tapped back a reply.

The boss is an absolute arsehole but other than that it's fine. What are you doing today? Xxx

A second later her phone, still on silent, vibrated in her hand.

'Hey you,' she said softly.

'Hey yourself,' Ben said. 'I thought I'd call. I was missing the sound of your voice.'

'Me too, but I can't talk for long. Mum thinks I'm in

the loo. Well, I am in the loo, but not going to the loo, if you know what I mean. Just sitting on it, talking to you. Where are you?'

'In my bedroom, thinking about you. Why is your boss an arsehole?'

'He told me off for having my phone switched on.'

'Wanker. Did you tell him where he could stick his job?'

'I wish I could but I can't. I need the money. And my mum would go apeshit. She works here, too, remember.'

'Probably not a good idea then. Can I see you over the holidays?'

Chloe paused. Ben had been badgering her to meet him since the open day in September. She loved hearing from him; the texts, the gifs, the funny memes. It was like a proper old-fashioned courtship, but instead of pouring out his love for her in wax-sealed letters, Ben wooed her with texts and phone calls and clips of cute cats. As the weeks passed, he'd gradually become more sure of himself. The stutter and awkwardness had disappeared, and he was funny and sweet.

Chloe had been out with enough boys at school to know that in real life, the first flush of infatuation didn't last long. Ben was like a virtual boyfriend, airbrushed and edited. And it worked both ways. He only saw the best bits of her, too. The only selfies she sent him were the ones when she was looking her absolute best. Newly-washed hair, lipgloss, eyeliner and a flattering Instagram filter. He didn't see her when she had her period, or her hair was greasy, or there was a spot the size of the Isle of Wight on her chin.

She'd told her friends they were dating. She'd also, somewhat to her shame, built him up to be a drop-dead gorgeous babe. Like the boys she usually went for, only more mature, shinier. Sporty, confident, good-looking boys who played football for the school. Cocky boys.

No, Chloe wasn't stupid. She knew that if they met in real life, Ben's stammer and geeky awkwardness would be a turn-off. That what appeared sweet behaviour on the phone would prove clingy in real life.

She enjoyed the attention, but she didn't want to see him for real. She liked keeping him in a box, separate from the rest of her life, because she was pretty sure that if she went on a date with him, there wouldn't be a second.

'I don't think I'm going to be able to,' she said. 'I'm going to be super busy, what with working here, and revising for my mocks. And my Uncle Rory's coming over from Australia for Christmas.'

'I could come and see you,' Ben said.

The faint wheedling in his tone was not attractive.

'That's a terrible idea,' Chloe said. 'Not that I don't want to see you,' she added, crossing her fingers. 'But I told you my mum doesn't want me to go out with anyone till I've finished my A-levels.'

Another lie. She would pay for them somewhere down the line.

'Oh, OK,' he said in a small voice.

She felt a flash of irritation. Taking a deep breath, she forced a smile. 'Look, I gotta go, otherwise I'm going to be in deep shit. But I'll call you in the morning, OK?'

'Sure,' he said, his voice hardening. 'Whatever.'

Chloe stared at the ceiling. The strip light was so

bright it hurt her eyes. She looked away, but the light still played on her retina. As the afterimage faded, so did her irritation. She reminded herself that she liked having Ben as a virtual boyfriend.

'Do you still love me?' she asked softly.

There was silence, and Chloe could hear her heart beating.

Then the exhale of breath and Ben's voice, sure and steady. 'Of course I do, Chloe. I will always love you.'

CHAPTER EIGHT

KATE

Kate stood in the arrivals hall at Heathrow and scanned the steady stream of passengers, looking for her brother's familiar mop of fair hair. The flight from Sydney had arrived half an hour ago, and its passengers were currently in baggage reclaim, according to the rows of information screens suspended in lines from the ceiling.

There was a tap on her shoulder, and Kate wheeled around, her arms outstretched.

'Where did you spring from?' she cried, and then took a step back, her hand flying to her mouth.

It wasn't her brother, weary and dishevelled after a twenty-three-hour flight from the other side of the world. It was a tall, distinguished-looking man in his early forties with cropped brown hair the colour of wet peat.

'Hello, Kate.'

For one disorientating second, Kate's mind went completely blank. She hid her discomfiture behind a smile.

'You don't remember me, do you?' he said. 'It's Adam. We met you and Chloe at Kingsgate Uni open day a while back? I was with my son Ben?'

Kate finally found her voice. 'Of course I remember! Adam! How lovely to see you! What a coincidence! How *are* you? How's Ben? What are you doing here?' she gushed.

Heads turned in their direction as families waiting for loved ones decided their conversation was far more interesting than the information screens. Mortified, Kate lowered her voice. 'Are you off on holiday?'

'This is the arrivals hall.'

'Of course. Silly me. Have you been anywhere nice?'

'Brussels for a legal conference. Dull as ditchwater. What about you?'

'I'm meeting someone.' Was she mistaken or did his smile falter? 'My brother,' she said quickly. 'He's flying in from Oz for Christmas. In fact,' she said, becoming aware that someone was yelling her name, 'that sounds like him now. He likes to make an entrance.'

Rory was waving frantically from the other side of the concourse. Happy he had her attention, he crossed the hall, abandoned his trolley and swept her into a bear hug.

'Good to see you, Katie,' he said, spinning her around.

'Put me down!' she shrieked, pummelling his back with her fists.

He let her go, and she shook her head in mock despair. Rory was a law unto himself, but she wouldn't change him for the world. She ran her fingers through her hair and smiled brightly.

'Rory, this is Adam. Adam, Rory.'

Adam held out a hand.

Rory glanced at his sister. 'You didn't say you were bringing anyone.'

'I'm not. I mean, we just bumped into each other.'

'For the love of God, I thought I told you that picking men up in airports would land you in a whole heap of trouble.'

Kate grimaced. 'Sorry, Adam. He thinks he's funny.'

Adam smiled. 'We met a couple of months ago at a university open day. The kids hit it off and have been texting each other daily ever since.'

They have? Funny how Chloe had conveniently forgotten to mention *that*.

'Young love,' Rory said, fanning himself theatrically.

'Quite. Well, I'll leave you in peace. It was lovely to see you again, Kate.' Adam took her hand and gazed into her eyes. 'You take care.'

'You too, Adam,' Kate said. 'Have a good Christmas.'

Kate and Rory had barely left the arrivals hall when he turned to her, his eyes wide.

'You're a dark horse. How come you never told me about the delectable Adam?'

'Because there was nothing to say. I met him once and bumped into him again today. End of story.'

'But you like him, don't you?'

Kate tried a nonchalant shrug. 'He seems nice enough. The car's over here.'

Rory was silent as he followed her to her mud-splattered Mini and stowed his luggage in the boot. But Kate could tell by his face that he had something to say, and he wasted no time once they had pulled onto the motorway.

'You should ask him out.'

Kate tapped her fingers lightly on the steering wheel. 'Ask who out?'

'Don't be obtuse. Adam. He seems like a nice guy.'

'I'm sure he is, but I don't want to go on a date with him. Or anyone else, for that matter.'

'Chloe would be cool with it if that's what's worrying you. We had a chat about it the last time I was over.'

'Did you indeed? Ever thought it might be none of your business?' Kate pulled out sharply to overtake a caravan dawdling in the middle lane. 'Bloody lane hoggers,' she muttered, glaring at the rear-view mirror.

'Chloe would love you to find someone nice. Someone who'd look after you. She's worried you'll be lonely when she goes.'

Kate resumed her tapping. 'As you said last Christmas, I have Pa to keep me company.'

'I was joking. You're not even forty. You can't spend the rest of your life on your own, spinster of this parish. Why won't you allow yourself a chance of happiness?'

'Happiness is over-rated if you ask me,' Kate said, instantly regretting it. She'd aimed to be flippant, but just sounded bitter.

Was that what she was? An embittered, dried-up old hag? Chloe was always telling her she was uptight, that she needed to chill, but that's what all teenage girls told their mums, right? Kate supposed she probably had become a bit set in her ways over the years. But she

45

wasn't complaining, was she? So why couldn't everyone else butt out?

'Speaking of happiness, how's Louis?'

Rory twisted the narrow platinum band on the third finger of his left hand.

'He's good. He sends his love. I'm sorry you and Chloe couldn't make the ceremony.'

Kate's voice softened. 'Me too. But there was no way Patrick would have given me the time off. August is always completely manic.'

'He takes advantage of you.'

'It's what bosses do.'

'Not the good ones.' Rory slipped the wedding ring off his finger and slid it into his wallet. 'I feel like a complete shit doing this.'

'Then don't do it. Tell Pa. It's about time. You're happy to lecture me on my non-existent love life, and you haven't even told your own father you're married. Pot and kettle.'

'I know. And I want to, Katie, I really do.' Rory stared out of the window, his jaw set. 'But you know how old school he is. I'm not sure his ticker would stand up to the shock revelation that his only son is a raving queer.'

CHAPTER NINE

CHLOE

Chloe emptied the books in her locker into her rucksack and hitched it onto her shoulder.

'Jesus, that's heavy,' she grumbled.

'I know. It totally sucks that we're gonna have to spend the whole frigging holidays revising,' her best friend Annie said. 'Is your Uncle Rory over for Christmas?'

'Yeah. Mum was picking him up from the airport this morning. He'll be there when I get home.'

'Cool.' Annie tilted her head. 'Is that your phone or mine?'

Chloe had felt her mobile vibrate in the pocket of her jeans. 'Mine.'

'Not lover boy again is it?'

She glanced at the screen and nodded.

'What does he want now?'

'I told him we were finishing early. He's asking what I'm up to this afternoon.'

Annie looked over Chloe's shoulder as she tapped a reply.

'Nothing much. Hanging at home. Will call you later. Smiley face. No kiss,' Annie read. 'He gave you three kisses. You gone off him or something?'

Chloe rubbed her face. 'He's getting a bit… intense.'

'So cool it off a bit. Don't tell him you're going to call. Don't answer his texts. He'll soon get the message.'

'I don't want to hurt his feelings. He's a nice guy but I don't fancy him.'

There. She'd said it.

'But you said he was hot. You said he looked like, like…' Annie clicked her finger and thumb and pointed at Chloe. 'That guy in Bodyguard. Richard Madden.'

Chloe pulled a face. 'I may have exaggerated a bit. He's OK. Not pig-ugly or anything. He's just not my type.'

'Now she tells us. I was dead jealous you'd found yourself a complete babe. In that case, I would definitely cool it. Give him the classic, "It's not you, it's me" line. Tell him you want to concentrate on your A-levels. He'll get over it.'

Was it that simple? Chloe felt a great weight lift from her shoulders. A weight she hadn't even realised she'd been carrying.

'You're right,' she said, linking arms with Annie. 'I'll text him tonight.'

As it was, she didn't have to wait that long. A sleek gunmetal-grey Audi was parked on the yellow zigzag lines outside the school gates. When she saw who was in the driving seat her stomach flipped, and she gripped Annie's arm.

'That's him,' she hissed out of the corner of her mouth. 'In the grey car.'

'The TT? Bloody hell, Chlo. Is it his?'

'Of course not. He's only seventeen. It must be Adam's.'

'Adam?'

'His dad. I knew Ben was having lessons, but he didn't tell me he'd passed his test. How does he even know where our school is? Quick, let's go down the alley before he sees me.'

'Too late,' Annie said, letting go of Chloe's arm.

Ben had wound the window down and was resting his elbow on the sill with studied nonchalance. But his eyes followed Chloe as she tramped through the gates towards him, Annie on her heels.

'What are you doing here?' Chloe demanded.

'You said you were finishing early.' Ben patted the car door and grinned. 'Want a lift home?'

Chloe fiddled with the strap of her bag. 'I guess. Annie, you coming?'

Was it Chloe's imagination, or did Ben's grip on the door tighten?

'Sorry, Chlo, but I promised Mum I'd mind Nathan this afternoon.' Annie glanced at Ben. 'But give me a ring when you get home, yeah?'

''Course.'

Chloe slung her bag into the footwell, climbed into the passenger seat and fixed her seatbelt. Ben adjusted the rear-view mirror and turned on the ignition. The engine roared into life, deep and throaty.

Chloe had only had a couple of driving lessons, but the mirror-signal-manoeuvre routine was the first thing she'd learned. She found herself repeating it under her breath like a mantra as Ben glanced in the mirror, waiting for a white van to pass before he slipped the car into first gear, indicated and pulled away.

'What did you say?' he asked.

'Nothing.' Chloe sat on her hands and stared at the dashboard with its complicated array of dials and buttons. 'Nice car.'

'It's completely wasted on Dad. He only uses it for "high days and holidays".' Ben tweaked his index fingers in air quotes as he gripped the steering wheel. 'He uses his Golf for work and shit.'

'Right.' She thought for a bit. 'It must have cost a bomb to put you on the insurance.'

'Yeah, about that.' Ben glanced at her and grinned.

A trickle of unease, as icy as a drip from a stone-cold shower, slid down Chloe's spine.

'You are insured, right?'

'Technically? No. I was insured for the Golf while I was learning to drive, but the cover stopped the minute I passed my test. How fucking stupid is that? The day you prove you can drive safely, they stop insuring you. Dad keeps promising to sort out proper cover when he's got a spare minute. But he never has.'

Ben stopped at a junction and drummed his fingers on the steering wheel. 'Which way?'

'Actually, I might walk from here,' Chloe said.

'What?'

She took a deep breath. 'I'm sorry, Ben. I don't feel comfortable with this. What if you hit someone?'

His eyes flashed dangerously. 'I won't.'

'OK, but what if someone hits you?'

A sharp blast of a horn made Chloe start. Ben frowned into the rear-view mirror.

'Prick,' he muttered, slamming the gear stick into first. The car leapt forwards then stalled, and the driver sounded the horn again. Ben gave him the finger. 'Which way?' he repeated, as he jabbed the ignition switch.

Chloe swallowed. 'Right.'

Mirror-signal-manoeuvre. The car pulled smoothly away.

'You worry too much,' Ben said. 'I'd never let anything bad happen to you.'

As they reached the outskirts of town Chloe decided she had no option but to go with the flow. She'd missed her bus and the next one didn't leave for another couple of hours. But instead of directing Ben onto the busy B-road that was the quickest route home, she guided him through the industrial estate and onto a much quieter back road that cut through a swathe of ancient woodland. With any luck, they wouldn't meet another car.

As the miles passed without incident, she felt herself relax. Ben was focused on the road ahead, his long, slender fingers tapping a beat to a song only he could hear.

'You're a good driver,' she said finally.

'Thanks. I passed first time. No minors.'

'Cool. How did you know where my school was?'

'That's for me to know and you to wonder.' He laughed and pointed to the dashboard. 'Satnav.'

Spotting a layby up ahead, he checked his mirror and indicated left.

Chloe's uneasiness returned. 'Why are we stopping?'

He smiled at her. 'You'll see.'

He pulled into the layby, turned off the engine and stared ahead. 'Pretty woods.'

'They're beautiful in the autumn. Not so much now,' Chloe said. Wet leaves clung to bramble bushes, and the winter-bare branches above them looked like twisted limbs against the late afternoon sky. She peered between the trees. 'Sometimes, if you're lucky, you see a deer.'

Ben unclipped his seatbelt and reached into the pocket of his jeans. He pulled out a small, ivory box with the word *Pandora* embossed on the top.

Chloe's heart crashed in her chest as he turned to her with a fervent expression.

'I want you to know that you are the best thing that's ever happened to me, Chloe Kennedy. I think about you all the time. I know you said we'd be together at uni, but I can't wait that long. This is for you.'

Chloe stared in horror at the box, as if it might suddenly snap open and nip the tip of her finger off. Ben prised it open.

'It's a promise ring. It's only silver and cubic zirconia, but it'll do until we're older and I can buy you the real thing.'

'A promise ring?' she said faintly.

'To show the world that I'm yours and you're mine.'

'But we're not even going out.'

His forehead puckered. 'We talk every day. We Face-Time. We've picked the same university so we can be together. I've told everyone you're my girlfriend. Of course we're going out.'

Chloe shook her head. 'It's not like that. We're friends, yes. But we're not boyfriend and girlfriend. You're not -'

'Not what?'

Chloe's hands closed around the seatbelt. Cool it off, Annie had said. And Annie was right. She didn't need this right now, not with Christmas a week away and her mocks looming. It wasn't her fault Ben had latched onto her like a drowning man clutches a lifebuoy. She didn't need the aggro. She took a deep breath.

'You're not my type.'

CHAPTER TEN

CHLOE

Ben flinched as if she'd hit him.

'W-what?'

'I'm sorry Ben. It's not you, it's me. But I don't want to go out with you.'

'But you said… '

'That it would be fun if we both went to the same uni because we'd have someone to hang out with. As *friends*.'

'You let me believe it was more than that. You led me on.' His expression turned ugly. 'There's a name for girls like you.'

She hung her head. 'I know. I'm sorry. I do care about you, honestly I do, but not like that.'

He snapped the ring box shut and leant over her. For one horrible moment she thought he was going to try to kiss her, but instead he opened the glove box and flung the ring inside.

'I'm really sorry,' she said again.

A muscle flickered in his jaw. He fastened his seatbelt and turned the engine on. Mirror-signal-manoeuvre. He swung onto the road and put his foot down. The engine growled as he worked his way up through the gears. Soon the trees were a blur as they raced along the road. Chloe picked at a strip of loose skin on her thumb.

'Please slow down, Ben,' she whispered.

Ignoring her, he started mumbling to himself. She had to strain to hear him over the guttural noise of the engine.

'I should have fucking known. Every fucking time. First Mum, then Lucy. Now Chloe. They all fuck off in the end. I'm a worthless piece of shit. I'm better off dead.'

He stamped on the accelerator and the car sped up. Chloe let out a small yelp and grabbed the edge of the seat with both hands.

'Ben! Slow down. Please!' she cried.

He eased his foot off the accelerator and she exhaled slowly.

'You know who you remind me of?' He didn't wait for an answer. 'My mother. You even look a bit like her. She was beautiful, too.'

'Was?' Chloe croaked.

'Still is, for all I know. She fucked off when I was a baby. Packed her bags one afternoon while I was having a nap and walked out leaving me in the house on my own. Dad said I was hysterical by the time he came home from work.'

Chloe's mouth fell open. 'That's awful, Ben. I'm so sorry.'

'Are you? Really?'

'Of course I am.'

'Yeah, well, shit happens. Dad and I do OK on our own.'

'You never hear from her?'

He shook his head. 'If she did try to get in touch I'd tell her to fuck right off. The bitch.'

The car lurched to the side as Ben accelerated around a tight right-hand bend. The contents of Chloe's stomach roiled unpleasantly.

'Who's Lucy?'

He laughed without humour. 'The proverbial girl next door.'

'She, like, literally lived next door to you?'

Ben nodded.

'Was she your girlfriend?'

'No. We were "just friends", as you would say.'

This time when he drew quote marks in the air he took both hands off the steering wheel. Chloe gasped as the car veered left, following the camber of the road. Ben, apparently unconcerned, seized the wheel with one hand and righted it before it hit the verge.

'What happened?'

'You don't want to know.'

'I'm not like Lucy. I'd like to stay in touch.'

'You would?' The undisguised hope in his voice filled her with shame. She'd meant it when she'd told Annie she hadn't wanted to hurt his feelings.

'Of course. We've a great thing going. As friends,' she added firmly.

She gazed out of the window as they passed the wrought iron gates to a country estate. They were fifteen minutes from home. Ben seemed less agitated, and her heart rate slowly began to return to normal.

And then, out of the corner of her eye, she caught a glimpse of a reddish-brown blur racing through the trees.

'Ben!' she cried. 'Look out!'

It took a second for Ben to register the massive stag hurtling towards them. He wrenched the steering wheel to the right, causing the car to lurch towards the verge. The stag was so close Chloe could see the whites of its eyes. Ben hauled the steering wheel to the left in a desperate attempt to straighten the car. But in his inexperience he overcooked it and the Audi span out of control.

The last thing Chloe remembered before they left the road was the sound of an explosion and the impact of the airbag on her sternum, knocking every ounce of breath out of her.

———

When she came to the car was nose down in a ditch twenty metres from the road and the stag had long gone. Ben was groaning quietly. She tapped him on the shoulder.

'Are you alright?'

He struggled to focus as he stared at her blearily.

'Think so.'

'Thank goodness.' Chloe felt as though someone had slammed a sledgehammer into her chest, but to her surprise she was clearheaded and purposeful. 'Ben, listen to me. We need to get out of the car, OK?'

Ben nodded. Chloe unclipped her seatbelt and tried the door handle. It swung open. Wriggling out, she staggered around to the driver's side.

'Come on,' she said, pulling the door open. As she bent down to undo Ben's seatbelt a wave of dizziness hit her and she had to grip hold of the roof to stop herself from keeling over. She breathed slowly, in through the nose, out through the mouth, until the dizziness passed, then released the seatbelt and hauled Ben out.

Once he was settled on the side of the ditch a safe distance from the Audi, she strode over to the road and gazed left and right. It was a grey ribbon of emptiness. Chloe pulled her mobile from her pocket and held her thumb over the home button. The phone sparked into life and she hit three nines.

There was a click and a man's voice asked, 'Which emergency service do you require? Fire, police or ambulance?'

She glanced over her shoulder. Ben was sitting with his legs crossed at the ankles and his head in his hands. His whole body was trembling. 'Ambulance, please.'

She held her breath as she was transferred to the control room.

'What's the telephone number you're calling from?' a woman asked.

Chloe relayed her number. 'We've had a car crash,' she said. 'We need an ambulance.'

'What's the exact location of the incident?'

'Um. Forge Lane, just past the gates to the Thornbury Estate.'

'Can you tell me what happened?'

Chloe pictured the hulking mass of the stag as it flashed past the windscreen. 'A deer ran out in front of us and we hit a bank when we swerved to avoid it.'

'How many vehicles were involved?'

'Just ours.'

'Make and model?'

'It's a grey Audi TT.'

'How many casualties?'

'One. He lost consciousness for a while. That's why I was worried.'

'But he's conscious now?'

'Yes. But I think he's gone into shock.'

'We'll dispatch a crew to you as soon as we can,' the woman said.

'When will that be?'

'Call volume is high but we hope to be with you within the hour.'

'An *hour*? But people die from shock!' Chloe could hear her voice rising. She took a deep breath and tried to calm herself.

'I'm sure he'll be fine,' the woman said briskly. 'But if you want to help him you can lay him down with his feet elevated and keep him warm.'

'Of course. I'll stay by the road so I can -'

A hand snaked around her side and grabbed the phone from her hand.

She yelped. Ben loomed above her, his face rigid with anger. He stabbed the end call icon and hissed, 'Who the hell were you calling?'

Chloe took a step backwards but he moved even closer.

'You better not have been phoning the pigs.'

'W-why?'

'Why d'you think, you stupid cow?'

The penny dropped. 'Because you're not insured.'

'That's right, because I'm not insured,' he mimicked. 'They'll crucify me.' His voice cracked and he rubbed his face with his hand.

'Anyway, I wasn't,' Chloe said. 'I was phoning for an ambulance. You need to get checked over, Ben. You were out stone cold for a while.'

'You definitely didn't ask for the police?'

'I didn't, I promise.' She held out her hand. 'Can I have my phone back?'

Ben shook his head. 'I need to phone my dad.'

Yes, Chloe thought. Adam would sort it.

Ben turned his back to her and stabbed a number into the phone. Cocking her head, Chloe heard the ring tone, a click, and a man's voice saying, 'Who is this?'

'Dad? It's Ben.'

CHAPTER ELEVEN

CHLOE

Dusk gave way to darkness as they waited in silence for the ambulance and Adam to arrive. Ben was still shaking but refused to lay down, and when Chloe tried to drape a coat over his shoulders he waved her away with an impatient hand.

Chloe paced back and forth between the ditch and the road. It kept her warm and used up some of the nervous energy zipping through her system. Occasionally they would hear the distant rumble of a car and Ben would stiffen, his head cocked to one side as it approached, only slumping down again once its headlights had disappeared.

'How will your dad know where we are?' Chloe asked.

'He'll find us,' Ben muttered.

'How long will he be?'

'Don't know.'

'My mum will be getting worried. I'm usually home by now.'

Ben staggered to his feet. 'For fuck's sake, do you ever shut up?'

Chloe took a step back. 'I'm sorry.'

'Text her you're going to be late.'

'And say what?'

'I don't know. That the bus broke down, or you stayed late at school, or you met a friend for coffee. You'll think of something. But please don't tell her what really happened. You owe me that.'

Ben's voice caught, and he crumpled to the floor. Guilt heavy on her chest, Chloe took out her phone.

Popped round to Annie's after school. Her mum's going to give me a lift home. Be back about 6. x

She didn't have to wait long for a reply.

No worries, but don't be too long. Uncle Rory's here, and he can't wait to see you! x

'I've done it,' she said tonelessly.

'Thank you.'

'What now?'

Ben stared at her with haunted eyes. 'We wait.'

Chloe's hopes rose when headlights approached. She stepped into the road and waved her arms frantically.

'Shit,' she muttered when the car indicated right and turned into the Thornbury Estate. She traipsed back to Ben. 'D'you think I should call the ambulance again? It's been nearly twenty minutes.'

'No,' Ben said through chattering teeth. 'Dad'll be here soon.'

Chloe resumed her pacing. A rustle in the undergrowth made her stop. Something big was moving through the trees, snapping twigs and swishing fallen leaves. Probably another deer, she told herself. But when a shadowy shape stepped out of the trees, she shrieked.

'Chloe,' the figure said, holding out a hand to quieten her. 'It's me, Adam.'

Her hand dropped to her side. 'Sorry,' she said, feeling foolish. 'I couldn't see in the dark. Where's your car?'

'I parked down the road. Where is he?'

'Over there.'

Adam approached her, his figure a silhouette in the soft glow of the Audi's side-lights. His face was in shadow as he took in the tyre marks that had sliced into the soft earth; the stoved-in bonnet; the tears streaming down his son's face.

'Jesus Christ.'

'I'm sorry, Dad.'

'Sorry? I should think you're sorry. You took my car without my permission - without insurance for Christ's sake - and you almost killed yourself. Not to mention Chloe. How the fuck would I have explained that to her mother? Jesus.' He ran his hands through his hair. 'I suppose you were showing off. Giving it all that in front of her.'

'I wasn't.' Desperation had squeezed Ben's voice an octave higher. 'It wasn't my fault, Dad. The accident, I mean. It was a deer. It ran out in front of us.'

Adam looked to Chloe for confirmation.

'He's right,' she said. 'There was nothing he could do.'

'Are either of you hurt?'

Chloe shook her head. 'I'm fine, but Ben was out cold for a few minutes after the crash. I think he must have hit his head. But don't worry, I've called an ambulance. They should be here soon.'

'What did you tell them?'

'Only that a deer had run out in front of us and we hit a bank.'

Adam massaged his temple. He glanced at the Audi and then back towards the road. 'And that's all? You didn't give them your names?'

'I was cut off before they asked.'

The distant wail of sirens sliced through the gloom and Adam raised an eyebrow.

'Talk of the devil. Chloe, go and sit with Ben. I'll handle this.'

Chloe's legs sagged as relief flowed through her and she collapsed on the bank beside Ben. The sirens grew louder and blue lights flickered through the trees. Ben gave a sharp intake of breath.

'What's wrong?' Chloe said.

'You bloody bitch. I thought you said you didn't call the police?'

Chloe flinched, stung by the vitriol in his voice. 'I didn't,' she stammered. 'I promise.'

'So why are they here?'

Chloe watched in horrified fascination as a police patrol car crunched over the loose dirt and came to a stop yards from the wrecked Audi. Two officers emerged, their faces inscrutable as they pulled on their hats. The taller of the two pulled a notebook from his top pocket while the other murmured into his radio.

'Evening, sir,' said the taller officer, nodding at Adam.

'We were expecting an ambulance, not the police,' Adam said.

'The ambulance control room informs us of all injury accidents, sir. It's standard procedure. Speaking of which,' he waved a hand at his colleague. 'Baz, check the ambulance ETA, can you?'

Adam smoothed his hair. 'I fear you've had a wasted journey, officer.'

The officer licked his thumb and flicked through his notebook. 'Control said the car collided with a bank when you swerved to avoid a deer. Was the deer hit?'

'Why?'

'Because if it was badly injured, we'd have to call out an armed response team to put it out of its misery. It's...'

'Standard procedure?' Adam said.

The police officer's eyes narrowed. 'Yes. So perhaps you'd like to tell me what happened?'

'It's all very boring, I'm afraid. The deer wasn't injured. My son and his girlfriend are both fine. No other vehicles were involved, and I'll phone my insurance company to arrange recovery. All's well that ends well, eh?'

'Apart from the car,' the officer said.

'Apart from the car,' Adam agreed. 'But it's only aluminium and steel. It could have been worse.'

Ben walked over to his father and tugged at his sleeve.

'I don't need an ambulance, Dad.'

The officer looked at Chloe. 'What about you? Are you hurt?'

Chloe scrambled to her feet and joined them. 'I'm absolutely fine. The airbag was brilliant.'

'Would you like us to cancel the ambulance?'

They all nodded.

'D'you hear that, Bazzer? Scrap the ambulance.' His colleague nodded and muttered into his radio again. The taller officer produced a pen. 'OK. I need to take some details then we can all be on our way. Registration number, please.'

Adam reeled it off, and the officer jotted down their names and addresses and the time of the accident.

'Just for the record, sir, who was driving?'

Silence for a beat, then Adam smiled. 'I was.'

CHAPTER TWELVE

CHLOE

Chloe felt as if the ground had disappeared from beneath her feet. What was Adam thinking, lying to the police? Had he lost his mind? She had to set the record straight. She stepped forwards, the truth on her lips, but before she could say anything, Ben put an arm around her shoulders and pinched the underside of her arm so hard she gasped.

The police officer stopped writing and looked at her with concern. 'Are you all right, miss? Are you sure you want us to cancel that ambulance?'

Chloe glanced at Ben. Beads of sweat lined his forehead even though she could feel him trembling with cold. Their eyes met for the briefest moment.

She swallowed. 'I'm OK.'

'Are you sure? Only you looked as though you wanted to say something?'

Ben increased the pressure on her arm, but she took a breath and kept her voice neutral. 'Honestly, I'm fine. I just felt a bit dizzy for a second.'

The officer nodded. 'If you're sure.' He turned back to Adam. 'Where were we?'

Ben steered her back towards the Audi while the officer finished taking details of Adam's insurance company. Minutes later, the two officers were climbing back into the patrol car and driving off. Chloe's heart thudded as the tail-lights disappeared into the night.

She pulled away from Ben and marched up to Adam. 'Why did you tell them you were driving?' she demanded.

Adam gave her a sorrowful smile. 'You see the predicament I'm in, Chloe. If we told the police Ben was driving they'd have realised pretty sharpish he had no insurance. They'd have been down on him like a ton of bricks. They'd probably have charged him with taking a vehicle without consent and dangerous driving, never mind driving without insurance. You said the accident wasn't his fault?'

'No. I told you, the deer came from nowhere.'

'And you and Ben are both OK.'

'I guess.'

'So there's no harm done, is there?'

'But lying to the police! We could get arrested for that!'

Adam gestured towards his son's hunched figure. 'Imagine for a minute what it would do to Ben if he were convicted. He'd have a criminal record and a tainted reputation. It could kill his chances of a career in the law. You wouldn't want to jeopardise that, would you?'

'I -'

'He thinks so highly of you, Chloe. You're all he ever talks about.'

'But -'

Adam took her hand and gave it a gentle squeeze. 'At the end of the day, does it matter who was driving? Think about it. No other cars were involved, and you and Ben are fine. The deer wasn't hurt, and I'll claim on my insurance for the damage to the Audi.'

Except Ben was driving, not you.

'Chloe?'

'If the police find out you're lying, they'd know I'd lied, too.'

'Who's going to tell them? Ben won't. I certainly won't. Just remember, I was driving, Ben was in the front passenger seat, and you were sitting behind him.'

Chloe jammed her hands in her pockets. She'd never broken the law before. She'd never taken drugs or shoplifted or even had a detention at school. In her mind, the law existed for a reason. Without legal systems, the world would descend into chaos. And yet here was an adult - a solicitor, for God's sake – willing to lie to the police.

She glanced at Ben. Remembered the desolation in his voice after she told him she didn't want to go out with him. Felt another pang of guilt that she'd led him on. He'd been agitated as he'd driven her home. Would he have crashed if she hadn't just dumped him?

One small lie. A little white one. More like twisting the truth. Would it hurt? Did it matter who was driving the bloody Audi?

She kicked a clump of mud with her toe.

'Have it your way,' she said finally.

Adam smiled. 'So if anybody asks?'

'You were driving.'

CHAPTER THIRTEEN

KATE

Kate poured three mugs of tea and pushed a plate of homemade flapjacks in Rory's direction. He was moaning about the cold, despite being wrapped in five layers.

'Don't you think it's about time you had a proper heating system installed, Pa? This is the twenty-first century, you know.'

Their father was still in shirtsleeves. 'Why would we want to do that when the storage heaters and immersion tank do a perfectly adequate job?'

Kate and Rory shared a smile.

'Anyway, never mind the heating,' their father said, turning a hawklike gaze on his son. 'When are you going to settle down and give me another grandchild?'

Rory choked on a mouthful of flapjack and Kate patted him firmly between his shoulder blades.

'Yes, when *are* you going to settle down, Rory?'

'Probably when you do, sister dear. How is the dating going, by the way?'

Their father raised his eyebrows. 'Dating? Ridiculous. First I've heard of it.'

'That's because Rory's winding me up. As usual.' Kate rolled her eyes, even though she secretly loved the way she and Rory slipped straight back into the easy banter they'd perfected as teenagers. She glanced at the clock above the Aga. 'I might text Chloe. See when she's going to be home.'

No sooner had she picked up her phone than the front door clicked open.

'There she is,' she said, pushing her chair back and calling, 'Chloe, love. We're in the kitchen.'

The door clunked shut, and footsteps thudded along the hallway. Chloe appeared in the doorway.

'Uncle Rory!'

Rory jumped out of his chair. 'Look at you, all grown up and more gorgeous than ever. Give me a hug.'

Chloe yelped as Rory pulled her close. He jerked back. 'You OK?'

She held her sternum. 'I collided with Hazel Matthews in double games. I think she bruised my ribs. Honestly, you should see her. Built like a brick shit-house.'

'Chloe!' Kate waggled her finger. 'That's enough, thank you.'

'Sorry Mum.'

'You're forgiven.' Kate made a fresh pot of tea and poured Chloe a cup. Her daughter's naturally pale complexion had the rosy bloom of someone who'd spent most of the afternoon outside.

'Must have been cold.'

'What?'

'Double games.'

'Oh. Yeah. It was.'

'It was kind of Annie's mum to drop you home. It's miles out of her way.'

'Yeah.' Chloe took a sip of tea and reached for a flapjack.

'You'll never guess who I bumped into when I was picking your Uncle Rory up from the airport,' Kate continued.

'Who?'

'Adam.'

Chloe's hand stopped mid-air. 'Adam?'

'You know. Ben's dad. Fancy the chances of that, eh?' Kate tried to keep her voice neutral. 'He said you kids have been keeping in touch since the open day.'

'We've been messaging a bit. As friends, you know?'

'Is the son as hot as the dad?' Rory asked, winking at his niece.

Chloe's flushed cheeks turned a shade darker.

Their father looked up from his crossword. 'For goodness sake, leave the poor girl in peace.'

'Chloe's been working at The Willows,' Kate said.

Rory grinned. 'Did your mum ever tell you about my one and only shift?'

Chloe shook her head. 'What happened?'

'He got as drunk as a skunk while he was in the glass room,' Kate said. The corner of her mouth twitched. 'He was drinking everyone's dregs.'

'You never were!'

Rory pouted. 'People were leaving glasses of perfectly decent fizz half-finished. It would have been criminal to waste it.' He leaned back in his chair. 'How's Patrick? As difficult as ever?'

'He's all right if you stay on the right side of him,' Kate said.

'Which I never did. He's the one who grassed me up to his mother and had me sacked, the sly little shit.' He tapped the side of his head. 'Something not quite right up here, if you ask me.'

'We didn't,' Kate said brusquely. 'Is there anything you want to do while you're over? Oxford Street? A show?'

'I'm quite happy with some walks in the country, a pub lunch or two, a spot of fishing and evenings in front of the fire, to be honest. Work has been full on this year. I could do with some downtime.'

Kate smiled. 'Downtime can be easily arranged.'

'Although -' Rory sat up straight. 'I've had a most excellent idea. Why don't we throw a bash?'

'A bash?'

'A Christmas party. Nothing too complicated. Some mulled wine and nibbles. Invite the neighbours over. It'd be a laugh.'

'That's a terrible idea,' Kate said.

'Why?'

'Because I'm the one who'll get lumbered organising the bloody thing, that's why. We've got half a dozen weddings on at work, I still haven't finished my Christmas shopping, and I haven't even thought about a tree or ordered a turkey yet. I've too much on.'

Their father finished his tea and hauled himself to his

feet. 'Then Rory and I will organise it. We haven't had a party for yonks. I'm in my twilight years, remember. I might not have another chance.'

Chloe looked up from her phone in alarm. 'Don't say that, Grandpa.'

'As Benjamin Franklin once said, Chloe dear, "In this world nothing can be said to be certain, except death and taxes." Don't you worry, I have a few years left in me. But we might not have the opportunity to have another shindig before you head off to university. I'll galvanise the neighbours and order some of those platters from Marks & Spencer. Rory, you can look after drinks and decorations.'

'Sounds good to me,' Rory said.

'Well, if that's sorted, I'll take my leave. I have back-to-back episodes of Eggheads to watch.' And with that, he helped himself to a second slice of flapjack and shuffled out of the room.

Rory turned to his sister. 'Before the house is filled with all the ancient neighbours, we need to think of a few people our age to invite. Otherwise, our party will be in danger of resembling bingo night at Age Concern.'

Chloe snorted.

'Is Pete still at The Willows?' Rory asked. 'We should ask him. He's a laugh.'

'Yes,' Kate said. 'But if we ask Pete we'll have to invite Patrick.'

Rory shuddered. 'If we must. Who else is there?'

'Most of the people we went to school with have long gone.'

Rory slammed his hand on the table. 'I know! What

about the delectable Adam and his son? What's his name again?' He looked at his niece, but it was Kate who answered.

'Ben. But I'm sure they won't want to come.'

'Of course they will. Adam clearly fancies the pants off you. And I'm sure Ben can't keep his hands off Chloe, either. Think what fun you two can have under the mistletoe. Although it could be weird if you did both hook up. Chlo, you'd be dating your step-brother.'

Chloe pushed her chair back and, muttering something about an English essay, tramped out of the room.

Rory turned to Kate with bemusement. 'What did I say?'

'Honestly Rory, you have the subtlety of a ten-tonne truck. Chloe bites my head off if I even ask about her day. She's not going to give you a blow by blow account of her love life, even if you are her favourite uncle.'

'An unfortunate choice of words, big sis, but fair enough. Let's decide on a date for our party, and you can hand over that business card I saw Adam slip into your pocket at the airport. I'll send him an invite.'

Kate reddened. 'How on earth did you notice that?'

'I see more than you think,' he said.

Kate stood outside Chloe's bedroom, wondering what to do. Usually, if the door was ajar, she knew she'd be welcome. But it was firmly closed. She tapped a couple of times and said softly, 'It's me. Can I come in?'

There was a sigh, and the sound of a chair leg scraping on the wooden floor. The door swung open. Chloe had dumped her school bag on the end of her bed, and the only thing on her desk was her mobile phone, blinking away with a constant stream of notifications. So much for the English essay, Kate thought, as she perched on the bed and smiled at her daughter.

'Don't take any notice of your Uncle Rory. He was teasing you.'

Chloe paced over to the window. Outside, the night was coal-black. Kate fought the urge to jump up and pull the curtains. Chloe never bothered. Said she liked waking up to natural light. Kate's warnings about draughts always fell on deaf ears.

'Do we have to have a party?' Chloe said, her breath misting the glass.

'You know what your Uncle Rory's like when he gets the bit between his teeth. And Grandpa seems quite taken by the idea. You never know, it might be fun.'

Chloe spun around and glared at Kate. 'You've changed your tune.'

'You know me. I hate surprises. But I have to say I'm coming around to the idea.'

'Well, I'm not. I'll stay over at Annie's, thanks.'

'Don't be silly, of course you won't. Annie can come to the party. I'm sure a couple of the kids from work will come, too. And we'll ask Ben. It won't all be old fogeys.'

Chloe rested her forehead against the glass. Kate tried another tack.

'I'll buy you a new dress.'

'I don't want a new dress.'

'What's wrong, Chlo? You normally love parties.'

Chloe took a deep breath, as if she was about to say something, then marched over to her desk. 'Fine. Have your bloody party. But don't expect me to be the life and soul, all right?'

CHAPTER FOURTEEN

KATE

K ate slammed the last tray of sausage rolls into the Aga and checked the time. Five to seven. Which meant she had precisely thirty-five minutes to shower, wash and dry her hair and do her make-up before the first guests arrived. And heat the mulled wine. And light the candles in the front room. And pour the vodka and prosecco into the Christmas punch.

Her father wandered into the kitchen wearing a double-breasted navy smoking jacket, black dress trousers, a pleated white dress shirt and a black silk bow tie.

Kate whistled. 'Look at you! Very dapper.'

'Found it in the back of the wardrobe.' He smoothed his hair. 'Do I pass muster?'

'You do indeed.' Kate pushed her fringe away from her face with a floury hand. 'Whereas I look like the wreck of the Hesperus. I'd better get ready. Can you take the sausage rolls out of the oven when the bleeper goes?'

'Consider it done.'

'Thanks, Pa. Where's Rory?'

'Still titivating.' He shook his head. 'He spends more time in the bathroom than Chloe.'

'You know Rory.' Kate stood on her tiptoes and pecked her father on the cheek. He smelt of talcum powder and mothballs. 'When he does make an appearance can you ask him to check there are enough beers in the fridge?'

Her father nodded. 'You run along and make yourself look pretty for this Adam chappie, eh?'

Swallowing the retort that was on the tip of her tongue, Kate ran up the stairs two at a time. She should be used to her father's outlandishly-dated views by now. In his eyes, women were somehow incomplete if they'd failed to find a husband before their thirtieth birthday and children were supposed to have both a mother and a father.

She could still remember the confusion on his face when she'd sat him down, poured him a hefty slug of whisky and announced she was pregnant. It was the hardest thing she'd done in her life.

'But I don't understand,' he'd said. 'You can't be. You're a child yourself.'

'I'm nearly nineteen,' she'd said, twisting the braids in her hair round and round her index finger.

'Who's the father?'

'I - I don't know.'

'Were you attacked? You can tell me, Katie. Because by God I'll have their guts for garters.'

She'd stared at the ground, wishing it would swallow her up. 'I wasn't attacked, Pa. There was a beach party. I was drunk. I don't remember much about it.'

That was a lie. Kate remembered every second. She'd

made friends with two girls from Melbourne staying at the same hostel in Phuket and had tagged along with them to a party on the beach. There had been a bonfire, too many bottles of Singha beer and snorkelling in the dark. Someone had been playing the guitar. She'd sat in her bikini next to a boy called Noah from California whose blond hair had been bleached ivory by the sun. A boy with laughing blue eyes, full lips, broad shoulders and a wash-board stomach and absolutely no idea he now had a seventeen-year-old daughter called Chloe.

He'd left for the Philippines the next day. He'd hugged her and said, 'It was good to meet you, English Kate.' And she'd never seen him again.

Her father had downed his whisky in one and wiped his mouth with the back of his hand. 'What do you want to do?'

'Keep it,' she'd whispered. She'd had no idea about anything else, but she'd been sure of that at least. 'I want to keep it.'

───

When Kate came out of the shower, Chloe was sitting cross-legged on Kate's bed, staring at her phone with a stony expression.

'What's up, love?'

'Annie's not coming. Her mum's car's broken down.'

'What about the bus?'

'The last one left town an hour ago.'

Kate began towel-drying her hair. 'I would offer to pick her up, but people will be arriving at any minute.'

Chloe drew her knees up to her chest and hugged them tightly. 'Do I have to come?' she asked again.

Kate dropped the towel on her bedroom floor and regarded her daughter. Chloe was wearing a tight red top and those tarty black boots Kate hated over her skinny jeans. Her long, golden hair, a few shades darker than her father's, tumbled down her back. Other than a sweep of eyeliner, a matt-black mascara and a slick of clear lipgloss, her face was bare. She had no idea how beautiful she was.

'Mum?' she wheedled.

Kate caved in. Anything for a quiet life. 'All right. Show your face for an hour or so, OK? Then you can hide out in the snug with Ben and the others if you like. Watch a film or something.'

'He won't want to do that.'

'Who won't?'

'Ben.'

'I thought you were friends.'

'We were. But Ben wanted to be more, and I told him I didn't. And so tonight's going to be totally awkward.'

Suddenly everything made sense.

'That's why you didn't want us to hold a party. Why didn't you tell me?'

'I don't have to tell you everything, Mum.'

'You used to.' The words tumbled out before Kate could stop them. She perched on the edge of the bed and touched Chloe's knee. 'Want to talk about it?'

'What's the point? It's too late now. He's coming, isn't he? Just because you fancy his dad. So I don't want to "hide out in the snug with Ben", because he hates my guts. Satisfied?' And she slid off the bed, huffed the way

82

only aggrieved teenagers can, and stomped out of the room, slamming the door.

'Give me strength,' Kate said, rolling her eyes. 'And I would like to point out that I don't fancy his dad,' she added.

Spraying herself liberally with the Paco Rabanne Olympea Eau de Parfum Rory had given her the previous Christmas, she crossed the room to her chest of drawers and ferreted through her underwear drawer until she found her only matching bra and knickers set.

CHAPTER FIFTEEN

CHLOE

Chloe slid her favourite silver bangle onto her wrist, tucked her hair behind her ears, checked her reflection in the mirror one last time and headed downstairs. Already the old house was alive with the murmur of voices and the regular chime of the doorbell as more guests arrived. The air smelt of pine needles and sausage rolls but, even though she hadn't eaten anything since breakfast, Chloe wasn't hungry. Her stomach was too busy tying itself in knots to worry about food.

When she reached the turn in the stairs, she paused, her hand gripping the bannister as she scanned the entrance hall and the drawing room beyond for Ben or his dad. Her grandfather was holding court by the fire. Rory was helping an elderly neighbour out of her coat. Next to the Christmas tree, Pete was chatting to her mum, a bottle of Becks in his hand. He looked different out of his chef's whites. More relaxed. Her mum, who was wearing a sapphire-blue dress Chloe hadn't seen before, was laughing at something he'd said. Not a polite chuckle but a proper belly laugh with her head thrown back and her neck exposed. At the base of her neck, a solitaire diamond necklace sparkled in the candlelight. Chloe was glad to see her mum had pinned her hair up. It suited her. Made her look sophisticated. Elegant. Most of her friends' mums were heading towards their fifties and had saggy faces and thickening waists. Her mum didn't often make an effort, but when she did, she looked amazing, and Chloe felt a flicker of pride.

Her eyes flitted over the rest of the room, resting on a dark-haired man standing at the bottom of the stairs, watching her mum and Pete. She could only see the back of his head from her vantage point, and for a second she thought it was Adam. Her heart fluttered anxiously. But when she looked again, she realised he was too short, too stocky. It was Patrick. She didn't know why her mum had invited him. He was as smug as he was smarmy, and she hated the way he ordered her mum around at work as if she was his personal servant.

Chloe pulled a face as Patrick blew into the palm of his hand and sniffed his breath, before crossing the room. He whispered something in her mum's ear, then took her elbow and guided her away from Pete towards the silver-plated bowl of mulled wine that sat on the sideboard like a witch's cauldron. After pouring a generous helping for her, they chinked glasses, Patrick's face cracking into a self-satisfied smile.

'Tosser,' Chloe muttered under her breath.

'You're not referring to me, I hope,' said a voice at her shoulder. She spun on her heels and came face to face with Adam. 'Sorry, I didn't mean to make you jump.' He dipped his head towards the stairs. 'I was looking for the loo.'

'The cloakroom's downstairs. The door opposite the kitchen.'

'Someone was in that one. Tell me, who's a tosser?' Adam asked, joining Chloe by the bannisters.

'Mum's boss. Patrick. The guy in the DJ.'

Adam followed her gaze. 'The little fella who has her virtually pinned to the wall?'

Chloe nodded. 'He thinks he owns her.'

'In that case, she needs rescuing by a knight in shining armour. Luckily, I know just the guy. But before I do, I wanted to check you're still all right with everything.'

Chloe looked over her shoulder to check no-one was listening. 'The accident, you mean?' she whispered.

'The accident,' he confirmed. 'What did you tell your mum?'

'That my friend Annie's mum gave me a lift home.'

'And she believed you?'

'She had no reason not to.' Because I never lie to her, Chloe almost added. Not until this.

'Good girl.' He placed a hand on her arm for the briefest of seconds. 'I'll go and rescue your mum from Patrick the Tosser, shall I?'

Chloe watched him jog lightly down the stairs. It wasn't until he'd reached the bottom that she thought to call, 'Where's Ben?'

Adam paused, his hand on the newel post. 'Here somewhere,' he said, waving a hand at the drawing room. 'But don't worry about looking for him. Knowing Ben, he'll find you first.'

Chloe made a beeline for the mulled wine. If she had to spend the evening with a boy she'd just dumped she needed a bit of Dutch Courage. She wasn't a big drinker, unlike some of her friends who seemed to treat the consumption of alcohol as a competition to win at all costs. She hated the room-spinning, stomach-flipping, befuddled sensation of being truly bombed. But she wasn't averse to the lightheaded, inhibition-busting merriness of a couple of drinks.

She used the silver-plated ladle to pour herself a glass, sniffed cautiously and took a sip. The mulled wine tasted of cinnamon, oranges and cloves. It was sweet and warm and actually not too bad. She took another slug, and another, enjoying the sensation of the alcohol burning the back of her throat. Before she knew it, her glass was empty, and she filled it again.

'Hello gorgeous,' said Uncle Rory, appearing by her side. 'You couldn't give me a hand with the canapés, could you?'

Chloe set her glass on the table and followed him into the kitchen. Plates of food covered every surface. There was enough to feed a small army.

'I think it's going all right so far, don't you?' Rory said, unwrapping clingfilm from a platter of blinis topped with smoked salmon and creme fraiche.

'I guess.'

'Your mum seems to be enjoying herself, anyway. The suitors are lining themselves up. I was rather hoping Patrick and Adam might hold a medieval-style duel to win her affections.'

Chloe pulled a face. 'I hope they don't. It would be so lame. And anyway, what about Pete?'

Rory popped a blini in his mouth and chewed thoughtfully. 'They're just good friends, aren't they? Unless there's something you're not telling me?'

Chloe shrugged. Rory was probably right. Pete and her mum had been friends since like forever. If he'd wanted to make a move, he would have done by now. 'Adam and Patrick then,' she agreed.

Rory picked up a tray of brie and cranberry filo tarts.

'Ready?' he asked.

'Why do I feel like I'm at work?' Chloe grumbled, picking up the platter of blinis and following him out of the kitchen. But she didn't really mind. It was better to have something to do. It would pass the time quicker. And the mulled wine was starting to work its magic, the alcohol pulsing through her veins, settling the butterflies in her stomach and bathing everything in a rosy glow.

Chloe painted a smile on her face and stepped into the drawing room.

CHAPTER SIXTEEN

CHLOE

After three circuits of the room, the platter was empty save for a forlorn frond of dill and a blob of creme fraiche. Chloe made her way back to the kitchen for a refill. Humming to herself, she pushed the door open.

Sitting at the table was a hunched figure, face hidden by a hood. Long, pale fingers curled around a bottle of beer. Chloe gave a little squeak of surprise.

'Hello Chloe,' Ben said, pushing the hood off his head and staring at her with emotionless eyes. 'How're things?'

'Um, fine thanks. You OK?'

'Oh, you know, I've been dumped by my girlfriend and dragged along by my dad to a crap party full of old biddies in the middle of fucking nowhere because he fancies my ex-girlfriend's mum. But otherwise, yeah, I'm absolutely fantastic.'

Chloe flinched at his naked hostility.

'Nice house, though,' he continued. 'You didn't tell me you lived in a manor house. No wonder you don't want to go out with me.'

'It's not our house. It's my Grandpa's. And it's basically falling down, anyway. But that's not why I don't want to go out with you. I don't care about stuff like that.'

She glanced over her shoulder, hoping Uncle Rory - anyone - would walk in and diffuse the tension in the room. But the hallway was deserted. Ben took a long draught of beer and wiped his mouth with the back of his hand.

'Can I have another?'

'Of course.' She darted to the fridge.

'I may as well get shit-faced. There's nothing else to do.'

'A couple of the guys I work with at The Willows are here somewhere. They're good for a laugh. I could introduce you?'

Ben shook his head. 'Sit and talk to me for a while, Chloe.'

She paused.

He tugged at the neck of his teeshirt.

'As friends. Please?'

'Sure.' What harm could it do? 'I'll get my drink. Won't be a minute.'

The buzz of conversation in the drawing room was growing louder. Someone - Uncle Rory probably - had turned off the main lights, so the fairy lights on the Christmas tree, the glow of the fire and a few strategically-placed candles illuminated the room. Chloe's glass of mulled wine was still on the table by the punch bowl. She downed it in one and poured herself another ladleful. That would be her limit. Any more and she'd pay for it in the morning. On her way back to the kitchen, weaving through the throng by the fire, she brushed past Patrick, accidentally clipping his elbow. His drink slopped over the top of his glass onto the sleeve of his dinner jacket.

He stopped mid-sentence and brushed furiously at his sleeve. Droplets of wine splashed onto the carpet.

'So sorry,' Chloe said, her hand flying to her mouth.

'I've just had the bloody thing dry-cleaned,' Patrick spluttered.

'Come here.' Chloe's mum stepped forwards and plucked the silk handkerchief from Patrick's top pocket. She dabbed at the small red stain on his sleeve. 'That's better.' She folded the handkerchief, popped it back in his pocket and patted his shoulder. 'No harm done.'

Patrick puffed out his chest like a cock pheasant. 'I suppose not. But watch where you're going next time, young lady.'

Chloe glanced at Adam, who had been watching the whole exchange with a look of amusement on his face. He met her eye, winked and mouthed, 'tosser'. Swallowing a giggle, she sashayed back to the kitchen.

Ben had finished his second beer, and Chloe fetched him another before plonking herself down at the table. Three glasses of mulled wine on an empty stomach had left her light-headed and giggly. She smiled brightly.

'How's school?' she asked Ben.

Her mind wandered as he launched into a convoluted story about his history teacher, who hadn't even started a module they needed to cover before their mocks in

January. She rested her chin in her hands and gazed at him. There was no doubt he would be as good-looking as his dad one day, but he was still in that awkward in-between phase when he was neither boy nor man. Narrow shoulders, a crusty-red spot on his chin that he'd obviously picked, a couple of blackheads between his eyebrows that her fingers itched to squeeze and dark brown, slightly too long hair that, frankly, needed a date with a bottle of Head and Shoulders. Chloe tried unsuccessfully to swallow down the snigger that rose in her throat. Ben's eyes narrowed.

'What's funny about the fact that my history teacher's a useless arse?'

'Nothing. Sorry. Just feeling a bit tipsy. I don't know why. I haven't had that much to drink.'

His face cleared. He pushed his chair back and reached into the fridge. 'I don't know why you're worried. Tipsy is good,' he said, handing her a bottle of beer.

'Yeah, tipsy is good,' she repeated, clinking her bottle against his, her earlier resolve melting like ice in a gin and tonic on a hot summer's day. She took a slug of the beer. After the aromatic, syrupy mulled wine, the lager tasted fizzy and sharp and ridiculously refreshing. She tipped the bottle back and drank deeply before smiling coquettishly at Ben. 'But drunk is better.'

CHAPTER SEVENTEEN

KATE

K ate leaned on a sideboard and surveyed the room. Neighbours and friends from the village, usually only ever seen in wellies and Barbours, were rosy-faced and brimming with bonhomie as they knocked back the booze. Her father, settled in his favourite armchair with a glass of brandy, watched the proceedings with a benign smile. Rory was working the room like a pro, topping up drinks and flirting indiscriminately. The kids from work had left shortly before nine, headed for a club in town.

Kate had finally managed to escape Patrick's clutches when he'd disappeared in search of a glass of water. Alone with Adam at last, her shoulders slumped when his phone rang. He listened to the voice on the other end with a set jaw.

He touched her arm, and she felt a fizz of desire.

'Everything OK?'

'Work crisis. I need to make a quick call.' His grip tightened a fraction. 'Don't disappear.'

She held his gaze. 'I'm not going anywhere.'

As she watched him leave the room, Rory appeared by her side with a fresh glass of prosecco. He led her to a small sofa in the window, and they sat in companionable silence. Kate slipped off her shoes and massaged her feet.

'See, everyone's having a whale of a time,' Rory said after a while. He dipped his head towards their father. 'Especially Pa.'

'Yes, you were right,' Kate said. 'It's been fun. Have you seen Chloe?'

Rory made a face. 'I think she might be a teensy bit the worse for wear.'

Kate's head snapped around. 'What d'you mean?'

'The last time I saw her, she was dancing in the kitchen. Trying to, anyway. Don't worry. I made her drink a glass of water and left her in Ben's capable hands.'

Despite her proximity to the fire, a chill ran down the back of Kate's neck.

'Ben?' she said sharply.

Rory nodded. 'Seems like a nice lad. Why are you looking at me like that?'

Because there's something not quite right about him. Because he's got a thing for my beautiful, golden daughter and she doesn't even realise it. Because he makes the hairs on the back of my neck stand up.

But it sounded ridiculous. Paranoid. Ben was a teenage boy with a crush, like a million other teenage boys with crushes the world over. She was over-reacting.

'Like what?' she said.

'It doesn't matter. Chloe's fine, I promise. If you're that worried, go and find her. But before you give her an earful, remember you were seventeen once, too. And not that long ago.'

Kate rolled her eyes, handed him her glass and marched off towards the kitchen. She didn't mind if Chloe was drunk as a skunk. But it was so out of character.

Ben was standing at the kitchen sink, staring out of the window with his hands in his pockets.

'Where's Chloe?' Kate barked.

He turned around slowly and gave a laconic shrug.

'No idea, mate.'

Mate?

She gave a tight smile. 'But she was here in the kitchen with you, wasn't she?'

'She was, and now she isn't,' Ben slurred.

He'd taken his hands out of his pockets and was holding onto the sink. Kate realised he was very, very drunk.

'Did she go to bed?'

He swayed slightly and lifted his bloodshot eyes to meet hers. 'Not with me.'

'What's that supposed to mean?' she snapped, any vestige of patience long gone.

He burped under his breath and turned back to the window. 'Nothing.'

Kate noticed tracks of dirt on his jeans. Clumps of mud on his trainers. 'Have you been in the garden?'

'Chloe said she was gonna puke, so I helped her outside. She was sick on the patio.'

'Is she still out there?' Kate was already halfway to the door with a growing feeling of dread. It was freezing out there.

'Nah.'

'So where the hell is she?' she said.

'She's in bed,' said a voice behind her. Kate whipped around. She opened her mouth to speak, but no words came out.

Adam stepped into the kitchen. 'It's OK, Chloe's fine. Just had a bit too much to drink.'

Kate gripped the back of the nearest chair. 'How did you...?'

'I went outside to make my call and found her in the garden. She'd been sick and had worked herself into a bit of a tizzy. I helped her upstairs and was coming down to find you.'

'I'd better go and see if she's all right.'

'I'll come with you,' Adam said. He turned to his son, who was swaying slightly. 'For Christ's sake, make yourself a coffee and try to sober up before we go home.'

As Kate followed Adam out of the room, she caught Ben glowering at his father, his middle finger raised in a drunkenly deliberate act of defiance.

'I tried to clean her up a bit,' Adam said as they headed upstairs.

'Stupid, stupid girl,' Kate muttered.

'Don't be too hard on her. Getting wasted is a rite of passage. She'll be fine once she's slept it off.'

The bedroom door was closed, but for once, Kate didn't bother to knock.

Chloe was curled on her bed, her hands clutching her

stomach, and her hair fanned out on the pillow. She was still fully clothed but was only wearing one boot which, Kate registered, was also covered in mud. Her pink plastic bin had been left on the floor beside her bed. The room was heavy with the scent of vomit.

Chloe raised her head slowly and when she saw her mum, burst into tears.

Kate, unsure whether she wanted to hug or throttle her daughter, took her hand. It was as cold as stone.

'I feel terrible,' Chloe moaned. She pulled herself to a sitting position. Her eyes widened, and she clamped her hand over her mouth. Quick as a flash, Kate whipped the bin off the floor. She rubbed Chloe's back as she emptied the contents of her stomach onto the balled up paper, pencil shavings and empty crisp packets lurking at the bottom.

'Is there anything I can do?' asked Adam, hovering in the doorway.

'A glass of water? And a flannel from the bathroom?'

He nodded and reappeared seconds later with a warm, wet flannel. Kate smiled her thanks.

'I'll get that water,' he said, disappearing again.

Kate wiped Chloe's face. 'Finished?'

'Think so,' she mumbled.

'Let's get you cleaned up.'

Kate couldn't remember the last time she'd undressed her daughter. Chloe had always been ridiculously independent, even as a toddler, insisting on choosing her own clothes and dressing herself. It made for some interesting sartorial choices. She teamed princess costumes with wellies and woolly hats, and tiny cream jodhpurs with ballet skirts. But if Kate tried to pick out an outfit, there would be tantrums.

This evening there was no resistance as she took off Chloe's boot, pulled down her jeans and eased her red top over her head. Stripped down to her bra and pants, Chloe shivered and wrapped her thin arms around herself.

That's when Kate noticed them. Two angry red marks wrapped around Chloe's wrists like cuffs.

CHAPTER EIGHTEEN

CHLOE

Chloe felt her mum's grip on her hand tighten. 'How did you get those?'

'What?'

'Those marks?'

Her mum held up her left hand. Chloe forced herself to focus on the red weal that circled her wrist. She shook her head slowly.

'Don't remember.'

She didn't like the way her mum was staring at her with a frozen expression on her face. 'Mum, what is it?'

She let go of Chloe's hand and pointed to her own collarbone. 'You've got a mark here, too.' She frowned. 'It looks like a -'

'Looks like what, Mum?'

She gave a little shake of her head. 'Nothing.'

Chloe shivered, and her mum stood up. 'Let's get you cleaned up properly. Can you make it to the bathroom?'

'What about the party?'

'Sod the party. Rory and Grandpa can look after everyone.'

Her mum helped her to her feet and held out her dressing gown. Chloe swayed as she wrapped herself in it. Her head was woolly as if it was stuffed with a whole packet of cotton wool balls, and her arms and legs felt as though they didn't belong to her.

'I feel dizzy.'

'Don't worry. I've got you.'

They made their way across the bedroom floor at a snail's pace. A small knock at the door made Chloe jump.

'It's all right. It's only Adam,' her mum said. 'Come in.'

He pushed the door open and set a glass of water on Chloe's desk. 'Anything else I can do?'

'Perhaps you could find Rory and explain what's happened? Tell him I'll be down as soon as I can.'

'Of course. Then we'd better be off. Ben's not looking too hot, either.' He gave Chloe's mum a rueful smile. 'Teenagers, eh?'

Chloe felt her mum stiffen, but her voice was light when she answered. 'Tell me about it.'

Her mum was treating her like she was about three, running the bath and pouring in copious amounts of bubble bath. Chloe wouldn't have been surprised to find a couple of plastic ducks lurking in the bubbles. She unhooked her bra, stepped out of her pants and peeled off her socks one by one. Slipping into the bath, she tipped her head back, so only her eyes, nose and mouth were above the water.

Her mum flipped down the lid of the toilet seat and sat down. Chloe pushed herself up and stared at the ceiling.

'Tell me what happened tonight, Chloe.'

'I told you. I can't remember.'

'But it's not like you to get drunk like that.'

She was silent because her mum was right. It wasn't.

'Those marks on your wrists,' her mum continued. 'I'm worried…'

Chloe closed her eyes, held her breath and disappeared completely under the water this time, only emerging when the pressure in her chest became unbearable. Her mum was staring at her, worry lines cutting deep furrows in her forehead. She took a breath, stopped, then blurted, 'Did someone hurt you?'

'Don't be ridiculous. Of course they didn't.'

'Are you sure? This is important, Chloe. Tell me what you do remember.'

She forced her mind back to the beginning of the evening. 'I had three glasses of mulled wine, and that was all I was going to have, honestly.' She glanced at her mum. 'Then, Ben wanted to hang out in the kitchen together. He gave me a bottle of beer.'

'And you drank that?'

She could still taste the sharp tang of the lager, the fizz of bubbles on her tongue. She remembered that all right. But then things were hazy. Disorientating. Random pictures flickering like an old black and white cine film…

Dancing around the kitchen table, feeling as though she was floating on air.

Her stomach lurching and a dash for the back door.

Grass squelchy beneath her feet.

Someone holding her hair back while she was sick.

A handkerchief pressed into her hand.

The taste of vomit.

Fingers slipping between her top and her jeans.

Hot breath on the back of her neck.

And then nothing until Adam found her crying in the garden and helped her upstairs.

'Chloe? Did you drink the beer?' her mum pressed.

'Yes.'

'And after? What happened then?'

Chloe chased the flickering images away. Her mind was playing tricks on her. Nothing had happened. She'd got drunk, blacked out and puked up, that was all. Nothing else. Nothing.

'Nothing,' she said, rearing up out of the bath.

Her mum scooped up her pants, socks and bra and dropped them in the wicker laundry basket.

Chloe grabbed the soap and a flannel and began scrubbing at her arms. A thumping headache and an overwhelming weariness had replaced the fuzzy feeling. All she wanted to do was curl up in bed, pull her duvet over her head and slide into oblivion.

'Sweetheart -'

'For God's sake, can you drop it? I was pissed, Mum. Probably fell over and battered my wrists myself. Or someone was helping me to my feet. I've learned my lesson, all right? I won't be getting drunk again anytime soon. So can you please stop fussing and leave me alone? Because. Nothing. Happened.'

Chloe closed her eyes and, to her relief, her mum finally took the hint.

'OK, I'll leave you in peace. But I'm not going to lock the door. And I'll be in my room if you need me.'

Chloe gave the tiniest of nods, and the door closed softly. Letting the water wash over her, she fingered her left wrist. It was red, yes, but it didn't feel sore. Remembering something her mum had said, she peered down at her chest. Just visible below her right collarbone was a reddish mark the size of a fifty pence piece.

Dozens and dozens of tiny burst capillaries under her skin.

A love bite.

Chloe shivered, despite the warmth of the bath.

She prodded it with a finger, hoping it would disappear, but it refused to fade. How the hell had that happened? Had she kissed Ben before she'd stumbled out into the garden to be sick? She ran her tongue over her lips and thought back. Ben had been antsy with her at first, for sure. But once he'd had a few beers, his animosity had disappeared, and they'd had a giggle. In fact, she suddenly recalled, it had been his idea to turn on the radio and dance. But she didn't remember kissing him. She didn't remember kissing anyone.

But that didn't explain the love bite on her collarbone.

A terrifying thought occurred to her. What if something had happened? What if she and Ben had…

A feeling of nausea flowed from her stomach into her oesophagus, and she clamped her hand to her mouth and breathed deeply. Think. But her mind stubbornly refused to co-operate. If she had any memories at all, they were buried so deeply she couldn't even begin to winkle them out.

Think. There would be other signs, wouldn't there? Evidence? The word was so clinical, so evocative of a criminal trial, of a courtroom, that Chloe's already pounding heart beat a little faster.

She tried to marshal her thoughts. She had red marks on her wrists and a love bite. Maybe she and Ben had shared a kiss and a drunken fumble. Ben's hot breath on the back of her neck. Ben's fingers slipping between her top and her jeans. It wouldn't be the first time she'd snogged a boy she hadn't fancied, and it probably wouldn't be the last. It wasn't the end of the world. As long as that was all it was.

Because she'd know if she'd gone all the way, right? Especially the first time. She'd feel different. And she didn't.

CHAPTER NINETEEN

KATE

K ate closed her bedroom door softly, leaned against it and closed her eyes. No matter how tightly she screwed them shut, she couldn't wipe out the expression on Chloe's face as she'd lain in the bath and claimed nothing had happened. She'd looked vulnerable. Hesitant. Lost. Kate stumbled to her bed and sank onto the covers. She had a bad feeling about this. A very bad feeling.

Did she believe Chloe only had a couple of drinks? She'd never had cause to doubt her before. She should have been keeping an eye on her, but she'd been too busy flirting with Adam.

Shame overwhelmed her as she remembered consciously mirroring his body language, laughing a little too loudly at his anecdotes and touching his arm a little too often. It was pathetic. Desperate. What must he think of her? And what kind of a mother was she? Too busy flinging herself at the first good-looking man to cross her path for years to realise her only child was drinking herself stupid and, even worse, was being mauled by a randy teenager.

Kate hoped to God that was all it was. But those marks on her wrists. That love bite. Kate raked her hands through her hair. How could Chloe not know what had happened? Even though Kate had been as high as a kite on that starlit beach in Thailand eighteen years ago, she remembered every kiss, every murmur, every touch.

A shrill toot-toot of a horn brought her back to the present. She walked stiffly to the window. Her father and Rory stood side by side on the driveway waving goodbye to the last of their guests, most of whom were staggering home guided by the beam of their torches. It was gone half eleven. Kate's shoulders drooped at the thought of the inevitable carnage downstairs. But it could wait. She had more important things on her mind.

She stepped out of her room and tapped on the bathroom door.

'Chlo, are you still in there?'

'I'm in my room,' came a muffled voice from further along the landing. Kate found a pair of pyjamas in the airing cupboard and let herself into Chloe's bedroom. Chloe was slumped on her bed, wrapped in a towel and her wet hair sticking to her shoulders like tendrils of seaweed.

'Clean jimjams,' Kate said, holding them out like a peace offering.

'Thanks,' Chloe muttered.

While Chloe pulled on the pyjamas, towel-dried her hair and slid under her duvet, Kate busied herself picking up tea-stained mugs and empty chocolate wrappers.

Chloe's heart-shaped face was bloodless, and there were purple shadows under her eyes as dark as bruises. Kate's eyes slid to the welts on her wrists, hoping she'd imagined them. But there they were, red and angry. Her mind made up, she perched on the edge of the bed and took Chloe's hands.

'How're you feeling?'

'A bit better, thanks. Think it helped, you know. Being sick.'

Kate smoothed Chloe's hair away from her face. 'Good. Now you've sobered up a bit have you remembered anything else about tonight?'

Chloe let out a long breath and shook her head. 'Not this again.'

'That beer Ben gave you.' Kate chose her words carefully. 'Did you watch him open it?'

Chloe frowned. 'Why?' She paused. 'Are you saying you think he drugged me?'

'Of course not!' Kate lied. 'I'm trying to understand why you got so drunk so quickly.'

'Oh my God, Mum. You should hear yourself. You sound totally paranoid. Of course Ben didn't try to drug me. He's a mate.'

Is that all? Kate's fingers traced the red band circling Chloe's right wrist. She looked her daughter in the eye. 'I think we should call the police.'

Chloe snatched her hand away. 'Are you *mad?*' she screeched.

'Just to talk things through with them. They have specialist officers who deal with this kind of thing.'

Chloe's eyes narrowed. 'What kind of thing?'

Kate leaned forwards and touched her collarbone. 'Sexual assault.'

Chloe threw her duvet off and stalked to the window. Her fists were clenched, and when she finally spoke her voice was tight.

'How many times do I have to tell you? Nothing happened. Nothing, nadda, zilch. Ben didn't drug me. He didn't touch me. We danced together, that was all. We were having a laugh. Having *fun*. I know that's a difficult concept for you to understand.'

Kate flinched. It wasn't like Chloe to be so caustic. 'I'm not judging you if that's what you think. You're almost eighteen. You're a young woman. It's up to you what you do with Ben or anyone else for that matter. But no-one should be putting pressure on you to do something that makes you uncomfortable. No-one should be hurting you. What if I rang the police on your behalf? You needn't speak to them. I could explain what happened and they could advise us on what we should do.'

Chloe folded her arms across her chest. 'I'm not doing anything.'

Kate pressed on. 'And if you still can't remember what happened, they could take blood and urine samples to see if you were given anything. I could probably still find the beer bottle. They could test that, too. Then we'd have proof that Ben...'

'Proof that Ben what? Drugged me? Touched me up? So what? It happens all the time. Boys get girls pissed. Boys get off with girls. It's no big deal.'

But Kate wasn't listening. An unwelcome thought had

occurred to her. 'I should never have let you have a bath,' she said.

'*What?*'

'The police doctor could have examined you. Taken swabs.'

'Jes-sus.' Chloe stretched the word to breaking point. Kate's head swivelled in her direction.

'What is it?'

'Are you actually listening to me? Good. Because I'm only going to say this one more time. Nothing bad happened tonight, and Ben would never hurt me. I'm the one who hurt him by telling him I wanted to be friends. So *please* stop going on about it, OK? And don't you dare phone the police.' Her blazing eyes met Kate's. 'Because if you do, I will never, *ever* speak to you again.' She clumped across the room and climbed back into bed. 'Now if you don't mind, I'd like to get some sleep. I'll see you in the morning.' She switched off her bedside light, pulled the duvet under her chin and turned her back to Kate.

'Don't be angry with me, Chlo. I won't call the police, I promise. And I won't go on about what did or didn't happen tonight. But please try to see it through my eyes. I want you to be safe, that's all. It's all I've ever wanted.'

As Kate hooked her little finger through the handles of two mugs they clinked together. The chocolate wrappers crackled as she balled them in her other hand. She nudged the door open with her foot and took one last look back at the huddled form of her daughter.

'Night, sweetheart. Love you,' she whispered into the darkness.

The reply was fainter than the beat of a butterfly's wings.

''Night, Mum. Love you, too.'

When Kate finally arrived downstairs, her father had retired to bed, and Rory was loading glasses into the dishwasher.

'You managed to get rid of everyone?' Kate said, pouring herself a glass of water from the tap.

Rory closed the dishwasher, and it launched into a wash cycle with a comforting rumble. 'They all took the hint once Lover Boy bailed. How's Chloe? Still pissed?'

'Sobered up a bit now.' To her horror Kate's eyes welled with tears. Chloe had looked so vulnerable curled up in her bed, her hair wet and her face bare of make-up, that Kate had wanted to wrap her arms around her and never let her go.

She drank deeply and stared out of the window, trying to compose herself. She couldn't betray Chloe's trust by sharing her suspicions about Ben, even though the desire to talk it over with Rory was immense. She had to pretend everything was fine. She dropped the glass into the washing up bowl and rubbed her eyes. 'I dare say she'll have a whopper of a hangover in the morning.'

'It already is the morning,' Rory said. 'Want a cuppa?'

'I should clear up first.' Kate gestured to the post-party detritus piled high on the kitchen table and worktops.

'It'll wait.' Rory flicked on the kettle and reached for two mugs.

Kate might want to forget the party had ever happened, but she couldn't tell Rory why. She pulled up a chair, swept a couple of baking trays and some paper plates to one side and sat down.

'So,' he said, handing her a mug of tea. 'You were quite the belle of the ball tonight.'

'Do we have to talk about me?'

'Three suitors no less. Adam, Patrick, and Pete.'

'Pete's not a suitor. He's a friend. And Patrick's my boss. He wanted to talk shop.'

'So that leaves the delectable Adam,' Rory said, smiling wickedly.

Kate took a sip of her tea, scalding her lips. Adam had been great, helping with Chloe. At the thought of her daughter she tensed.

'I should check on Chloe.'

'She'll be fine. Talk to me about Adam.'

Kate knew from experience Rory wouldn't shut up until she did. She scratched the back of her neck and sighed. 'He's not interested.'

'He is. Take my word for it. I know a man on the prowl when I see one, sweetie. Did he ask you out?'

'Nope.'

'I'm sure he would have if it hadn't all kicked off with Chloe. Question is, would you have said yes?'

With a denial on the tip of her tongue, Kate paused. Why couldn't she admit to her own brother that Adam stirred feelings in her she'd thought had been buried for years? She was tired of being on her own. She wasn't a bloody nun. OK, so meeting a man hadn't been top of her list of priorities for the last eighteen years - Chloe had always come first. But now Chloe was about to fly the nest, leaving her on her own. Perhaps it was time she put herself first.

She wrapped her fingers around her mug and gave Rory a sheepish smile. 'I think so, yes. If he'd asked. Which he didn't,' she added.

Rory patted her shoulder.

'Don't worry. He will.'

CHAPTER TWENTY

CHLOE

Chloe spent a fitful night tossing and turning, her dreams full of faceless strangers chasing her through woods, waiting for her to trip and fall so they could pin her down by the wrists and...

At half-past three she woke with a start, her legs tangled in the duvet, her hair plastered to her sweaty forehead and her mouth as dry as sandpaper. Desperate for a drink, she pulled on her dressing gown and padded downstairs in search of a glass of water. Max lifted his head as she tiptoed into the kitchen, his tail thudding on the floor. He heaved himself to his feet, tottered over to the back door and whined softly.

'Five minutes,' she told him, unlocking the door and taking an involuntary step back as an icy blast hit her in the face. The security light flicked on as Max made his way to the area of longer grass by the vegetable patch where he preferred to do his business.

Chloe stood at the sink and watched him as she sipped her water. He cocked his leg on the wheelbarrow, then started nosing through the grass before picking up a scent. Soon he was crossing the lawn back and forth like a zigzag stitch on a sewing machine. Grandpa had bought Max as a puppy from a local gun dog breeder who was selling him for a song because he was afraid of loud noises. He might give the appearance of a milk chocolate-coloured predator chasing down his prey, but Chloe suspected that if he ever came face to face with a rabbit he'd run a mile.

'Crazy dog,' she said, downing the last of her water and refilling the glass. Her head was still pounding. She crossed the kitchen to the drawer where they kept all their medicines, rootling through until she found a packet of paracetamol. She popped two out of the blister pack and swallowed them one by one. The security light flicked off, plunging the back garden into darkness, which meant only one thing. Max had followed the rabbit's scent through the hole in the fence into the woods at the bottom of the garden. Chloe slipped her feet into her grandfather's enormous Hunter wellies, picked up the torch by the back door and headed into the night.

'Max!' she called softly, not wanting to wake everyone. As she stepped onto the patio, the security light flooded the garden. Her eyes scanned the lawn, but there was no sign of the labrador.

'Max!' she called again. Still, he ignored her. For a dog that hated loud noise it was ironic he had been blessed with selective hearing. Swearing under her breath, Chloe clumped onto the lawn, her feet sliding like skates on an ice rink in the giant-sized wellies. Gripping the torch in her right hand, she peered into the gloom. 'MAX!'

In the witching hour, the towering pine trees that guarded their house by day loomed like menacing spectres, dark and foreboding. Hearing a rustle to her right, Chloe spun around and trudged towards the sound. As she did, the security light switched off again. 'Bloody light,' she muttered, shining the wavering beam of her torch into the trees. 'Bloody dog.'

She called him again. Another rustle, this time directly ahead. She swung the torch towards the sound, straining to see the dog's outline in the shadows. Nothing. But she could have sworn she'd heard him crashing through the undergrowth with all the grace of a baby elephant. A movement caught her eye, off to the left where a wide grassy track led to the lane behind the house. A shapeless shadow of a figure, bent low. She froze. Who would be in the woods at this time of night? A burglar, come to case the joint? A poacher after Grandpa's rainbow trout? Did people even poach these days? Easier to pop to Sainsbury's, surely? All these thoughts raced through her mind as she stared into the trees, the light of her torch growing weaker as the batteries faded.

Suddenly she was startled by a swishing sound, and something careered into her legs, almost knocking her off-balance. A panting face. Warm, smelly breath. The smiling, solid bulk of their chocolate labrador.

'Jesus, Max. You frightened the life out of me,' she said, grabbing hold of his collar. He licked her hand and then stiffened, his eyes fixed on the trees. His hackles lifted like spikes on a porcupine, and he growled into the darkness. Chloe tightened her grip on his collar, switched the torch off, gave it a shake, and switched it back on again. The struggling beam fell on a squat rhododendron bush, its evergreen leaves glossy in the torchlight, before the batteries finally died.

Letting out a breath she hadn't even realised she'd been holding, Chloe hugged Max. 'It's only a bush, you silly sod.' She tugged the cord from her dressing gown free, looped it through Max's collar and headed towards the house.

All evidence of the party had been removed when Chloe finally emerged from her bedroom, yawning and tousle-haired, shortly after eleven. Her mum was sitting at the kitchen table with a coffee, staring blankly at her phone. She jumped to her feet when Chloe wandered in.

'How are you feeling, sweetheart?'

The concern on her mum's face rankled and Chloe pressed her lips together. 'Fine.'

'Have you remembered anything?'

'Here we go again,' Chloe said under her breath. She marched over to the kettle and flicked it on.

Her mum's gaze settled on Chloe's wrist as she tipped a spoonful of coffee into her favourite mug. Chloe tugged down the sleeve of her dressing gown and glared at her. 'Have I remembered anything about what?'

'Last night.'

'Nope. Where are Grandpa and Uncle Rory?'

'Don't change the subject.'

'Mum, for pity's sake can you please shut up? You're driving me mad.'

Her mum flinched as if she'd been struck. Chloe was immediately contrite.

'I know you're worried about me but honestly, I'm fine. So don't go on about it. Please?'

Her mum sighed. 'All right. But if you do want to talk about it...'

'I don't. But if I do, you'll be the first to know, I promise.'

Her mum nodded, sat down and reached for her mobile.

Chloe narrowed her eyes. 'Why are you staring at your phone as if it's about to spontaneously combust?'

She shifted in her seat. 'I'm not.'

'Is it because you're waiting for a call from someone, by any chance? A *man*?'

'Of course not!'

Yeah, right. Chloe had no idea why her mum was so cagey about Adam. Any idiot could see they had the hots for each other. And Adam was a nice guy. A really nice guy. He'd looked after her last night when she'd been off her head, without patronising or judging her, which was pretty cool when you thought about it.

Chloe poured Shreddies into a bowl. 'You didn't find my bangle when you were clearing up, did you?'

'The silver one?' Her mum shook her head. 'Sorry.'

'I've lost one of my boots, too. I wondered if Max might have taken it.'

Her mum frowned. Chloe sighed. 'I shouldn't have said anything. It's probably under my bed anyway.'

'But -'

Chloe held up a hand. 'Don't start.'

Her mum flung her phone on the table and pushed her chair back. 'I'm just worried about you, but that's fine. Have it your own way. Why don't you take a look outside? Your bangle and boot probably fell off last night *while nothing was happening*. And while you're at it, perhaps you could hose your vomit from the patio? I'm not accidentally stepping in that when I take Max out for his bedtime wee, thank you very much.'

Chloe pulled a face. 'Oh Mum, do I have to?'

'Don't whine. You're seventeen, not seven.' She gave Chloe a tight smile. 'Apparently you're too old for me to care. In which case you're too old for me to clear up after you, too. You can bloody well do it yourself.'

Chloe wrinkled her nose, turned on the outside tap and, holding the nozzle of the hose at arm's length, pointed it in the general direction of the puddle of puke. There was a surprisingly large amount of it, considering she'd hardly eaten anything all day.

Once the jet of water had washed the paving slabs clean, she edged closer, scouring the ground for a glint of silver or the shiny black leather of her missing boot. But there was no sign of either. Just a scrap of white silk caught on the thorns of a rose bush.

Chloe had a sudden recollection of someone pressing a handkerchief into her hand as she'd emptied the contents of her stomach. She remembered the satin-smoothness of it as she'd rubbed it between her thumb and forefinger. Without thinking, she lunged forwards and snatched at the piece of fabric. It was crinkly and stained and smelt unmistakably of vomit.

A feeling of dread clutched her heart, and she gasped.

Because if the handkerchief had been real, maybe the other memories were, too.

CHAPTER TWENTY-ONE

KATE

Two weeks later Kate packed away the last of the Christmas decorations and treated herself to her first bunch of daffodils of the year.

Rory's flight was booked for the following morning, and she was dreading him leaving. He'd kept her sane during that strange period between Christmas and New Year, when everything had seemed out of kilter, and she couldn't put her finger on why.

Not that she'd been home for much of it. Weddings on Christmas Eve and Boxing Day and a party for almost two hundred people on New Year's Eve had meant she'd spent much of the holiday at The Willows. Patrick, whose unpredictability was the only predictable thing about him, had been more capricious than ever. Last-minute changes to menus and seating plans and drinks orders and staffing rotas meant more work, and Kate bore the brunt of it.

At least she'd been so busy she'd had little time to brood about Adam and the fact that she hadn't heard a peep from him - not even a thank you text - since the party. She'd been so close to calling him. Now she was glad she hadn't.

Chloe had spent most of the break in her bedroom, revising for her mocks. Whenever Kate had ventured in, she'd been hunched over her desk with her textbooks open, scribbling furiously. If Kate suggested she take a couple of hours off, Chloe would start ranting about how much work she needed to put in to achieve the three As she needed for university.

Kate hadn't dared mention the night of the party. It was easier to back out of the room and leave her to it.

Her father had also seemed a bit subdued over Christmas, and Kate wondered if he was as worried as she was about Chloe leaving home. She said as much to Rory as she sat on his bed watching him pack.

'You're probably right,' Rory said, expertly folding a shirt and wrapping it in tissue paper before placing it in his suitcase. 'She's going to leave a big hole.'

'Tell me about it.' Kate was silent for a moment, then said, 'Have you noticed he's getting short of breath? And what about that chest pain he had after lunch on Christmas Day? I'm worried it might be angina.'

'The chest pain that miraculously disappeared after he took some anti-acid tablets? He's fine, sis. I'm always telling you he's as strong as an ox. But if you're worried, book him an appointment with the quack.'

'What's the point? He won't go.'

'True.' Rory laid a couple of books on the top of his clothes and zipped up the case. 'All done.'

Kate gazed forlornly at her brother. 'I wish you didn't live so far away.'

He sat on the bed beside her. 'Is that all it is?'

'What d'you mean?'

'You've seemed so down since the party. Still no word from Adam?'

She shook her head. 'Not a dicky bird. He isn't interested.'

'How do you know until you ask? Maybe he's worried you'll give him the brush-off. Why don't you text him and see if he'd like to meet you for a drink? If he doesn't reply or makes an excuse, then I'll admit I'm wrong and shut up about it. But at least you'll have tried. Nothing ventured and all that.'

Kate shook her head.

'One text,' Rory said.

'I don't want to.'

Rory tapped his fingers together as if reaching a decision.

'OK, here's a deal. If I tell the old man about Louis, will you ask Adam out for a drink?'

Kate's eyes widened. 'You'd tell Pa you're married? That you're gay? So I ask Adam on a date?'

'Not just because of that. It's time he knew. I can't keep wimping out.' Rory's voice softened. 'It's not fair on him, and it's not fair on Louis. I don't want to spend another Christmas apart.'

'If you told Pa, you could bring Louis with you next year,' Kate said.

'Or you could all come to us.'

'Christmas on the beach. That would be nice.' She smiled wistfully. 'What the hell. I'll text Adam if you tell Pa. Deal.'

She held out a hand. Rory shook it.

'When are you going to tell him?'

'I'll take him for a pint before lunch. At least he can't start shouting at me if we're in the pub. And they've got one of those defibrillators outside the village hall in case his ticker does give up the ghost.'

***

'Turns out he'd suspected for years,' Rory said, shaking his head in disbelief as he helped Kate lay the table. 'Just because I never had girlfriends at uni and because I spend an inordinate amount of time preening myself in the bathroom.'

Kate burst out laughing. Rory pursed his lips.

'He was quite affronted that I thought he'd be upset. He had a couple of friends during National Service who "batted for the other side", apparently.' Rory raised his eyebrows. 'His words, not mine. And despite that, they were "excellent chaps".' He cleared his throat and launched into an uncannily accurate impression of their father. '"Rory, m'lad, I've heard stories in court that really would make your toes curl. If you prefer men, that's your prerogative. I'm only sad you felt you couldn't tell me sooner."'

Kate squeezed his hand. 'So, at the grand old age of thirty-four, you're properly out. How does it feel?'

Rory grinned. 'Fucking fantastic. And now it's your turn.' He mooched over to the dresser, unplugged Kate's phone from its charger and handed it to her.

'But I need to get lunch.'

'Lunch can wait. We had a deal, remember.'

Kate held her thumb over the home button and opened her contacts. Adam's name was at the top. She chewed a nail.

'What should I say?'

'I don't know. How about, "Hi Adam. It's Kate. Fancy a shag?"'

She tutted. 'Don't be an arse. C'mon Rory, help me out here. I've never asked a man out in my life.'

'Whereas I, my sweet, have asked out dozens. Give me the phone,' he instructed.

Kate watched nervously as he tapped away. 'Show me before you send it!'

He grinned again. 'Too late.'

'Rory!'

She grabbed the phone and stared at the blue speech bubble, an anxious knot forming in the pit of her stomach. What the hell had he written? To her relief, the text was reassuringly banal.

Hi Adam, Kate here. I wanted to wish you and Ben a happy New Year and to see if you'd like to meet up for a drink sometime. Kate.

'Short and to the point,' Rory said. 'Perfect.'

'I guess.' She slipped the phone into her back pocket. 'But I bet I don't hear back from him.'

She was wrong. The phone buzzed as she strained a pan of new potatoes, making her jump and sending a splash of scalding water over her fingers. Yelping in pain, she ran her hand under the cold tap until they stopped throbbing, dried them on a tea towel and stared at the screen.

Hey Kate, you must be a mindreader. I was just thinking about you. A drink sounds perfect. Is 7pm Friday any good? I know a great wine bar. I'll send you the address. Maybe we can grab something to eat afterwards? Adam.

Kate's face broke into a smile, her burnt fingers forgotten.

CHAPTER TWENTY-TWO

CHLOE

Chloe flicked through her economics textbook until she found the chapter she was looking for: *The Measurement of Macroeconomic Performance*. Today, even reading the title gave her a headache. Usually, she loved economics; intellectually demanding, it suited her analytical mind. To excel at the subject, you had to learn the economic theories and apply them to real life. You had to understand human nature and the principle of cause and effect. It was logical and rational. Increase supply and prices will fall. If prices fall, demand will go up. Stick to the theories and everything else will slot into place.

Only real life wasn't that simple, was it? The economy might be mostly reliable, but people were emotional and unpredictable. They hadn't read the textbook, and they didn't follow the rules. They went off-piste and did what the hell they liked. They were a bloody nightmare.

Take Ben. Ever since the party he'd been texting at least a dozen times a day. The first had arrived the morning after when she'd been feeling paranoid and liverish.

Hey Chlo, hope you're not too hungover. xxx

Without thinking, she'd tapped a reply and pressed send before she had thought through the consequences.

I'm sure I'll survive, she'd said, with a grimacing face emoji.

Poor baby. Thinking of you. xxx he'd replied.

And just like that, he was back in her life.

It didn't matter if she told him she was busy or if she ignored him altogether. Still the texts came, as unstoppable as an incoming tide. He seemed to think they were going out, which was scary. Terrifying, in fact. Because she'd made it crystal clear they were nothing but friends when he'd driven her home from school before Christmas, and he was acting like the conversation had never taken place. Sometimes she wondered if the knock to his head had affected his memory. But he'd remembered the night of the party, hadn't he? So why did he think they were back on?

Chloe stared glumly at the textbook. Getting pissed with him hadn't been her finest hour. Dancing with him -

what had she been thinking? If only she'd left the mulled wine untouched, turned down that bottle of beer. Maybe she'd remember what had happened next. Had they kissed? Was it Ben who'd given her a handkerchief and held back her hair while she'd been sick? Was it his hand she'd felt, sliding round her waist? The truth was she didn't know. She'd tried so many times to piece together the shattered fragments of her memory, but her brain refused to co-operate. The evening was still a blur.

Sometimes she wondered if she should come straight out and ask him what, if anything, had happened between them. Common sense told her it must have been Ben and that was why he now assumed she was his girlfriend.

So why didn't she pick up the phone and ask him outright?

Perhaps it was easier not to know.

Guilt stopped her from dumping him again. What if he flunked his A-levels and it was all her fault? She didn't want that on her conscience. And she couldn't risk the inevitable fall-out impacting her own grades. Kingsgate had sent her a conditional offer, and she needed three As. She knew she could get them, too, if she worked hard and stayed focused. What she didn't need were any distractions.

What harm would it do if she let him carry on believing they were an item until the exams were over? It was only for five months. She could cope with the text messages. If he suggested meeting up, she'd tell him she was too busy revising. Which would be true. Then, once their exams were over, she could dump him properly. Problem solved.

Her mind made up, Chloe set her phone face down on her bedside table, far enough away that she wouldn't be tempted to keep checking for notifications. She picked up her pen, wrote MACROECONOMIC INDICATORS in her notebook in capital letters, and underlined it twice. She twirled a strand of hair around her finger and then recited every indicator she could remember. 'Real GDP; real GDP per capita; retail price index; measures of productivity and unemployment; the balance of payments.' She scribbled them down, checked them against the textbook and nodded her head in satisfaction.

She had no problem remembering her schoolwork. It was a shame she could remember sod-all about the night of the party.

An hour later there was a tap at the door, and her mum poked her head into her room.

'You busy?'

Chloe put down her pen and massaged the palm of her writing hand.

'No more than normal. Why, what's up?'

Her mum pushed the door closed behind her, and sat on the bed.

'I feel like I've barely seen you all weekend. How's the revision going?'

'Slowly.' Chloe looked pointedly at her notes, but her mum didn't take the hint.

'Rory's texted to say he's landed.'

'That's good.'

'And he sends his love.'

'Mmm.'

'I'm going to miss him.'

'Me too.' Chloe picked up her pen and started doodling in the margin of her notebook.

Her mum paused, then stared at her nails.

'And I can't remember if I told you that I'm out Friday night.'

'Working?'

'I'm meeting Adam for a drink.'

Chloe's head jerked up. 'You definitely didn't tell me that.'

'You don't mind, do you?'

'Why would I? He's a nice guy.'

Her mum gave a self-conscious smile. 'He is. What d'you think I should wear?'

Chloe sighed. A girly chat with her mum was the last thing she needed. 'I don't know. Your black jeans with the teal cardi and that scarf Rory bought you for Christmas?'

'I wondered if you fancied a shopping trip tomorrow. I'll treat you to a new outfit if you help me find something to wear.'

Chloe gestured at her notes. 'Sounds great but I can't. You know my mocks start next week. I'm already so behind with my revision.'

'A couple of hours' shopping isn't going to make a difference,' her mum said. 'A break would do you a power of good. You're working too hard.'

How else was she supposed to get three As, exactly? It was so bloody frustrating. Everyone assumed that because she was bright, she didn't have to put in the work. If only.

Across the room, her mobile buzzed with an incoming call. Her mum glanced at the screen as she reached for the phone and handed it to Chloe.

Chloe knew by the way her mum's eyes widened that it was Ben, and her heart sank. She ignored her phone's entreaty to 'slide to answer' and pushed it to the back of her desk.

'Aren't you going to answer that?'

'I told you, I'm *trying* to revise!'

'Why is Ben calling you?'

She shrugged. 'No idea.'

Her mum frowned. 'You told me you were friends.'

'We are.'

'But at the party -'

Chloe's voice hardened. 'What about the party?'

'You and he…'

'Nothing happened. You know that.'

'So why's he phoning you?'

'For God's sake, Mum, I don't know. Maybe he wants to talk about the fact that you and his dad are going on a date and that he might end up being my step-brother.' She let out a strangulated noise, halfway between a snigger and a sob, before she could stop herself.

Her mum gave her a pained look. 'It's just a date, Chlo. You said you didn't mind.'

Chloe felt a wave of irritation rise up inside her. Why couldn't everyone leave her alone? All she wanted was to keep her head down, ace her exams and take up her place at Kingsgate University. Was that too much to ask? She drew a long breath in and released it slowly.

'Of course I don't mind.'

Her mum nodded, smiled briefly, and stood. 'I'll leave you in peace.'

Once she was safely out of the door, Chloe picked up her phone and glared at the screen and the missed call icon from Ben.

'And you can fuck right off, too,' she growled, powering the phone off and hurling it onto her bed.

CHAPTER TWENTY-THREE

KATE

The prospect of walking into the wine bar on her own sent the knots in Kate's stomach writhing like eels. She hadn't been this nervous in years. What if Adam wasn't there? What if he stood her up? She'd have to nurse a solitary glass of wine and stare at her phone while conversations hummed and laughter rang out around her. It would be mortifying. She peered harder through the window, willing Adam's familiar features to swing into focus. But an opaque layer of thick condensation made it impossible to see anyone. She had no idea if he was there or not.

Only one way to find out. Her hand closed around the door handle. As she gave it a push, she felt a hand on her shoulder, and she gasped.

'Did I make you jump?' Adam said, his eyes searching hers.

'Of course not.' She smiled. 'I was worried I was late. I couldn't find anywhere to park.'

'You're here now.' He reached up and held the door

open while she scuttled inside. 'I've asked Marco to reserve a table in the window for us.'

Kate shrugged off her coat and pulled off her gloves, finger by finger. A man greeted them and showed them to a round table in the bay window.

'Marco, this is my friend Kate. Marco owns the place.'

'For my sins.' Marco winked at Kate and produced a navy leather-bound wine list which he offered to Adam. 'What can I get you?'

'Kate, what d'you fancy - red or white?'

'Red would be lovely, thanks.'

Adam waved the wine list away and leaned back in his chair. 'I think tonight is a cause for celebration, don't you? Let's push the boat out. What do you recommend, Marco?'

The restaurateur's eyes crinkled. 'You want something extra special?'

'Why not?'

Marco smiled. 'Adam likes to think he's a bit of a connoisseur.' He raised an index finger. 'I have just the thing. I'll be right back.'

'A connoisseur, eh?'

Adam laughed. 'He means I'm good for business. My office is down the road, so I tend to use the place for client lunches.'

'And dates?' she asked, suddenly curious.

Their eyes met, his gaze lingering for a second longer than felt comfortable. 'Occasionally, yes.'

Kate fiddled with a coaster on the table. *Serves you right for asking*, said the voice inside her head. Of course he dated women. Not only was he charming, funny and ridiculously good-looking, but he was educated and articulate to boot. He had his own law practice and, she suspected, had brought up his son single-handedly. She was both astonished and flattered that he'd looked twice in her direction, let alone wanted to meet for a drink.

Marco reappeared with a starched white napkin draped over one arm and a bottle of red wine with a buff-coloured label in the other.

'The 2015 Masseto,' he said reverentially, holding the bottle for Adam to inspect.

Adam raised his eyebrows. 'I wasn't expecting *that*.' He turned to Kate. 'It's one of Italy's Super Tuscan wines, made from Merlot grapes grown on the Masseto vineyard, a seven-hectare former clay quarry on the Tuscan coast. Aged in French oak barrels and blended by the famous winemaker, Axel Heinz, if I remember correctly.'

Marco nodded, and Kate gaped.

'How do you know all this?'

'Wine is a bit of a hobby of mine. I've been a collector for the last five years or so. I've been drinking it a lot longer than that, of course. But I've never been lucky enough to taste *this*.'

'And is tonight the night for the Masseto?' Marco asked.

'Tonight is indeed the night,' Adam said, smiling at Kate until she flushed with pleasure.

For the next few minutes, Marco busied himself fetching glasses and making a show of opening the wine. He poured an inch into a glass and Adam swirled the dark red liquid around before taking a sip. Closing his eyes, he sighed in appreciation.

'Well?' Marco asked.

'Complex and fruity with notes of cherry and... mulberry,' Adam said. 'Exquisite.'

Marco's head bobbed up and down. 'Exquisite, yes. Or as we Italians would say, squisito.' He picked up Kate's glass.

'A small one for me, thanks, Marco. I'm driving.'

'I could order you a taxi?' Adam offered.

'That's so kind, but I need my car in the morning.' She sipped her wine. It was smooth and soft, but whether she could tell it apart from a £10 bottle of Merlot from Waitrose in a blind tasting was another matter.

Realising Adam was looking at her expectantly, she smiled. 'Delicious.'

'Good.' He nodded his approval. 'Marco? We'll have a platter of antipasto, please.'

The restaurateur bobbed his head again and headed towards the bar. Conscious that they were finally alone, Kate fished around for something interesting to say that didn't involve weddings, grumpy teenagers or cantankerous octogenarians, which was, after all, her life in a nutshell.

Luckily Adam saved her.

'So, I'm curious. Why did you decide to have a baby instead of going to university?'

She winced. 'It doesn't sound great, does it?'

'I'm not judging,' Adam said.

'It wasn't a conscious decision.' She shrugged. 'Chloe wasn't exactly planned.'

He watched her steadily. 'I guessed as much. What happened?'

'I met someone in Thailand when I went travelling after my A-levels.'

'Do you still keep in touch?'

'It was a... one-night stand. I never saw him again.'

'He doesn't know about Chloe?'

She took another sip of wine. 'No.'

'And you've never tried to find him? For Chloe's sake?'

'There's not much to go on. All I know is that he was called Noah, and he was from California.'

'And there are probably more than a few Noahs in California,' Adam said.

'Exactly. And Chloe's never said she wants to track him down. My dad and Rory are a big part of our lives, so it's not as though there aren't any male role models. I know we're hardly a conventional family, but it seems to work. Most of the time, anyway.'

They were silent as Marco arrived with a huge oval plate of creamy mozzarella balls, artichokes in olive oil, cherry peppers stuffed with anchovies and tuna, slivers of prosciutto and salami, green and black olives as shiny as exotic jewels and garlicky bruschetta.

Olive oil dribbled down Kate's chin as she bit into an artichoke. She brushed it away with her napkin and asked the question that had been niggling her for weeks. 'What about you? Is Ben's mum on the scene?'

Adam cleared his throat, put down his fork and picked it up again. 'She left me when he was eight months old. Walked out one day and never came back.'

Kate caught her breath. 'That's terrible.'

'It was a lucky escape if I'm honest. Daisy had always been mentally fragile, but after Ben was born the anxiety took over her life. She became completely paranoid and delusional. I tried to help her as much as I could. They put her on anti-anxiety medication and she saw countless therapists, but nothing made a difference. Turns out some people either can't or don't want to be helped.' Adam's eyes glassed with unshed tears. Kate touched his hand.

'That's terrible. It must have been awful, coping with that and a newborn baby.'

'You don't know the half of it. Every time I came home from work, I wondered what I'd find. Would she have managed to drag herself out of bed? Would there be any food in the house? Was Ben still wearing the babygrow I'd left him in that morning? Would they even be there?' His jaw tightened, and he shook his head as if chasing the memory away. 'Anyway, let's not spoil a very expensive bottle of wine talking about that crazy bitch.' He speared a cherry pepper and smiled at Kate. 'Let's talk about us.'

She smiled back. 'Is there an us?'

He clasped her hand across the table. His touch was like a jolt of pure electricity that sent her senses reeling.

'I'd like there to be,' he said softly, tracing circles on the inside of her wrist with his thumb, round and round until she was dizzy with longing. She couldn't remember the last time she'd felt so alive. He increased the pressure on her wrist. 'If that's what you want?'

'I do,' she said breathlessly.

CHAPTER TWENTY-FOUR

KATE

The house was in darkness as Kate let herself in the front door just after midnight. She was far too wired to sleep, so she made herself a camomile tea and sat at the kitchen table wishing she had someone to analyse her date with other than a slightly overweight labrador who thought everyone was amazing, even the vet. She counted on her fingers. Midnight here meant it was eleven in the morning in Sydney. If she was lucky, she might catch Rory at home.

She propped her phone against her mug and Face-Timed him. He answered on the third ring.

'How did it go?'

'Hello to you, too, brother dearest.'

'Never mind that. How did it go?' he said again.

'Um. All right, I think.'

'You think?'

She shrugged her shoulders. 'I'm a bit out of practice, aren't I?'

'Well, you'd better tell me all about it, and I'll decide.'

'Have you got time?'

'Of course I've got time. I'm waiting for Louis to finish working so we can pop out for brunch.' He swivelled the phone around to Louis, who was tapping away at his laptop. He looked up and waved.

'Hey, Kate, how's it going?'

'Good, thanks Louis,' she said, blowing him a kiss.

Rory's face reappeared on the screen. He raised a quizzical eyebrow. 'Come on then. Tell all.'

'Well, the wine bar was nice, and we had some lovely antipasto, and Adam ordered a posh bottle of wine. He's a bit of a connoisseur.'

'Oh yeah?' Rory also held pretensions of being an expert because he'd once signed up to a wine plan with Laithwaites. 'What was it?'

'Um, it was Italian and began with an M.' Kate pictured the buff-coloured label. 'Masseto, that was it.'

'Flash git,' Rory said. 'That must have cost at least five hundred quid.'

The colour drained from Kate's face. 'Are you having a laugh?'

He shook his head. 'One of the senior partners in London bought a crate of the stuff as an investment a few years ago. Six bottles set him back over three grand.'

'Bloody hell.'

'Bloody hell indeed. He must really want to get in your knickers.'

'Rory!'

'What did you talk about?'

'The usual stuff. Our favourite books and films, his

job, the kids, Kingsgate Uni. Did I tell you he went there, too?'

'No. But it all sounds rather dull.'

'Not at all. He's a really interesting man. He's done so much. Much more than me, anyway.'

'Don't do yourself down. So, after you'd sunk the bottle of very expensive wine, did he call you a taxi?'

'I was driving so I only had one glass. He offered to, though. And he walked me to my car.'

'He didn't invite you home to show you his legal files?'

'No, he didn't!'

'And he didn't kiss you?'

Kate was silent.

'But you wanted him to, right?'

'Tell him it's none of his business!' came Louis' disembodied voice.

Kate smiled. 'It's none of your business,' she agreed. 'But yes, I did.'

'Did he ask you on another date?'

The smile slid from her face, and she shook her head. 'Do you think I did something wrong?'

'I'm sure you didn't. He's probably playing it cool. But two can play at that game.'

'Christ, it's like being sixteen again, only I've forgotten all the rules. Are you saying I shouldn't contact him?'

'Absolutely not. Men attach value to people and things they perceive to be unattainable. They are goal-focussed and like a challenge. Don't worry, he'll be in touch. And when he does, pretend you're busy. He'll be as keen as mustard, mark my words.'

Kate stifled a yawn. 'I need to hit the sack. Thanks for

the chat. I had no idea you were such a relationship guru, but I'll take your advice and let him do the running. At least I can blame you if it all goes horribly wrong.'

Rory tutted. 'Don't be such a pessimist. You're allowed to have some fun. Let me know when he calls you, OK?'

They ended the call, and Kate rinsed out her mug. She felt curiously deflated. It had been a lovely evening, and she'd enjoyed Adam's company. He was charming and erudite, the kind of man she'd have probably ended up marrying if she'd trained as a solicitor and had a proper career. If she hadn't met a beach bum called Noah and had a baby at nineteen.

Would she have been any happier if she'd chosen a more conventional path, she wondered as she followed Max into the moonlit garden, dew soaking the toes of her suede boots. It wasn't that she was unhappy. But as Chloe grew up and needed her less and less, she was feeling increasingly unfulfilled. Stuck in a rut, still living in her childhood home with a job that bored her witless. And she was *lonely*.

Trying hard not to wallow in self-pity, she locked up and turned off the kitchen light and, clutching a hot water bottle, made her way upstairs. As she did, she passed the collection of photos she'd taken of Chloe every September on the first day of the school year. They were as familiar to Kate as the touch of the smooth oak bannister or the squeaky tread on the second to last stair. She passed them dozens of times every day as she carried baskets of washing downstairs or piles of ironing back up.

She paused by the photo of Chloe on her first day at primary school. Staring at her daughter's impish grin, she was transported back in time. The day was etched in her memory. Plaiting Chloe's hair, boiling an egg and cutting toast soldiers for her breakfast, making sure she remembered her Dora the Explorer lunchbox. Even aged four, Chloe couldn't wait to start school while Kate had been filled with trepidation, wondering how she would fill the empty hours between nine and three.

Chloe had always lived life to the full. It was in her genetic make-up. Noah's genes, Kate supposed. Because Chloe's sense of adventure certainly didn't come from her.

She carried on up the stairs, past pictures of Chloe through her primary school years when her smile was wide and uncomplicated. Throughout her tweens, with the unmistakable hint of teenage rebellion in the way she stared at the camera, one hand on her non-existent hips. Her first day at grammar school, in a blazer two sizes too big because Kate was skint and needed it to last.

Chloe had been a grade A student throughout secondary school. One of those kids who found everything easy and took life in their stride. Other mums told Kate they wished their daughters were 'more like Chloe'. Kate counted herself lucky that her daughter's unconventional start to life hadn't held her back.

Thirteen-year-old Chloe had train-track braces and livid red spots. Fourteen-year-old Chloe had discovered Clearasil and realised a heavy fringe didn't suit her. Fifteen-year-old Chloe spent half an hour every morning straightening her wavy hair, so it fell in a sleek, shiny curtain over her shoulders. Sixteen-year-old Chloe would rather spend longer in bed, so had learned to love her curls. Seventeen-year-old Chloe…

Kate stopped abruptly, staring at the space where the photo of seventeen-year-old Chloe should have been. She checked the floor in case it had fallen off the wall. It hadn't. She peered at the gap on the wall, half expecting to see a hole in the ancient plaster where the picture hook and Rawlplug had fallen out. But the picture hook was still there, and when she gave it a tentative tug, it didn't move a millimetre. Had the photo been there on her way out? She hadn't noticed. Her head had been too full of her date with Adam.

The grandfather clock in the hallway struck one with a melancholy chime, and she shivered with unease. She clutched the hot water bottle and told herself there was probably a perfectly simple explanation. Perhaps the photo had blown off in a draught and her father had picked it up and put it somewhere safe. Perhaps Chloe had taken it down to copy for a Throwback Thursday Instagram post.

Because there was no other explanation for a photo of Chloe to go missing. Was there?

CHAPTER TWENTY-FIVE

CHLOE

The darkness was suffocating, so dense, so *absolute*, that it threatened to swallow her up. Chloe sprinted through the trees, terror granting her super-human speed. Branches whipped her face, stinging like the slash of a thousand knives, and her breath came in short, panicky gasps. Behind, the shapeless figure who haunted her nightmares crashed through the under-growth. Ahead, she could see a pool of yellow light. If she could reach the light, she would be safe.

A hand grabbed her shoulder. She screamed, but no sound came out. The grip on her shoulder tightened, and as her eyes snapped open, she recoiled in shock.

'Chloe, are you all right?'

'Jesus, Mum, you scared the living daylights out of me.' Chloe sat up in bed and pulled the duvet up to her chin, her heart still pounding in her ribcage. 'Why are you waking me up? It's Saturday.'

'You're working, remember. You're starting at ten. You know what Patrick's like if you're late.'

'Shit.' Chloe had forgotten she'd signed up for an eight-hour shift at The Willows. It had seemed like a good idea when she was flat broke after Christmas. Now she'd rather eat her own toenail clippings.

'Shit,' she said again, shooting her mum a filthy look as if it were all her fault. 'Shit, shit, *shit*.'

'Think of the money.'

'The money's crap. Four pounds thirty-five pence an hour. It's slave labour. After Patrick's docked me half an hour for lunch I'll barely make thirty-two measly quid.'

'I did say you should have got a job at the pub,' her mum said evenly. 'But you knew best. I'll leave you to it.' She picked up a dirty pair of leggings from the floor and stopped by the door. 'By the way, you know your latest school photo? The one I took on your first day in Year 13?'

'What about it?'

'It's not on the wall. Have you taken it?'

'Why would I have taken that? It's terrible.'

'Right. It must have been Grandpa. I'll ask him.' Her mum gave her a bright smile. 'Would a boiled egg and soldiers cheer you up?'

'Christ Mum, I'm not three! I'll do myself some toast, all right? But let me have a sodding shower first.'

A pained expression crossed her mum's face. She marched out of the room, muttering something about teenagers under her breath.

Chloe reached for her phone and scrolled half-heartedly through her Instagram feed. The fact that all her friends seemed to be having a way better time than she was, drinking shots at parties and snogging boys, did nothing to improve her mood. Annie had updated her profile picture with a cryptic photo of two pairs of feet resting on a coffee table. Her eyes narrowing, Chloe stabbed out a text.

Seen your new Insta profile pic. Is there something you need to tell me????

She didn't have to wait long for a reply.

You know that lad Luca from the high school? He and I hooked up at Liv's party the other night.

What party?

I'm sure I told you about it?

Chloe was sure she hadn't, but she probably wouldn't have gone anyway so close to their mocks. She was still way behind with her revision.

Yeah, you probably did. So are you guys going out or what?

He hasn't actually asked me, but we're going to the cinema

and Nando's tonight, so I think so, yeah. Followed by three laughing emojis.

Cool, Chloe typed. Then, not wanting to sound as churlish as she felt, added, You go, girl! Xx

She threw off the duvet and padded across the room to the radiator to retrieve her towel. Her phone pinged again, and she glanced at the screen.

Thought you should know that bloke Ben is following me on Insta. But not just me. Liv and Meera too. He's liking and commenting on loads of our posts like he's our bestie or something. It's all a bit creepy TBH. You defo dumped him, right?

Chloe hesitated before she replied, Yeah, I did.

Not sure he's got the message! Be careful, hun. He's a right nutjob if you ask me. xx

Chloe's bad mood had deepened by the time she stalked up the drive to The Willows an hour later. Annie's words rang in her ears. *It's all a bit creepy... Be careful.* She was blowing it out of all proportion, of course. Ben was about as dangerous as a kitten, but she was right about one thing. He hadn't got the message.

When he'd tried to FaceTime her while she'd been drying her hair, Chloe had been so overcome with fury she'd been a beat away from hurling her phone at the wall. If it wasn't for the fact that it was only a few months old and wasn't insured she would have done, no question. Instead, she'd turned it off and left it in a drawer. Out of sight, out of mind.

And now, as if things couldn't get any worse, she had eight hours of bobbing and bowing like a bloody skivvy to a load of entitled, pissed-up wedding guests ahead of her. She'd be too knackered to get any revision done afterwards, so she'd probably fail all her exams and lose her place at Kingsgate. Which would mean she'd be stuck at home in a dead-end job for the rest of her life, like her mum. Full fucking circle.

Aware she was already five minutes late, Chloe chanced her arm and slipped in through The Willows' imposing front door. Checking the coast was clear, she crept through the vast entrance hall, past the Great Hall and towards the kitchens in search of the wedding planner, Lola.

Before she'd taken a couple of steps, she almost collided with the puffed-up chest of Patrick. He drew himself up to his full height - about five foot eight, Chloe thought bitchily - and glared at her with his piggy eyes. Today was obviously a Shirley day.

'You're late.'

'Sorry,' Chloe muttered. 'I'll make it up at the end of the shift.'

'You will,' he agreed, appraising her. He took a step forwards and reached for her neck. Before she had a chance to react, he straightened her tie and murmured, 'That's better.' He was so close she could smell the spearmint on his breath. She shivered with revulsion and backed up against the wall. The chalky plaster was cold against the palms of her hands.

'Where's Lola?'

'Lola?' Patrick echoed, still staring at her.

Chloe's skin crawled. 'I should tell her I'm here. See what needs doing.'

Patrick finally stepped out of her way. 'She's in the storeroom,' he said shortly.

Chloe resisted the impulse to leg it out of there. Instead, she turned slowly and walked along the hall to the fire doors at the back of the house.

As she heaved the doors open, Patrick bellowed after her. 'Make more of an effort next time, Chloe. And don't let me catch you sneaking in through the front doors ever again.'

CHAPTER TWENTY-SIX

KATE

K ate's father stared at her with knotted eyebrows.
'Why on earth would I have taken a photo of Chloe off the wall?'

'Because it's not there and I haven't touched it, and Chloe hasn't touched it, and you're the only other person apart from the dog who lives here,' Kate said, trying and failing to hide the impatience in her voice. She breathed slowly. 'I wondered if it had fallen down and you'd put it somewhere safe.'

He shook his head slowly. His hair was rumpled, and flecks of white stubble gave his jowls a stippled appearance. Sitting in bed with his faded dressing gown draped over his shoulders like a shawl and the creases of sleep yet to leave his face, he looked frail and old. She probably shouldn't have marched into his room unannounced and given him the fourth degree about the photograph. But she'd spent all of Saturday fretting about it and hadn't been able to sleep for worrying about who might have taken it... and why.

'It's all right, Pa. I'm sure it'll turn up.' She laid a hand on his shoulder. 'Would you like a cup of tea?'

'That would be nice thank you, Katherine. Perhaps you could bring me the paper while you're at it?'

As she crossed the landing, Kate knocked on Chloe's door.

'I'm making Grandpa a cup of tea. Would you like one?'

'Yes, please,' came a faint answer.

Kate pushed open the door. Chloe, still in her pyjamas, was already at her desk, which was cluttered with a pile of revision notes.

'Early start?' Kate said.

'Yeah, well, yesterday was a complete wash-out, wasn't it?'

One of the other waitresses had called in sick, and Chloe had ended up working till ten. When she'd arrived home, she'd been in a foul mood. Kate had stayed out of her way.

'When's your first exam?'

'Economics, tomorrow.' Chloe groaned, dropping her head in her hands. 'I'm so not ready for it.'

'You always say that, and you always do brilliantly. You'll be fine. And even if you're not, they're only mocks. You still have four months until the real thing. Why don't you have a shower while I make you some tea and a bacon sandwich and you can have a working breakfast.'

Chloe raked her fingers through her hair. She'd bitten her nails to the quick.

'Thanks, Mum.'

Downstairs, Kate let Max out for a wander in the

garden and busied herself making tea and bacon sandwiches. As she made her way back upstairs with the breakfast tray, she stared at the gap on the wall where Chloe's photo should have been and did her best to ignore the flutter of anxiety in her chest.

The hum of the electric shower seeped through the walls of the old house. She pushed open the door to Chloe's bedroom without knocking and set the tray on the floor while she shifted a couple of books on the desk to one side. A text notification lit up Chloe's phone. Before she could stop herself, Kate's hand shot out. Her eyes widened as she read the message.

ARE YOU THERE? the text demanded in angry capital letters. Without thinking, she pressed her thumb to the home button but she was met with a warning that her fingerprint was not recognised and an instruction to enter the passcode.

Bugger.

As Kate held the phone, another text message dropped onto the screen.

WHY WON'T YOU TALK TO ME???

And another.

YOU HAVE NO IDEA WHAT YOU'RE PUTTING ME THROUGH.

. . .

And another.

I'M GOING THROUGH HELL HERE.

The screen lit up with a dozen more messages, each more desperate than the last.

IT'S KILLING ME.

YOU'RE RIPPING MY HEART IN TWO.

JUST PICK UP THE FUCKING PHONE!

BECAUSE YOU KNOW I LOVE YOU CHLOE.

AND I KNOW YOU LOVE ME TOO.

The door creaked open, and Kate dropped the phone onto the desk. She shoved it under a pile of books and bent down to pick up the tray, glad to be able to hide her face. Chloe, dressed in her favourite jeans and an oversized jumper, groaned.

'That smells delicious. I hadn't realised how hungry I was. Thanks, Mum.'

'It's no trouble,' Kate said. 'Your phone was buzzing away. Someone must be trying to get hold of you.'

Chloe stiffened, and her eyes darted to the desk where her phone was half-hidden under a history textbook. 'Did you see who?'

Kate paused. The texts were disturbing, to say the least, and it was glaringly obvious who'd sent them. They had to stop and stop now. But Chloe would have a fit if she knew Kate had been snooping. Perhaps there was another way she could tackle this without losing her daughter's trust.

'No,' she said before she could change her mind. 'I didn't.'

At the door she stopped, her hand on the frame. 'Chlo, you would tell me if you were worried about anything, wouldn't you?'

Their eyes met for a second before Chloe looked away.

'You know the only things I'm worried about are my exams. So, if you don't mind, I'd better get on with my revision.'

If Chloe had been about to confide in her, the moment was lost.

'I'll leave you to it,' Kate said.

'Thanks. And Mum?'

'What, love?'

'Thanks for the bacon sarnie. It's lush.'

Not caring that Rory would wholeheartedly disapprove, Kate composed a text to Adam.

Hi Adam, it's Kate here. First, I wanted to thank you for a lovely evening. I had a great time. Second, I was wondering if I could return the compliment. Our local pub does a mean steak and ale pie. Friday night? My treat this time!

She added a smiley face and pressed send before she could change her mind.

Max whined softly in his basket. Kate scratched his ear.

'I refuse to sit and stare at my phone like a lovesick kid waiting for Adam to text back,' she told the dog, as he gazed adoringly into her eyes. 'Come on, Maxie, let's go for a walk, shall we?'

Max leapt out of his bed and circled round her in a frenzy of excitement. Shrugging on her coat, Kate found his lead and pulled on her wellies. She followed Max across the back garden and through the broken fence into the woods.

After endless wet and windy days, the sun had finally made an appearance in a cloudless sky so blue it reminded Kate of the sapphire in her mother's engagement ring.

She felt her spirits lift as Max bounded through the trees, his tail tracing circles in the air as he sniffed out rabbity smells. Old Man's Beard festooned bramble bushes, and underneath a twisted yew tree, a clump of snowdrops had pushed their way through the decaying leaves.

Kate reached into the back pocket of her jeans for her phone to take a picture of the delicate white, bell-like flowers, but realised she must have left it on the kitchen table. Would Adam have texted her by the time she returned, she wondered. Did he even want to meet her again? She thought the evening had gone well, but it was hard to know for sure. He hadn't suggested a second date, nor had he tried to kiss her. Not even a chivalrous peck on the cheek. And Rory was right. She'd been disappointed he hadn't.

Perhaps he liked her as a friend, nothing more. But that was fine by her. Sex only complicated things anyway. And she had other more important things on her mind. Like Ben, for instance. Ben, who had latched onto Chloe like a leech, who had got her drunk so he could...

Kate threw a stick for Max, who tore after it like an ungainly gazelle.

If Adam did get in touch, should she mention her concerns about Ben? And if so, what the hell would she say? *Your son's infatuated with my daughter. Please tell him to back off.*

At first, she'd dismissed Ben as harmless. A teenage boy with an innocent crush. But what really happened the night of the party? Chloe swore Ben hadn't assaulted her. Was she telling the truth, or protecting him? And the texts had left Kate feeling increasingly uneasy. At what point did a crush become an obsession?

Chloe said she liked Ben as a friend, nothing more. The irony wasn't lost on Kate. Maybe that's how Adam felt about her. Max dropped his stick at her feet and woofed excitedly. She hurled it through the trees, her shoulder muscles screaming in protest. The stick landed in the middle of a rhododendron bush. Max dived in after it until only his tail was visible.

'Max!' she called, worried his collar would catch on one of the branches. He gave a muffled woof and wiggled out of the bush backwards. 'Come here, you silly dog.'

He scampered over and dropped something on the ground by her feet. Not a stick, but a boot. A high-heeled, black leather boot with a silver buckle on the side. A boot they hadn't seen since the night of the party.

Chloe's missing boot.

CHAPTER TWENTY-SEVEN

CHLOE

'Chloe, have you got a minute?' her mum called, as Chloe sat at her desk, summoning the energy to open her history textbook.

Sighing loudly, she pushed her chair back and slouched into her mum's room.

'What is it?'

'I don't know what to wear tonight. What d'you think, my velvet dress or this?' Her hands fluttered over the black jeans and embroidered jersey smock top she was wearing.

'Definitely the dress,' Chloe said.

'You don't think it's too dressy for the pub? That it'll make it look like I'm trying too hard?'

Isn't that precisely what you're doing? Chloe stopped herself from saying out loud just in time. Instead, she smiled, shifted a pile of discarded clothes out of the way and sat on the bed. 'Not at all. Anyway, men like women to make an effort, don't they?'

'Christ, whatever happened to feminism?' muttered

her mum, reaching into her wardrobe for her damson-red velvet dress. 'I suppose I could wear it over my jeans.'

'That'd look ridiculous. Wear it with your long black boots and a nice necklace.' Chloe remembered her mum's words the morning of the open day at Kingsgate, and she arched an eyebrow. 'It's pretty. It suits you. And you want to make a good impression, don't you?'

If her mum spotted the dig, she didn't say anything. 'I guess.' She stripped down to her underwear and pulled the stretchy velvet dress over her head. She was fiddling with the clasp of a necklace when the doorbell chimed, and Max let off a volley of barking. She froze in horror.

'Shit! He's early. I haven't even done my make-up or hair yet. Will you let him in?'

'Can't Grandpa?' Chloe grumbled.

'He had a migraine, so I sent him to bed. Please Chlo, Adam can't see me like this.'

Chloe stared at her mum, who looked totally normal, and huffed. 'All right then. But don't be long. I have a heap of revision to do.'

Her mum shot her a grateful look. Chloe clattered downstairs, grabbed hold of Max's collar and opened the door. Adam was standing on the doorstep with a bunch of pale pink roses. His face broke into a smile.

'Hello, Chloe, how's it going?'

'Good thanks. Come in. Mum won't be long.'

Adam stepped past her into the house, ruffling Max's head and handing her the roses. Chloe breathed in their heady scent.

'These are gorgeous. I'll put them in some water.' She

remembered her manners as she headed for the kitchen. 'Would you like a drink while you wait?'

'Depends how long your mum's going to be.'

'At least ten minutes, I should think.'

'In that case, I'll have a coffee.' Adam pulled up a chair.

'How's Ben?' Chloe asked, watching Adam's face carefully as she arranged the roses in a vase.

'Ben's Ben, you know what he's like. Did he tell you he's had an unconditional offer from Kingsgate?'

'No. Ouch!' Chloe said as a razor-sharp thorn embedded itself in the pad of her thumb.

Adam jumped up. 'Are you all right?'

'I'm fine. It's just a thorn.'

'Let me see.' He held her thumb up to the strip light and squeezed it gently. A bead of blood appeared, and he wiped it away with a handkerchief. 'I can't see anything in there, but you'd better hold it under the tap to make sure.' She followed him over to the sink and winced as the icy water ran over her hand and trickled down her wrist.

'Lucky Ben to have an unconditional offer.'

Adam nodded. 'He would have struggled to get the grades otherwise. He's more than capable if he puts the work in, but he seems so distracted at the moment, always on his bloody phone.'

Texting me, Chloe thought bitterly. After a string of forlorn messages, she'd taken to leaving her phone switched off. But she knew that wasn't the answer. And then there was the mystery of her missing boot. Max had found it in the woods, not far from the house. Judging by the expression on her mum's face, she thought malevolent forces were at work.

'Don't you think it's odd?' she'd said, holding the boot by the tips of her thumb and index finger as if she was worried about smudging fingerprints.

'Nope,' Chloe had scoffed. 'There's bound to be a perfectly reasonable explanation. Like Max took it and left it there so he could retrieve it later. It's what dogs do.'

'He's a labrador, not a retriever, and he's never stolen a shoe in his life.'

'He chewed up Grandpa's favourite slippers one time and hid them behind the sofa,' Chloe reminded her.

'When he was a puppy,' her mum retorted. 'You lost your boot on the night of the party. Do you remember going into the woods?'

Chloe's face was mutinous. 'I told you I don't remember anything about the party. Stop fussing for God's sake. It's driving me mad.'

'Have you had any offers?' Adam asked, bringing her back to the present.

'An unconditional offer from Kent, but only a conditional offer from Kingsgate and that's where I really want to go.'

Adam led her over to a chair and wrapped a clean piece of kitchen roll round her thumb. 'Plasters?'

'Second drawer by the fridge.'

Adam found a box of Elastoplasts. 'There you go,' he said. 'Good as new.'

'Thanks.'

'My pleasure. Can't have you bleeding out from one of my roses.' He sat down, his head bent to one side. 'The head of the law school at Kingsgate is an old friend of mine. I could put in a word for you, if you like?'

Chloe remembered the head of faculty giving her presentation at the open day all those months ago. Professor Jan Steel, if she remembered correctly. She had impressed Chloe with her quiet confidence. Softly-spoken but with a commanding presence.

'You know her?'

'We were cohorts. Jan stayed on at Kingsgate for her masters while I went to law school. We've kept in touch ever since. I'm sure if I spoke to her...'

'It's very kind of you, Adam. But I want to get in on my own merits, you know?'

'Fair enough, and I admire your integrity,' Adam said. 'But if you change your mind, let me know.' He took a sip of coffee. 'Changing the subject, how's Patrick the Tosser?'

Chloe's mouth turned down. 'Worse than ever. He slagged me off for using the front door the other day. We servants - sorry, waiting staff - are only supposed to use the back entrance, you see. Honestly, it's so demeaning.' She shivered. 'And he's such a creep. All the girls hate him. I found out the other day that a waitress accused him of sexual harassment years ago. His parents paid her off so she'd keep quiet.'

Adam frowned. 'And your mum doesn't mind you working there?'

Chloe liked the way his voice was brimming with fatherly concern. She shrugged. 'She says it's just idle gossip and he's harmless. All talk and no trousers.'

Adam sat forwards in his chair. 'You should still be careful, Chloe. Men like him have no respect for women. None at all. Promise you'll tell me if you have any problems with him?'

Chloe nodded.

He sat back again. 'Good. Oh, look, here's your mum.'

Chloe turned almost guiltily as her mum swept into the kitchen in a haze of Paco Rabanne perfume.

'So sorry to keep you waiting,' she said breathlessly.

Adam waved her apology away. 'It's fine. Chloe has been looking after me.'

'Adam brought you flowers,' Chloe said, pointing at the vase of roses.

Her mum's face was wreathed in smiles. She was as easy to read as a Ladybird book. 'How beautiful!' she gasped. 'Thank you so much.'

'My pleasure.' Adam stood up. 'I guess we'd better make a move?'

'Our table's booked for half seven.' Her mum picked up her keys and phone from the worktop and shrugged on her coat. 'Ring me if you need anything,' she said to Chloe. 'We won't be late.'

'I'll be fine. Have a nice time.'

Adam followed her mum out of the room. At the door, he stopped and turned back to Chloe. 'Take care of yourself. And if you change your mind about Professor Steel, let me know. Promise?'

She smiled. 'I promise.'

CHAPTER TWENTY-EIGHT

KATE

The pub was warm and cosy, with a roaring fire, the hoppy smell of real ale and fat ivory candles on the tables. A barmaid showed Kate and Adam to their seats and handed them menus.

'I'm driving tonight so you can enjoy a drink,' Adam said. 'Red or white?'

Kate flexed her toes under the table. 'Red, please.'

As the barmaid ran through the wine menu, Kate surreptitiously checked Adam out. He was immaculately dressed as always, this time in a neatly-pressed navy and white checked shirt and a pair of chinos. The top two buttons of the shirt were undone, showing a glimpse of chest hair. Kate found she couldn't tear her eyes away and gave a little start when he placed his hand on hers and asked what she was going to eat.

'I usually have the steak and ale. It's famous around these parts,' she said in a mock-country accent.

He smiled. 'It's steak and kidney for me. Ben doesn't do offal in any shape or form.'

'That's offaly boring,' Kate said with a straight face. Adam smiled indulgently, and she flushed with pleasure.

The barmaid arrived with a bottle of Australian shiraz and poured two glasses. Kate took a slug. 'That's lovely.'

Adam raised an eyebrow. 'Not as lovely as the Masseto, I trust?'

'Of course not. That was...' she paused as she remembered his words, 'exquisite.'

'It was. So, tell me about your week. What have you and Chloe been up to?'

'Nothing much. It's always quiet at The Willows this time of year. Not many brides want a January wedding.'

'But Chloe worked last weekend?'

'We had a small wedding on Saturday.'

'She told me she's been having a few problems with Patrick.'

'She did?' It was the first Kate had heard about it.

'He seems to be giving her a hard time. And he has a reputation as a bit of a sleaze, I hear.'

Kate laughed. 'Don't believe everything she tells you. She's got it in for him because he dared to tell her off for having her mobile phone with her on her very first shift.'

'You're not concerned?'

Kate shook her head. 'Patrick wouldn't dare lay a finger on her if that's what's worrying you. He'd have me to answer to if he did. And anyway, the world is a big, bad place full of sleazeballs and misogynists. Chloe needs to know how to handle them, don't you think?'

'You want her to be independent?'

'I guess I do.'

'But you're dreading her leaving home?'

Kate grimaced. 'Is it that obvious?'

'Only to me.'

'I am,' she admitted. 'The house is going to feel empty without her. What about Ben? Is he looking forward to uni?'

'Who knows? I'm afraid Ben is a law unto himself.'

Kate stopped tracing her finger round the rim of her glass and stared at Adam. 'What d'you mean?'

Adam glanced at the pub's timbered ceiling. 'He's had a few issues with anxiety over the years. All related to his mother walking out when he was a baby, if you ask me. He finds it difficult to make connections with people, but when he does, it's hard for him to untangle himself.'

Kate chose her words carefully. 'He seems to have become quite attached to Chloe.'

An emotion Kate couldn't read flickered across Adam's face. Resignation? Concern? He rubbed his chin and said finally, 'Yes, he does.'

'He texts her a lot.'

'I know.'

'The thing is, Chloe likes him as a friend,' Kate began.

'But not as a boyfriend?'

'No. And she's trying to concentrate on her exams at the moment.'

'So she could do without any distractions?'

Kate nodded gratefully.

'You want me to have a word with him?' Adam asked.

'Would you?'

'Of course. I'll talk to him tonight.'

'You won't tell him I asked?' Kate said, aware that Chloe would go mad if she knew she was having this conversation.

'Of course not.' Adam was quiet for a moment. 'The thing you have to understand about Ben is that he only sees things in black and white. Unless Chloe has told him point blank to back off, he'll think she's still interested. Don't worry. I'll sort it.'

'Thank you,' Kate said, feeling pounds lighter as if she'd shrugged off a heavy rucksack. She wondered if now was the time to broach the party. She could ask Adam if he'd seen what had happened in the garden. Share her suspicions that Ben had got Chloe drunk on purpose and lured her outside so he could try it on.

But how would Adam react if she practically accused his son of sexual assault? Because once the words were out, there was no taking them back. She didn't want to jeopardise their fledgling relationship if that's what it was. And did she need to, anyway? Adam was going to tell Ben to stop bothering Chloe. He'd promised to sort it. And Chloe was adamant nothing had happened in the garden anyway.

As Kate wavered, the barmaid arrived with their food. By the time she'd warned them the plates were piping hot, had re-filled Kate's empty wine glass and brought a jar of mustard for Adam, Kate had made up her mind. Mentioning the party would serve no purpose other than upsetting Adam and incriminating Ben in something he may or may not have done. Because it was, Kate realised, entirely possible that Chloe had lied about how much she'd drunk and had slipped over in the garden. And Ben had been nothing but courteous in pulling her to her feet.

'How's your pie?' she asked Adam instead.

'Good. Yours?'

'Lovely. I hadn't realised how hungry I was.'

Adam dabbed the corner of his mouth with his napkin. 'Chloe tells me she still wants to go to Kingsgate.'

'She's got her heart set on the place. That's why she's so worried about her exams.'

'I've told her I'm more than happy to put in a good word with Jan Steel, the head of the law school.'

Kate speared a green bean. 'You know her?'

'From way back. We were at Kingsgate together. She might be willing to make Chloe's offer unconditional. Then she wouldn't have to stress about her A-levels.'

'I thought the university admissions teams made the offers.'

'And you don't think the heads of faculties have the final say? Sometimes, even the most able students slip through the net through no fault of their own. All I'd be doing is making sure that didn't happen in Chloe's case.'

'That would be so kind of you.'

'But Chloe's asked me not to. She said she wants to get there on her own merits.'

Kate sighed in frustration. 'That sounds like Chloe. As pig-headed as her grandfather.'

'Perhaps you could have a word with her because I'm more than happy to give Jan a ring. Maybe even set up a meeting between them.'

Kate touched his hand. 'You are one amazing man, Adam Sullivan.'

He shrugged. 'Plenty of people helped me when I was Chloe's age. It's nice to pay it forward.'

'In that case, I'll see if I can talk some sense into her.'

CHAPTER TWENTY-NINE

CHLOE

Chloe knew something was wrong the minute the usual babble of voices fell silent as she walked into the sixth form common room. Two Year 12 boys, all testosterone and bum fluff, leered at her. A diffident girl from her economics class made to approach her, then apparently thought better of it and backed away towards the water cooler.

Chloe scoured the room for Annie as she headed for her locker, but her best friend was nowhere in sight. A wolf whistle from a far corner of the room stopped her in her tracks. She spun on her heels and glared at the perpetrator, a barrel-chested boy called Kyle she'd known since primary school.

'Simmer down, Kyle,' she said, injecting as much scorn as possible into her voice, despite her growing sense of unease.

His mouth turned down in a sneer as he nudged the boy standing next to him and said in an undertone, 'I would, wouldn't you?'

'Would what?' Chloe said, marching over to him. The room was so quiet she could hear the blood pounding in her ears.

Kyle stepped forwards until their faces were barely a few centimetres apart. 'I'd give you one,' he said, puffing out his chest as a nervous titter spread through the room like a bush fire.

'In your dreams,' Chloe snapped, pushing past him to the lockers. She felt the heat of a dozen pairs of eyes on her back. What was wrong with everyone? It was as if the entire sixth-form was playing a huge prank and she was the only one who wasn't in on the joke. Perhaps they were all hyper because their mocks started today. Perhaps she'd gone to sleep and woken up in some weird parallel universe where all her classmates had been taken over by zombies. Perhaps she was still asleep…

Fingers shot out and grabbed her arm. She whipped around, her hand raised in the air.

Annie caught her wrist.

'Chloe, you need to come with me,' she said, pulling her towards the girls' loos.

'What the hell's going on?' Chloe cried as Annie pushed open the door and the smell of urine and bleach filled her nostrils.

Annie reached in her coat pocket for her phone and handed it to Chloe.

'There's something you need to see.' The grave expression on Annie's face should have been warning enough, but the shock still hit Chloe like a kick in the stomach. She briefly registered the yellow Snapchat logo before her gaze fell on a photo of her naked body, hands on hips and staring at the full-length mirror in her bedroom.

'It's you,' Annie said unnecessarily. 'And it's already gone around most of the school.'

Chloe's legs turned to water and she leaned against the wall for support. 'Shit.'

Annie took the phone back. 'Someone called *No1fanbuoy* posted it last night. He must have taken it from your back garden, the bloody perv. He's zoomed in to your bedroom window, see?'

Chloe did not want to see.

'When was it sent?' she asked.

'Last night. I took a screenshot to show you before it disappeared.'

'Why didn't you tell me last night?'

'I didn't want to worry you. I was hoping *No1fanbuoy* had just sent it to me. But when I arrived this morning, it was all anyone was talking about. I'm so sorry, Chloe.'

Chloe buried her face in her hands. Her eyes felt hot and she rubbed them. Annie handed her a length of toilet roll from the nearest cubicle and gave her a sympathetic smile.

'I can call your mum if you like?'

Chloe shook her head.

'No way. She'll go ape. She's always nagging me to draw my curtains.' Another thought pummelled her. 'What if my Grandpa sees it? It'd kill him. No,' she said decisively, 'they must never know about this.'

'You should still report it to Snapchat, though. Get them to take it down.'

'What's the point? Fatheads like Kyle Johnson will

have already saved it and sent it on to God knows who.' A sob rose in the back of her throat. 'What if it goes viral?'

Annie wrapped her arm round Chloe's shoulder. 'I'm sure it won't. Looking on the bright side -'

'There is one?' Chloe muttered.

'Looking on the bright side,' Annie continued. 'At least everyone's saying how hot you look.'

Chloe and Annie waited in the toilets until the bell for registration sounded before they made their way to the hall for their first of three economics papers.

'What if we see anyone?' Chloe said.

'Brazen it out. If people think you don't give a toss, they'll soon stop giving a toss, too.'

Chloe supposed it made sense. But it wasn't true. She did give a toss. She felt violated as if she'd caught someone rifling through her knicker drawer. As if someone had stared into her soul and seen every atom. Her faults, her failings and her darkest secrets. Everything.

Nevertheless, she took Annie's advice, and when they passed a gaggle of boys outside the sports hall, she held her head high and stalked past, ignoring their wolf whistles and dirty laughs.

But inside she was bleeding.

Chloe sat towards the back of a row of identical desks all

facing the stage. She laid out her clear plastic pencil case, her watch, her bottle of water and the one mascot she was allowed - a wallaby keyring from Uncle Rory.

Crossing her ankles, she stared at the exam paper face down on the desk in front of her. The main invigilator stepped onto the stage. Clearing his throat, he announced that they were now under exam conditions.

'If you have a question at any time you must raise your hand and wait until an invigilator comes to you,' he said.

Chloe held her head in her hands and tried to blink away the Snapchat image, but it refused to disappear.

The invigilator glanced at the clock and rocked forwards on his toes. 'It's nine o'clock. You may open your question papers and begin.'

Chloe turned over the paper and picked up her pen. She scanned the first question.

In 2015 a report by Public Health England recommended the imposition of a 20% tax on the sale of soft drinks that contain high levels of sugar. Evaluate the likely microeconomic effects of such a tax.

She took a deep breath and reread the question. But the harder she stared at the lines of text, the more the words unravelled, like tiny lengths of squid ink spaghetti on a plate, twisting and spiralling until they became meaningless.

She sat on the edge of the hard plastic chair and looked around. Everyone else was writing furiously. A rustle of paper to her left caught her attention. She stared, astonished, at a boy two rows along who was already turning onto a fresh sheet of paper, his right hand gliding over the lines as if it had a life of its own. How on earth could he write so quickly? They'd barely sat down. But when she checked her watch, she gasped in horror. Thirty-five minutes had already passed, and she hadn't written a single word.

Christ, this couldn't be happening. She was Chloe Kennedy, all-round nice girl and grade A student. Polite, conscientious, never put a foot wrong. And yet in the space of a morning, naked photos of her were spreading like a virus through the internet, as unstoppable as a pandemic, and she was about to fail an exam for the first time in her life.

Chloe's chest tightened, panic rising in time with the flush creeping up her neck. She dropped her pen, earning her an irritated look from Amber Jackson, sitting to her right, as it clattered across the desk. Her heart skipped a beat, and she clutched her chest, wondering if she was having a heart attack. Reason told her she was too young and fit and healthy. But a little voice in her subconscious whispered a memory of Megan Wright's brother who'd been just nineteen when he'd dropped down dead in the middle of a football match. No-one had any idea he had a congenital heart condition until it was too late.

A wave of dizziness sent Chloe's stomach swirling. She closed her eyes and was transported back to the night of the party, chill air hitting her face like a slap as she tottered outside in her high-heeled boots. Squelchy grass. The taste of bile. Her fingers worrying at a square of silky cotton. And then a new memory. A male voice, soft in her ear. 'I'll look after you.' And the feel of warm flesh on her goosebump-cold skin.

Chloe gripped the edges of the desk until her knuckles

turned white. She took a long gulp of air and willed herself to forget the party. It didn't matter. None of it mattered. All she cared about were her A-levels; her ticket to Kingsgate. If she went, she could leave all the shit behind.

She breathed slowly and picked up her pen. She reread the question, trying to dredge up some form of an answer about indirect taxes and the social cost of sugary drinks, but her mind remained blank. The pen felt slippery in her sweaty palm, and underneath the table, her knees trembled.

Panic rose like a tidal wave and this time she succumbed to its force. She set her pen down at the feet of the beady-eyed wallaby and held her hand in the air.

CHAPTER THIRTY

KATE

Kate wandered through the Great Hall, checking glasses for smears, re-arranging place cards and straightening cutlery. She'd been at The Willows since nine, helping Lola lay the twelve tables under Patrick's watchful eye. It was a lavish reception for over one hundred and twenty people and was costing the happy couple almost forty grand. More than double her annual salary, she thought, brushing a wayward anemone petal off the top table.

Pete was in the steaming kitchen putting final touches to the canapés - local chipolatas with red onion chutney, bitesize goats' cheese tartlets and satay chicken skewers.

The sound of *Love is all Around* was playing in the background as the wedding ceremony began in the all-weather marquee behind the main house. Kate checked the time. Midday. The waiting staff were starting to arrive in dribs and drabs. As it was a big wedding party, Patrick had brought in two teams. Kate still needed to allocate hands and run through the order of the day so they would be ready to serve champagne and canapés the minute the ceremony was over, but she still had time to touch up her make-up, and headed to the poky staff room.

Unlike the rest of the lavishly-decorated mansion, it was no-frills, with a trestle table surrounded by six plastic chairs, and hooks along one wall strung with cheap cardigans and thin coats from Primark and H&M. Bethany and Shannon, two of the younger waitresses, were sitting at the table on their phones. Kate found her bag hanging on the furthest hook and scrabbled around for her brush and lipstick.

Patrick liked all his 'girls', as he proprietorially referred to them, to look well-turned-out at all times. He was a stickler for it. His mother had been the same. Legend had it that she'd once sent a girl home after spotting a star-shaped henna tattoo on her neck. Only Kate knew it wasn't a legend - she'd been there when it happened. The girl had walked in as cocky as you like and left in tears after the dressing down of her life.

Kate stood in front of the only mirror and reapplied her lipstick, brushed her hair and retied her ponytail. She ran her tongue over her teeth, as even a touch of lipstick on a tooth was enough to prompt a sarcastic comment from Patrick. Satisfied she would pass even the most critical of inspections, she put the lipstick and brush back in her bag, just as her phone vibrated.

Nothing was guaranteed to wind up Patrick more than staff using phones on his time, so she left hers on silent at work and usually never bothered to check it. But now her heart missed a beat. Perhaps it was Adam, suggesting a third date. Smiling to herself, she gazed at the screen.

Five missed calls and one voicemail message, all from Chloe's school. The smile slipped from her face as she gripped the phone tightly. Had something gone wrong in Chloe's exam? Maybe she'd forgotten her pencil case and had asked the school to phone Kate to run it in. But no, that was silly. Chloe would have phoned herself or borrowed a pen from a friend.

It must be something else. Kate remembered a call from Chloe's primary school, not long after she'd started. One of the other reception kids had thrown a stone which had hit Chloe and cut the soft skin above her eye. When Kate had arrived at school, she found Chloe sitting pale-faced outside the school office holding a wet flannel to her forehead. Kate had almost passed out when she'd seen her daughter's uniform drenched in blood.

Head injuries, even minor ones, always bled a lot, a nurse in the local minor injuries unit had reassured her. A couple of stitches later, Chloe was as right as rain. Kate had gone home and poured herself a generous glass of wine.

She listened to the voicemail.

'This is Mrs Stanton in the school office. Please could you ring as soon as you pick up this message?' She paused momentarily and added almost as an afterthought, 'It's about Chloe.'

'When are we having the run-through?' Bethany asked.

Kate, still staring at her phone, said, 'I have to make a quick call.'

She dialled the school, clamped the phone to her ear and listened to a recorded message. No, she didn't want to report an absence, and she already knew the bloody term dates were on the website. Why was the number to actually speak to someone always last on the list? Eventually, she was connected to one of the secretaries.

'It's Kate Kennedy. You left a message about my daughter, Chloe, in Year 13 and asked me to ring.'

'Mrs Kennedy.' Kate didn't bother to correct her. 'Thanks for calling back. Chloe wondered if you would be able to pick her up. She's a bit… upset.'

'Why, what's happened? Is she ill?'

'Not ill exactly. Just a bit… under the weather.'

'I'm at work at the moment. Is she well enough to catch the bus?'

There was a pause, and the secretary said, 'She's right here. I'll ask.'

Kate stared at the ceiling as a muffled conversation took place on the other end of the line.

'She'd like to have a word. I'll pass you over.'

Kate's grip on the phone tightened as her daughter came on the line.

'Mum?'

'What is it, Chloe? You sound awful. What's wrong?'

'I… I almost passed out.'

'Passed out?'

'In the middle of the exam. I thought I was having a heart attack! Mrs Bentley reckons it was probably a panic attack, but what difference does it make? I've completely screwed up.'

'Calm down, Chloe. It's not the end of the world. It's only a mock. I'm sure they'll let you re-sit. Are you feeling better now?'

'Not really,' Chloe said. 'Please will you pick me up?'

'I'm at work, Chlo. Canapés are in,' she glanced at her watch. *Shit*. 'Fifteen minutes. Can't you catch an early bus?'

'*Please* Mum.'

Kate felt a tightness in her throat. When did Chloe ever ask for anything? She was always so fiercely independent. She made a split-second decision.

'I'll be with you in half an hour. You hang in there, sweetheart, OK? I'm on my way.'

'Holy crap, Patrick's going to lose his shit if you go now,' Shannon said, her eyes wide.

'He'll survive,' Kate said, more bravely than she felt. She grabbed her coat and hitched her bag onto her shoulder. 'I have to go.'

'Good luck,' Bethany said. She let out a titter of nervous laughter. ''Cos you're gonna need it.'

Twenty-five minutes later, Kate pulled into the quiet residential street that led to the school. Parents were banned from parking in the school grounds, and the caretaker policed the rules like an autocratic leader of his own small state. Kate cruised slowly down the road towards the entrance, looking for a place to pull in.

She was so intent on finding a space that she didn't see the grey hatchback speeding towards her until it sounded its horn. Not a polite *toot-toot* but a long and angry blast. She stamped on the brakes, expecting the other car to do the same, but it kept coming, bearing down on her Mini like an unstoppable force.

For a second she froze, then adrenalin kicked in and, checking nothing was behind her, slammed the car into reverse. The Mini's engine whined as she twisted around in her seat and backed up the road. Narrowly missing the wing mirror of a parked Freelander, she swerved into a bus lay-by and stared in disbelief as the grey car raced past.

'Tosser!' she yelled, banging her palm on the steering wheel. 'Absolute bloody wanker!' she added for good measure. She looked around to see if anyone else had witnessed the unbelievable display of dumb-ass driving. But the street was empty apart from two collared doves, who were sitting side by side on a telegraph wire, watching her.

Glancing in her rear-view mirror, she pulled back onto the street. Finding a small space just past the school entrance, she parked up and sat for a minute until her breathing returned to normal, then gathered her coat and bag and went in search of her daughter.

CHAPTER THIRTY-ONE

CHLOE

Chloe hugged her schoolbag to her chest and gazed out of the car window.

'D'you want to talk about it?' her mum asked, keeping her eyes on the road.

'Not really.'

'It might help.'

'What's there to say? My life is a grade one shitshow.'

'Come on, Chlo, that's a little over-dramatic, don't you think? You heard what Mrs Bentley said. You won't be the first student to have a panic attack in the middle of an exam, and you certainly won't be the last. She's going to let you resit next week, and she's promised to help you with some coping strategies in the meantime. It's not the end of the world.'

You don't know the half of it, Chloe thought, fighting the tears that had formed a hard mass at the back of her throat.

'I used to suffer terribly with nerves. Couldn't eat a thing on the morning of an exam. It's a wonder I didn't pass out,' her mum continued. 'Maybe you had low blood sugar.'

Chloe snorted. 'Hardly. I had a massive bowl of porridge for breakfast and a banana on the bus. Anyway, can we please change the subject?'

Her mum was quiet for a bit, then said, 'I almost had a prang outside school. Some prat in a Golf driving like an idiot. My life flashed before me, I'm telling you.'

Chloe couldn't care less, but at least the spotlight was off her - for now.

'A man or a woman?'

'Hard to tell, they were driving so fast. Some kind of boy racer. You know the sort, baseball cap and shades, trying to look cool.'

'That's very sexist of you. And ageist,' Chloe said.

'And probably true,' her mum retorted, turning on the radio.

Chloe loathed Radio 2, but in that moment she was happy to let the banal chatter and the stream of vanilla pop songs wash over her, like piped music in a lift. As they neared home, her mum laid a hand on her knee.

'I'm going to have to go back to work this afternoon. Will you be all right at home?'

'I'll be fine, Mum.'

'Good. Grandpa's there if you need anything, and I'll try to get off straight after the wedding breakfast. Patrick owes me a couple of hours.'

'I bet he was delighted when you told him you had to pick me up.'

Her mum pulled a face. 'I didn't tell him.'

'Mum!' An unpleasant thought occurred to Chloe.

Could Patrick have taken the picture of her through the window? He was such a sleaze. He'd virtually touched her up the other day. And he only lived around the corner. She pictured him crouching in their garden, his camera trained on her bedroom window, and shivered.

'Are you cold?'

'A bit,' Chloe lied, turning the heater up a couple of degrees. 'Is Patrick on Facebook?'

'That's a strange question.' Her mum laughed. 'Why, are you thinking of friending him?'

'No-one under the age of twenty is on Facebook, Mum. It's for old people. And anyway, he'd be the last person I'd friend. No, I was wondering if The Willows uses it to promote weddings and stuff.'

'They've got Facebook and Instagram accounts, I think, but Lola manages them. Patrick doesn't do social media. It's all a bit beneath him.'

Chloe nodded. That would make sense. But if he didn't do Facebook, it's unlikely he'd be on Snapchat. It wasn't exactly the social media channel of choice for the over-forties. He probably hadn't even heard of it. No, she decided, it couldn't be him. And if it wasn't him, there was only one person it could be.

Before she could explore that train of thought any further, they pulled up outside the house. Chloe unclicked her seatbelt and jumped out.

'Text if you need anything. I'll make sure I check my phone,' her mum said.

Chloe nodded. 'I will.'

Her grandfather had left a note propped against the pepper grinder on the kitchen table announcing he'd gone fishing. Craving fresh air and some of his old school advice, she whistled to Max, grabbed his lead, pulled on her parka and wellies, and headed outside.

She found Grandpa in his favourite spot under a weeping willow a short distance downstream from their house. Bundled up in his old Barbour jacket, bucket hat and a checked scarf, he was sitting in his dark green camping chair, his fishing rod resting lightly on his lap. When Chloe kissed his cheek, it was as cold as marble.

'Grandpa, you're frozen! Should you be out here?'

'Don't fuss. You sound like your mother. I'm fine, despite the rather inconvenient fact that the fish aren't biting this afternoon. How did your exam go?'

Chloe crouched down beside his chair. 'On a scale of one to ten, it was about a minus five.'

Her grandfather chuckled. 'That doesn't sound good. What happened?'

'I had a panic attack, Grandpa. I thought I was having a heart attack. I couldn't breathe. It was *horrible*.'

His bushy eyebrows knotted together. 'That's not like you. Do you know why?'

Chloe desperately wanted to tell someone about the Snapchat photo; someone who would take her side and reassure her that she shouldn't feel ashamed and it wasn't her fault. To report the matter to Snapchat and order them to take it down before it spread any further. To be the grown-up and take control, because Chloe felt like a helpless child.

She stared at the muddy bank of the river and

wondered how to start. Then she glanced at her grandfather, at the deep lines that furrowed his forehead and tracked across his weathered cheeks, at the slight tremor in his hand as he held his fishing rod. He was almost ninety. She couldn't worry him with something like this.

'Chloe?' he said gently.

'I guess I've been putting too much pressure on myself. I so want to go to Kingsgate. And if I don't get the grades...'

The rod slipped from his grip, and he clasped Chloe's hands.

'Chloe, love, if I've learned anything in this life, it's that you have to be kind to yourself. You know you've worked hard. Trust yourself. It'll all come good, I promise.'

'I hope you're right, Grandpa.'

'I'm always right.' He struggled to his feet. 'I've had enough of those damn trout laughing at me. Why don't you give me a hand back to the house and we'll light the fire and have tea and crumpets and a board game?'

At the mention of crumpets, Max gave an excited woof.

Chloe smiled in spite of herself. 'Max is right. Crumpets do sound nice.'

He rubbed his hands together. 'Then that sounds like a plan. I might even let you beat me at Scrabble.'

Her grandfather was as good as his word, letting Chloe win at Scrabble while they demolished a pot of tea and a packet of crumpets between them. Then he wandered upstairs for a nap, leaving Chloe in front of the fire watching a re-run of *Come Dine With Me* with Max snoring softly by her feet.

When her phone rang, she jumped. It was a mobile number she didn't recognise and, as her finger hovered over the green accept button, she felt a creeping sense of disquiet. What if the photo had gone viral and some freak had managed to track her down? She stared at the phone until it stopped ringing. A red dot appeared on the phone icon. She pressed it cautiously. Someone had left a message. Telling herself that freaks didn't generally leave voicemails, she forced herself to listen to it.

'Could you give me a quick call? It's Adam. Nothing to worry about.' He gave his number, even though it was logged in her call history. 'I'll try again later, but if you pick up this message first, call me.'

Chloe threw another log on the fire, sat back down and dialled his number. He answered on the second ring.

'That was quick. Were you screening calls?' There was a teasing note to his voice, and Chloe found herself smiling.

'I did wonder how you had my number.'

'Ben used your phone to ring me after the accident.'

Chloe had forgotten.

'That's the reason I was calling, actually. About the accident.'

Chloe hitched her feet up until she was sitting cross-legged on the sofa. 'What about it?'

Adam paused, then exhaled a breath. 'I'm afraid we have a bit of a problem.'

CHAPTER THIRTY-TWO

CHLOE

Chloe's mind raced. She should never have gone along with Adam's story. Everyone knew lies tripped you up in the end. She blinked. 'What sort of problem?'

'It's nothing to worry about, really. The insurance company is going to ask for a statement from you, that's all.'

'Me?' she said faintly.

'It's a formality because it's such a big claim, but obviously, I'm conscious we need to have our stories straight.'

A log shifted in the grate, sending a spark onto the brick hearth where it glowed red then died.

'Chloe, are you there?'

She nodded, forgetting he couldn't see her. 'Is that normal? I mean, for them to want statements from everyone in the car?'

'There were no other witnesses, you see. All you need to do is tell them exactly what happened. Just remember I was driving, Ben was in the front passenger seat, and you were sitting behind him. You do remember, don't you?'

Chloe was silent. She still felt guilty she'd strung Ben along for so long because it had suited her. She also felt she was partly to blame for the accident because he probably wouldn't have crashed if he hadn't been so distracted and angry.

And then, at the party, she'd led him on again. So *stupid*. And suddenly he was back in her life, constantly texting, trying to FaceTime, leaving earnest messages declaring she was the love of his life, which she did her best to ignore. Although, weirdly, he'd not texted or called since Saturday.

Had he finally got the message?

Then over the weekend, someone had sent that photo to half of her year. Revenge porn, they called it. Could it have been Ben? Was he trying to even the score?

And now Adam was asking her to lie on record to make sure Ben didn't end up with a criminal conviction, and a tainted reputation. To cover up for him so he could take up his place at Kingsgate, the university Chloe was so desperate to attend. Was that even fair?

No.

What if she told the truth? The insurance company and the police would want to know why she'd changed her story and, knowing her luck, she'd be the one in trouble. The lies she'd already told would tangle her up.

Chloe knew deep down that the moment she promised Adam she would go along with his deceit she was complicit. There was no way she was jeopardising her future for Ben. Lying would save his skin, but it would also save hers. She saw that now.

'Chloe? Did you hear what I said?'

'Yes. I'll tell them you were driving, like you said.'

'Good girl. I'm sure they'll email you in the next couple of days asking for a statement. Call me if you're not sure what to say. You have my number.'

'Fine.'

'And if there's anything I can do for you - *anything* - let me know, all right?'

Chloe swallowed hard. She was helping Adam. Perhaps he could help her, too. 'Actually, there is something.'

'Name it.'

'But my mum mustn't know.'

He paused for a beat. 'It's OK, I'm good at keeping secrets.'

'You know Snapchat?'

'Of course. Ben's on it all the time.'

I bet he is. 'Someone sent a photo of me to some kids in my class. An... an inappropriate photo.'

'Inappropriate?'

She licked her lips.

'I need to know if I'm going to help, Chlo,' he said so gently that she felt a stab of tears behind her eyes. Is this what it felt like to have a dad who could magically make everything better?

'It was a... picture of me getting undressed in my room.'

'Right.'

'And it's gone around half the school.'

'Have you reported it to the police?' he asked.

'No. I don't want Mum or Grandpa to find out.' She rubbed her face. 'I just want it to go away.'

'Sure, I can make that happen. It's the least I can do.'

He sounded so confident she felt a flicker of hope. 'You can?'

'I've represented a few clients who've been the victims of this type of thing. It's not as unusual as you might think, unfortunately. Mostly disgruntled ex-partners posting explicit photos on social media. If it was without your consent it's a criminal offence.'

'It was taken through my bedroom window. Of course it was without my consent,' Chloe said, then bit her lip. 'Sorry, I didn't mean to snap. I just feel so *vulnerable*, you know?'

'There's no need to apologise. I can't begin to imagine what you're going through. But I can make it go away. Do you have a screenshot of the photo?'

'No, but my friend Annie does.'

'Can you get her to send it to me? I'm afraid I'll need to see it, so I know what we're dealing with.'

The thought of Adam seeing the photo made Chloe's toes curl, but if that's what it took to get it taken down, it was worth the embarrassment. Besides, almost everyone at school must have seen it by now. It was too late to be prudish.

'I'll text her now.'

'If Snapchat is slow to act, I can make an application for a Right to be Forgotten, which, in layman's terms, is the right to have your name removed from online search results,' Adam said.

'You think if people google my name, the photograph will come up?'

'We should cover all bases to be sure,' he said.

'Thank you,' Chloe said in a small voice.

'It's the least I can do.' He let out a long breath. 'Do you have any idea who might be behind this?'

Ben, she wanted to tell him. Because there wasn't anyone else who knew where she lived, who'd infiltrated her friends on Instagram, who had a score to settle. But what if she was wrong? Falsely accusing the son of a solicitor would be crazy. He'd probably sue her.

'No,' she said finally. 'I have absolutely no idea.'

CHAPTER THIRTY-THREE

KATE

It was gone nine o'clock when Kate slipped in through the back door. She found Chloe in the snug, in her pyjamas and dressing gown with Max at her feet and her laptop balanced on a cushion on her lap. Love Island was on in the background, the volume set so low the contestants' voices were little more than a murmur.

Kate sat beside Chloe, pulled off her shoes and rubbed her feet.

'God, that was a long shift. Where's Grandpa?'

'Gone to bed.' Chloe angled the laptop away from Kate, but not before she caught a glimpse of a map of California.

'I thought you were going to get off early?'

'I did try, Chlo, but Patrick had already agreed to let one of the other girls go at seven. I had to stay. You've been all right though, haven't you? No more funny turns?'

'Panic attacks, Mum, not *funny turns*. I'm not a bloody geriatric. Christ.'

'Sorry. Silly me.' All Kate seemed to do these days was

apologise to Chloe. 'Why were you looking at a map of America?'

'I wasn't.'

'I thought I saw it on your computer.'

Chloe folded her arms across her chest. 'I don't think so.'

Kate was too tired to argue. 'If you say so. I'm going to make myself a hot chocolate. D'you want one? I think I have a packet of marshmallows somewhere.'

'Yes, please.' Kate was halfway through the door when Chloe said, 'I was looking for my dad.'

Kate stopped. 'Your *dad*?'

'Noah the surfer. I wanted to see if I could find him, if you must know. But it turns out that California is a pretty big state. The third biggest in America. It's almost nine hundred miles from Mexico to Oregon, and almost forty million people live there. I'm becoming a bit of an expert.'

She sounded like a tour guide, reeling facts from a crib sheet. Only Kate detected a tiny catch in her voice, so subtle you could easily miss it. Deciding the hot chocolates could wait, Kate sat back down, so close their hips were touching.

'What's brought all this on?'

Chloe picked at the skin around her thumbnail. 'I don't know. I suppose I was wondering what it would be like to have a dad. And it got me thinking about Noah, about whether we could try to find him.'

'You've never wanted to before. Why now?'

Chloe stopped picking and stuffed her hands into the pockets of her dressing gown. 'I don't know.'

There's something you're not telling me, Kate thought. 'Is it something to do with the panic attack?'

'No,' Chloe said, a little too quickly.

'Are you missing Uncle Rory? Is that it?'

Chloe gave a fleeting nod.

'Oh sweetheart, me too.'

'I looked on Facebook for Noahs from California. There are, like, literally hundreds of them. Will you tell me the story again? About the night you two met? There might be some clues we've missed that could help us narrow down the search.'

Before Kate could wonder whether or not this was wise, Chloe had turned off the television and was sitting cross-legged facing her, an expectant look on her face.

'So, I'd been travelling round South East Asia for about eight months when I rocked up in Thailand. I was a seasoned backpacker by then. As brown as a berry with braids in my hair and henna tattoos on my ankles. I thought I was pretty cool.'

Chloe raised an eyebrow. 'Debatable. I've seen the photos.'

'Thailand was beautiful,' Kate said, ignoring her. 'I loved everything about it: the beaches, the jungles, the food, and the people.'

'One person in particular...'

'Do you want me to tell you the story or not?'

Chloe nodded. Sitting with her legs crossed and her chin resting on her closed hands, she looked like a Buddha's pale and skinnier alter ego.

'I did all the usual gap year clichés. I rode an elephant through the jungle in Chiang Mai, went to a full moon party in Koh Phangnan and visited the place where they filmed The Beach on Phi Phi Island. I ended up in a hostel in Phuket. I wanted to spend a couple of weeks there before flying to Laos.'

'Is that where you met the two Aussie girls?'

'Yes.' Kate had been telling Chloe a squeaky-clean version of this story since she was about five. She trotted it out every time Chloe asked about her dad, which, come to think about it, hadn't been for years. It was probably time to tell her the unabridged version.

'They had the room next to mine. I wish I could remember their names, but it was so long ago. Anyway, they'd heard about a party on a beach further up the coast and invited me along.'

'And that's where you met Noah?'

Kate nodded.

'What was he like? Tell me everything you remember. Everything.'

There was a hunger in Chloe's eyes that tugged at Kate's heartstrings.

'He was tall. About six foot two. And his hair was even blonder than yours.' She picked up a strand of Chloe's hair and twisted it around her fingers.

'What colour were his eyes?'

'Dark blue, like new denim. And he had a dusting of freckles across his nose.'

'Like me,' Chloe said.

Kate nodded.

'What did you talk about?'

'We swapped stories about our travels. Noah was a

couple of years older than me and was taking his gap year after college, before he started work.'

'What did he major in?'

Kate cast her mind back. Although they'd talked about travelling, they hadn't discussed their lives back home. No self-respecting backpacker liked to be reminded that on their return they'd have to step back into the real world, where degrees had to be studied for, jobs found, rent paid. It was easier to forget about it. Out of sight, out of mind.

'I'm sorry, Chlo. I don't think he told me.'

'Did he say where in California he was from?'

Kate let her memory transport her back to that sultry Thai beach, a cold bottle of beer in one hand, her other entwined with Noah's and the sound of the waves lapping at the shore a few feet away. A heavily-tattooed boy with ginger dreadlocks and an Australian accent had taken an acoustic guitar from a dusty black case smothered in travel stickers and had started strumming.

'*Do You Know The Way To San José*,' Kate said softly.

'What?'

'The song. By Dionne Warwick, I think. There was a lad at the party playing it on his guitar. Noah said that's where he lived. San José. I've just remembered.'

Chloe grabbed her laptop and began typing. 'San José, capital of the Silicon Valley,' she read. 'Close to San Francisco. It has a Mediterranean climate and a population of more than a million.' Her face fell. 'That's still loads.'

'Try googling Noah and San José.'

As Chloe's fingers flew over the keyboard, Kate felt her pulse quicken. What if, after all these years, they did find Noah? Would she have the courage to contact him? Tell him he had a daughter he knew nothing about? Would he even remember her, a girl he'd made love to on a starlit beach so many years ago?

'There's a pizza restaurant in San Jose called Noah's,' Chloe said. 'Look, here's the website.' She swivelled the laptop around so Kate could see and clicked on the *About us* tab. There was a photo of the owner, Noah Bianchi, smiling in front of his pizza oven. He had a shiny bald pate, twinkling brown eyes and a generous paunch. He was sixty if he was a day. Even allowing for the chance that Kate's Noah had really let himself go, there was no way this was him. Kate shook her head.

'Thank goodness for that,' Chloe grinned. She returned to the search results. 'There's a pro ice hockey player called Noah Sanders who plays for the San José Sharks. It would be cool if he was my dad.' She pointed to a photo of a square-jawed, black-haired man with the physique of a heavyweight boxer, wearing a turquoise team jersey with a shark emblazoned on the front.

'He's not much older than you,' Kate said.

'He could be our Noah's son? My half-brother.'

'Why would he call his son Noah?'

'They do in America, don't they? This could be Noah Junior.'

Kate pretended to study the photo, even though she'd known from one glance there was no resemblance. Chloe was motionless, like a sprinter in the blocks waiting for the starter's gun.

'I'm sorry, Chlo, but he looks nothing like him.'

'Are you sure? Take another look.'

Kate closed the laptop and placed it carefully on the

coffee table. 'I know it's not what you want to hear, sweetheart, but the fact is Noah could be anywhere in America. He could still be backpacking around the world for all I know.'

'Why didn't you think to get his contact details so you could keep in touch?' Chloe wailed.

'I'm sorry. And if I could turn back the clock... ' Kate stared at her hands, which still smelt faintly of the white vinegar solution they used to clean the cutlery at work. 'But I can't. Like it or not, it's you and me, Chloe. Isn't that enough?'

'It used to be, Mum,' she mumbled, so quietly Kate had to bend her head to hear. 'But I'm not sure it is any more.'

CHAPTER THIRTY-FOUR

CHLOE

Chloe stood outside Patrick's office and knocked.
'Come in,' he called.

Steeling herself, she pushed the door open. Patrick was sitting in his black leather office chair with his hands clasped behind his head. On the desk was a silver fountain pen, an unopened pad of paper and an old-fashioned blotter that looked like a seesaw in a children's playground.

'Kaz said you wanted to talk to me,' Chloe said, playing with the straps of her apron.

Patrick jumped to his feet, darted around the desk and pulled out a chair. 'I did,' he said jovially. 'Please - sit down. There's something I wanted to discuss.'

Chloe did as she was told, perching on the edge of the low-slung seat, designed, no doubt, to give anyone visiting the office a height disadvantage.

'Coffee?' he asked, popping a pod in the Nespresso machine on the antique walnut sideboard before she had a chance to answer. 'No sugars, I'm guessing,' he said over his shoulder. 'You're sweet enough as it is.'

Chloe mimed a gagging action then stuck her tongue out behind his back. As he busied himself with mugs and milk, she wondered why he'd summoned her. Kaz had found her in the kitchen where she'd been helping Pete prep the individual sticky toffee puddings for that afternoon's wedding breakfast.

'Patrick wants to see you in his office, Chloe. Something about the rota for the next quarter?' she'd said.

'Are you sure he didn't mean Mum?' Chloe said, bemused.

'He definitely asked for you,' Kaz had said.

Pete had taken the tray of puddings from her and given her a reassuring smile. 'Don't worry. He probably wants to check whether you'll be doing any shifts during your A-levels. You know how busy we get in May and June.'

'Of course,' Chloe said, her face clearing. 'That must be it.'

Patrick was full of bonhomie as he handed her a mug of coffee and sat back down behind his desk. Perhaps today was a Henry day, Chloe thought.

'Two things I wanted to discuss,' he said, steepling his fingers and watching her carefully. 'First, I fear we may have got off on the wrong foot. I get the impression you feel a little… uncomfortable around me.'

Chloe's eyes widened. She hadn't been expecting this. 'Not at all. It's my first job, and I'm a bit shy,' she said, inwardly berating herself for not having the guts to stand up and say, *Yes, you do make me feel a bit uncomfortable. In fact, you're a total sleazeball.*

'Good, good.' Patrick said. 'I like my girls to enjoy

working at The Willows. I wouldn't want anyone to feel awkward.'

The silence stretched between them like a taut elastic band until Chloe could stand it no longer. 'And the other thing?' she asked.

'That's a rather more delicate matter,' Patrick said. 'Adam Sullivan. What do you know about him?'

'Adam?'

'You met him at a university open day, I believe?' Patrick picked up his pen and twirled it in his fingers like a majorette's baton.

Chloe nodded. 'He was there with his son.'

'And he latched onto your mother?'

'Not at all, he just -'

'And suddenly he's taking her out to dinner and wooing her with expensive wines and acting like the big I Am. To be perfectly frank with you, Chloe - and I hope I can be, because I know we both have your mum's best interests at heart - I'm worried for her. She's led a very… sheltered life.'

'She has?' Chloe thought about her mum backpacking across South East Asia when she was still a teenager. Spending the night on a beach in Thailand with a boy she'd just met.

'She's unworldly and impressionable. This Adam Sullivan has wormed his way into her affections in the blink of an eye. Yet I seem to be the only one with misgivings. Because I'm worried about her, I really am.'

'He seems genuinely fond of her,' Chloe began.

'He's a player.' Patrick stabbed his fountain pen on the desk as if ramming home his point. 'I can spot them a mile off.' He pushed his chair back and gave a businesslike smile. 'So you'll have a word with her?'

'A word?'

'I doubt she'd listen to me. She'd think it was sour grapes on my part, even though I've known her since she was your age and my feelings for her are purely fraternal.'

Chloe almost choked on her coffee. *Yeah, right.*

'I'm not sure she'd listen to me, either.' Chloe placed her mug on Patrick's desk, stood, smoothed her apron and made her way to the door. She turned to him and smiled sweetly. 'But even if she did, I wouldn't try. Adam's lovely. He's the best thing to happen to her for years. So why don't you butt out of her life for once and let her be happy?'

Chloe was still seething as she walked home at the end of her shift. How dare Patrick think he had the right to dictate who her mum could and couldn't date? He didn't own her. It was jealousy, pure and simple.

Her phone buzzed. She glanced at the screen. Talk of the devil...

'Chloe? Can you talk?'

'Yes, of course.'

'Thanks for sending the photo,' Adam said. 'I wanted to let you know that I've been onto Snapchat's head office and they've agreed to take the picture down.'

Chloe closed her eyes. 'Thank you.'

'And I've made an application for a Right to be Forgotten. I thought I might as well fight the fire on all fronts.'

'That's so kind of you.'

'It's nothing, honestly. I'm glad I can help.'

'Well, I really appreciate it. You've restored my faith in human nature.'

'Oh dear, that sounds serious. Is something wrong?'

'It's Patrick being a tosser again.' The words tumbled out before she could stop them.

'Why, what did he do now?'

Chloe was quiet.

'You can tell me, you know.'

The desire to confide in Adam was overwhelming, but Chloe could hardly tell him that Patrick, a man whose reputation as a sleaze preceded him, thought he was a bad 'un who was going to break her mum's heart. Adam would, quite rightly, be furious. Best not to say anything.

'Chloe? What's wrong?'

'Nothing,' she told him. 'Everything's fine. I'm over-reacting as usual. He hasn't done anything.'

CHAPTER THIRTY-FIVE

CHLOE

Chloe stomped up the drive, her head tucked into her chest and her hands deep in the pockets of her coat. Her mum was right. She should have stayed well clear of The Willows and got a job at the pub instead. Patrick had some neck, slagging off Adam of all people. Adam had been brilliant, contacting Snapchat and making sure she didn't show up on any search engines. She wasn't naive enough to think there weren't still photos of her circulating, but the fact that he was looking out for her made the knot of anxiety in the pit of her gut unwind itself a fraction.

A little way ahead the gravel crackled. Chloe stopped and listened, her head cocked to one side.

'Who is it?'

Her call was answered by a low woof. Max bounded out of the dark, his tail wagging. He thrust a wet nose between her legs, and she gave his ear a playful tug.

'Are you supposed to be out?' It was nine o'clock, and he wasn't usually let out for his last wee until ten.

Ignoring her, he wandered over to a hebe and cocked his leg. Chloe whistled, and he followed her, tail still wagging, to the back of the house. The security light flashed on and Chloe was surprised to see the back door wide open.

'Mum? Grandpa?' Chloe yelled, kicking off her loafers and shrugging out of her coat. The kitchen was empty and bitterly cold, and the air was thick with a sickly-sweet smell that Chloe recognised but couldn't place. Her eyes fell on a bunch of Cellophane-wrapped flowers on the counter. A huge bouquet of lilies the same ivory-white as the bride's wedding dress at The Willows that afternoon. So much for Patrick's misgivings about Adam.

A floorboard in the hallway creaked, and her grandfather appeared in the doorway in his dressing gown and slippers.

'Hello, favourite grandchild. How was your shift?'

'Only grandchild,' Chloe automatically corrected him. 'Deadly dull. Grandpa, did you leave the back door open?'

His unruly eyebrows knotted. 'I don't think so.'

'It must have been Mum. Where is she?'

'She disappeared into the bathroom an hour ago, muttering something about clay face masks and waxing strips. I haven't seen her since.'

Chloe giggled. 'She does have it bad. I'm guessing the flowers are from Adam?'

'What flowers?'

Chloe crossed the kitchen and picked them up. 'These flowers. You can hardly miss them.'

Her grandfather frowned. 'They weren't here earlier.'

'Are you sure?'

He looked round him, a baffled expression on his face. 'I think so.'

'Don't worry. They were probably delivered before Mum had her bath.' Chloe fished around for the small, square envelope half-hidden in the waxy petals, careful not to get pollen on her fingers. Bewildered to see it was addressed to her, she ripped the envelope open and skimmed the typed message inside, her eyes growing wider.

My beautiful Chloe, it said. *More perfect than any flower.* And then a quote. *'I loved her against reason, against promise, against peace, against hope, against happiness, against all discouragement that could be.'*

Anger swept through her, her fingers itching to hurl the flowers into the bin and tear the envelope and its contents into a hundred tiny pieces. But, aware her grandfather was watching, she left the bouquet on the counter and slipped the card and envelope into the pocket of her work trousers.

She forced a smile. 'Just as I thought. They're from Adam. Mum'll be blown away.'

'He does seem as keen as mustard,' her grandfather agreed. He held up a mug. 'Bournvita?'

'No thanks, Grandpa. I'm going to head up. I'm shattered.'

It wasn't until she was safely in her room with the door closed, that Chloe let out a howl of frustration. Bloody Ben and his bloody lilies! When would it sink into his thick skull that she didn't want to go out with him?

But the more she said no, the more he chased her. And now this. It was beyond belief.

She reread the quote. She was sure she recognised it. It tugged at her memory, like a lyric from a long-forgotten song. She typed it into the search engine on her phone. Of course. It was from *Great Expectations*. Pip, talking about the beautiful Estella. The book had been one of the texts for her English Lit GCSE, and she'd used the quote in an essay on unrequited love in the exam. Ben must have studied the book, too.

Without considering the consequences, she found his number and called him.

'Ben, this has to stop. Now.'

'Chloe? What are you talking about?'

'The lilies, Ben. Why are you sending me flowers when you know I don't want to go out with you? It's creepy, and it's wrong, and I don't want you to do it ever again.'

'But I didn't -'

'Don't lie, Ben. I'm not stupid. First, you spy on me, then, as if that wasn't bad enough, you send a picture of me to all my friends, and then you send me a bunch of bloody lilies. I'm not having it.'

'Chlo,' he began.

Chloe's voice rose. 'Don't "Chlo" me, Ben Sullivan. Because of you, I've messed up my mocks, I'm a laughing stock at school, and I've had a shitty day at work with Patrick up to his usual tricks. The last thing I need is more hassle. So take a hint and piss off. Otherwise, I'll call the police and have you arrested for stalking, all right? Take the hint and leave me alone!'

She ended the call, slammed the phone on her desk

and massaged her throbbing temples. A knock at the door made her start.

'Chloe?' said her mum. 'Can I come in?'

'I guess.'

Her mum padded in, bringing with her a waft of cocoa butter body lotion with faint undertones of Veet. 'I thought I heard raised voices. Everything all right?'

'Fine.'

'So, who were you talking to?'

'Annie.' The lie tripped off her tongue. 'She wanted to check when our history essay needed to be in.'

'At half-past nine on a Saturday night? She's keen.'

Chloe shrugged.

'How was work?'

'Boring.'

Her mum sighed. 'Well, as long as you're all right, I'll leave you in peace. Night night.'

'Did you know some more flowers have been delivered?' Chloe asked as her mum was halfway out of the door.

She shook her head. 'Grandpa must have taken them in while I was in the bath.'

'He said he didn't. And the back door was wide open when I arrived home.' Chloe fiddled with the seam of her duvet. 'Have you noticed how he keeps forgetting things lately?'

'Don't be fooled by the wily old fox. Your grandfather has a selective memory, same as his selective hearing. It's funny that he never misses an episode of Eggheads but can't remember which day is bin day. Were they for me?'

'What?'

'The flowers?'

'Yes. They're from Adam, your not-so-secret admirer, in case you were wondering,' she lied.

Her mum was positively glowing. 'How lovely! I guess I'd better go and find a vase.'

CHAPTER THIRTY-SIX

KATE

Kate would have liked to have drifted through the next week daydreaming about her future as the next Mrs Sullivan, but she never had the chance. On Saturday, The Willows was the venue for its first high-profile celebrity wedding.

'Celebrity is overstating it somewhat,' Pete said in an aside to Kate as they sat in Patrick's office on Thursday morning, checking menus and table plans for Pippa Harrington-Jones and Edison Cooper's nuptials one last time.

'Six million people watched Edison win Love Island,' Kate countered, 'including Chloe and me. It's my one guilty pleasure,' she added, seeing his pained expression. 'And Pippa is a mega social media influencer.'

'What in God's name is one of those?' Pete asked.

'Someone who has more than fifty-thousand followers on Instagram,' said Patrick, who was stepping in as wedding organiser while Lola celebrated her thirtieth birthday on a beach in the Maldives. She'd booked the holiday eighteen months previously and had refused point-blank to cancel, much to Kate's dismay. Saturday was going to be stressful enough without Patrick micromanaging everything. He was already on edge. By Saturday morning he would be a nightmare.

Patrick handed Pete a copy of the menu. 'It's vital you take this wedding seriously, Peter. Pictures of Edison and Pippa's wedding will be pored over by thousands of people. This kind of publicity is priceless. That's why every single detail has to be faultless. How are you getting on sourcing those organic quails' eggs?'

As Patrick and Pete discussed the menu, Kate let her mind wander. She'd been so busy since the weekend checking and rechecking table decorations, planning staff rotas and overseeing a deep clean of the whole venue that she hadn't had a chance to see Adam. Not that he'd actually asked her on a third date. But he was also snowed under at work. No peace for the wicked, he'd said in a text the previous day, with a winking emoji and two kisses that had made Kate's heart beat a little bit faster.

'I said, have you had a final count-up of napkins?' Patrick said.

Kate consulted her clipboard. 'Sorry, yes. I've checked napkins, tablecloths, cutlery and glasses. The florist is delivering the displays for the tables first thing on Saturday, so I was going to arrange the tables and chairs on Friday night.'

Patrick nodded. 'Kaz can give you a hand. How many tables?'

'Two hundred guests with a top table of eight means sixteen tables of twelve.'

'Two waiting teams?'

Kate nodded. 'And we have four extras to be on the safe side.'

'Excellent.' Patrick gave them a businesslike smile. 'The helicopter is bringing the groom, best man and ushers at eleven. I want perfection from the moment they arrive. Understood?'

Kate and Pete nodded dutifully.

'Understood,' they said in unison.

At a quarter to four on Friday afternoon, Kaz texted Kate to say she'd come down with the flu and couldn't work that evening.

'Going on the piss with your mates, more like,' Kate said, swearing under her breath. Arranging the tables and chairs would take hours on her own. She dashed off a quick text to Chloe, whose bus was due in at four.

Fancy earning some cash? I need an extra pair of hands for a couple of hours this evening. Mum x

Chloe texted straight back.

My time is precious. What's it worth?

. . .

Kate rolled her eyes.

We can stretch to time-and-a-half.

She'd have to pay the extra, but she was so knackered she didn't care.

Double time or nothing, came back the response.

'Cheeky little minx,' Kate said, typing back, All right, just this once. Come over as soon as you're home.

Chloe appeared, in jeans and her favourite Abercrombie and Fitch hoody, at half-past four.

'Is Patrick here?' she asked without preamble.

'Hello to you, too. No, he's gone to pick up the meat order. Why?'

'No reason.' She rolled up her sleeves. 'Where shall I start?'

They spent the next couple of hours hefting tables into place and making sure each chair was spaced evenly like the numbers on a clock. Chloe passed the time speculating what famous guests might turn up. Kate, who had a copy of the guest list, would have loved to have told her, but had been expressly forbidden by Patrick to divulge a single detail. The happy couple had imposed a blanket ban on anyone posting anything on social media as they'd sold exclusive rights of the ceremony and wedding breakfast to a celebrity magazine.

A bit rich for a couple who'd built their fortunes on the lucrative foundations of Instagram, but as the magazine fee was probably paying Patrick's over-inflated prices, and Patrick paid Kate's under-inflated wages, who was she to argue?

Once the final chairs were in place, they laid the tablecloths and hung a length of bespoke bunting featuring the bride and groom's names on the wall behind the top table. Satisfied they'd done as much as they could, Kate jingled her keys.

'Great job. Let's go home and eat. I don't know about you, but I'm starving.'

'I'm just going to wash my hands. They're filthy,' Chloe said.

'OK. Take the keys and lock up. I'll see you outside.'

Kate lobbed the keys to Chloe, who caught them one-handed.

'Remember to double-lock the main doors.'

'I know how to lock a door, Mum. I'm not stupid.'

Kate sat on a wrought iron bench in front of the water fountain that was a popular spot for wedding photos. Hoping Adam might have texted, she checked her phone but found only a WhatsApp message from Lola and a picture of a deserted beach with white sand and a cornflower-blue sea. With a pang, Kate was reminded of Thailand and Noah. Her spine tingled.

. . .

How's everything going? All set for the big day? Lx

Why? Afraid we won't cope without you?! You enjoy your holiday and don't worry about us. Everything is sorted, and it's all going to run like clockwork. We're going to give everyone a day they'll never forget. See you soon. K x

CHAPTER THIRTY-SEVEN

KATE

The alarm on Kate's phone wrenched her from sleep early the next morning. Even though the ceremony wasn't due to start until one, she knew from bitter experience that time had a habit of running away with itself. She needed to be at The Willows by eight at the latest.

Showered and dressed, she headed downstairs. Her father was already in the kitchen, sitting at the table flicking through a seed catalogue, which amused her given he never lifted a finger in the garden.

Max wandered over, biffed her thigh with his head and stood by his bowl, looking at her expectantly.

'He's been out,' her father said. 'And the kettle's just boiled. Cup of tea?'

'That would be lovely, thanks.' Kate fixed Max's breakfast and poured herself a bowl of bran flakes. 'I have a feeling it's going to be a long day. Patrick wants everything to be perfect.' She pulled a face.

They sat in companionable silence while Kate finished her breakfast, thinking about the day ahead, mentally double-checking they'd covered every eventuality. It was important for The Willows that the wedding went without a hitch.

She placed her bowl in the dishwasher, gathered her bag and coat and patted her pockets. 'You haven't seen my work keys, have you, Pa?'

Her father looked up from his seed catalogue. 'Aren't they on the hook?'

Kate peered at the key rack by the back door, scanned the dresser and double-checked her pockets. 'Nope.' She riffled through a pile of papers and magazines on the table and glanced underneath the fruit bowl.

'Say a prayer to my namesake.'

Kate looked blankly at her father.

'Saint Anthony, the saint for lost objects,' he said.

Kate turfed the contents of her handbag onto the kitchen counter. She picked through her scuffed red leather purse, hairbrush, a small tub of Vaseline, a packet of tissues and a few receipts. But no keys. She raised her eyes to the ceiling. 'Saint Anthony, can you please tell me where my bloody work keys are?' She raked her hands through her hair. 'I can't be late today of all days.'

Her father patted her shoulder on his way to the sink. 'Work backwards. When did you last see them?'

'When I locked up last… Wait a minute, Chloe locked up for me. They're probably still in her pocket. Thanks, Pa, you're a lifesaver.' She brushed her lips against his stubbly chin as she flew out of the kitchen and up to Chloe's room.

Kate eased the door open and poked her head around the frame. Chloe was fast asleep, her hair fanning across the pillow like spun gold. She gave a small sigh and turned over to face the wall. Her coat was hanging on the back of her desk chair. Kate crept into the room and felt in each pocket. A lip balm, more tissues but no keys. *Shit*.

'Chloe, it's Mum. Can you remember where you put my work keys last night?' she said, shaking Chloe's shoulder gently.

Chloe groaned and buried her head in the pillow. 'What time is it?'

'Half seven. What did you do with my keys? I need to get to work, and I can't find them anywhere.'

'I left them on the dresser.'

'They're not there now.'

Chloe muttered something under her breath, then said, 'Grandpa's probably put them in the fridge or something. I told you he's getting more and more confused. I caught him putting Stork margarine on his toast the other morning. Yuck.'

'That's because we'd run out of butter,' Kate said. 'Are you sure that's where you left them?'

Chloe sat up in bed. 'Of course I'm sure!' she snapped.

'Fine. I'll look again. Go back to sleep, and I'll see you at two.'

Kate checked the dresser in the kitchen again and glanced inside the fridge, just in case Chloe had been right about her grandfather. Not that Kate thought he'd do anything so absentminded.

'No luck?' he asked.

She shook her head. 'I'll have to hope Pete's already in the kitchen and use the spare set today. I'd better go. I won't be home until late. Can you make your own tea tonight?'

'I'm sure I'll manage. Good luck with today.'

'The way things are going so far, I'm going to need it.'

To Kate's relief, Pete's pickup was already in the staff car park. She scurried into the kitchen and found him laying out two hundred small plates in the prepping area.

'Is Patrick around?' she asked breathlessly.

'I haven't seen him yet. Luckily for you, I was the first to arrive. I found these,' he said, reaching into his pocket and dangling a set of keys on his finger, 'left in the back door.'

Kate frowned. 'But we went out of the front door last night. Are you sure they're mine?'

He held them out to her. 'No-one else I know has an elephant keyring.'

Kate took the keys. Sure enough, there was the little silver elephant she'd bought from a market stall in Chiang Mai nineteen years ago. Chloe must have let herself out the back, accidentally left the keys in the lock and then come around to the front of the house. Silly girl. Head in the clouds half the time. She'd give her a rocketing later. Imagine if someone had found the keys before Pete? The thought sent a frisson of fear down Kate's spine. She shook her head. Don't dwell on it, she told herself. No harm done.

'Thanks, Pete, you're a lifesaver,' she said, slipping the keys into her back pocket.

He grinned. 'No worries.'

'Has the florist been?'

He picked up another pile of plates. 'I haven't been into the house yet, but I've not seen her car.'

Kate strode through the kitchen, heading for the main part of the house. She stopped at the fire door. There was a smudge of crimson on the white paint, as if someone had cut themselves and touched it with bloodied fingers. Wrinkling her nose, Kate pulled a length of blue roll from the dispenser over the sink, ran it under the tap and dabbed at the smear. It didn't rub off.

Not blood then. She touched it with her index finger, drawing back as if she'd been burnt. It was tacky, like fresh gloss paint. But they hadn't been decorating. Her scalp prickled as she pushed the door open, fearing the worst.

CHAPTER THIRTY-EIGHT

KATE

A t first glance, everything seemed fine. The tables and chairs were where Kate and Chloe had left them. The large easel displaying the seating plan was in its place and the cake stand was ready and waiting for the cake. Kate let out a long breath and turned back into the kitchen in search of the napkins they'd folded the night before.

She loaded them on a trolley along with two hundred sets of cutlery. Laying the tables would take a couple of hours, but it was her favourite part of the day. She loved the mathematical precision of it all: working outwards from the main knives and forks, getting everything just so.

She could have waited for the first couple of waitresses to arrive so they could help, but no-one took as much care with the plate settings as she did. It was easier to do it herself.

She wheeled the trolley over to the top table where the bride, groom, and their parents would be sitting, along with the best man and chief bridesmaid, a Premier League football player and an up-and-coming actress, widely tipped to become the next big thing. Kate made a mental note to remind the staff not to gawp. Patrick had already warned them he'd be locking their phones in his office, removing the temptation to snatch an illicit picture of the happy couple.

Kate counted out eight napkins and laid them on the table. That's when she saw the scrawl of red graffiti on the white linen tablecloth, right where the bride and groom would be sitting. Her stomach clenched as she read the words, *Patrick Twyman is a dirty paedophile.*

She shot a glance over her shoulder as if the culprit might still be lurking somewhere in the building, but the huge hall was empty. Her eyes were drawn to the tablecloth. The red paint matched the smudge on the kitchen door. The meaning behind the words was clear. But who would have done it, and how the hell had they got in?

With a swooping sensation in her stomach, she remembered the lost keys. *Shit.* Someone must have found them, let themselves in and...

'Kate!' Patrick barked from somewhere in the belly of the house. 'Have you seen the box of wedding favours?'

Kate froze. They ought to call the police to report the graffiti, but in less than three hours Pippa and Edison would be arriving, bringing their whole entourage with them. And she could hardly tell Patrick. He'd go ballistic. Kate gazed around the room, checking nothing else was amiss, but the sixteen other tablecloths were pristine, and everything else was in its place. The only damage was to the table linen on the top table. She had freshly-laundered spares in the storeroom. There was still time to clear up the mess.

'Kate!' Patrick hollered again.

Kate wavered for a second then came to a decision. Bundling up the defaced tablecloth, she stuffed it onto the bottom shelf of the trolley as Patrick swept into the room.

'I've been calling you for the past ten minutes,' he grumbled. 'Have you seen the favours? Pippa's been on the phone. She's just found out one of the guests has a nut allergy and wants us to take out the sugared almonds.' His eyes narrowed. 'What's happened to the tablecloth on the top table?'

Kate forced a smile. 'The favours are in the prep room, where they always are. And there was a red wine stain on the tablecloth. I'm on my way to get a clean one.'

Patrick huffed. 'I've a good mind to swap laundry services. That's the second time they've delivered dirty linen.'

'Leave it to me,' Kate said hurriedly. 'I'll have a quiet word with them on Monday.'

He gave a curt nod. 'Is everything else on schedule?'

'I think so. Is that all?'

He nodded.

'Right, well, I'd better get on.'

With the rolled-up tablecloth under her arm, Kate headed out of the kitchen and across the staff car park to the storeroom, her heart still beating uncomfortably fast in her chest. She shoved the cloth in a black rubbish sack which she double-knotted and stuffed into a corner behind some broken chairs. A glance at her watch sent her pulse even higher. It was almost half-past eight, and she hadn't even made a start on the tables. She called Chloe, who answered on the third ring.

'Triple time if you come over to help me now.'

'I'm trying to revise.'

'Please Chloe. I wouldn't ask, but I'm really up against it.'

'Triple time, you say?'

'And I'll let you have Netflix.'

'Deal. I'll be there in ten minutes.'

———

Kate was laying the dessert cutlery when Chloe arrived. She handed her a bag of small forks and a pair of white gloves.

'Put the forks under the spoons like this.' Kate demonstrated on the nearest table. 'Put the gloves on so you don't smear the cutlery. And remember, keep everything nice and straight. Everything needs to be -'

'Perfect. I know. I've heard Patrick going on about it enough. Where is he, by the way?'

'Why?'

Chloe jerked her head back. 'Don't jump down my throat. I was only asking.'

'Sorry. I'm a bit on edge. There's still so much to do. Listen, Chlo. You know last night I left you to lock up? Are you sure you came out of the front door?'

'Yes. Why?'

'Because Pete found my keys in the back door when he arrived this morning. You must have left them there.'

Chloe stared at Kate. 'No, I didn't. I left them on the dresser at home, I swear. Anyway, you saw me come out of the front door. You were there waiting for me.'

'I was texting Lola. I didn't see.'

'You don't believe me.'

Kate paused. 'Of course I do. But how else do you explain why the keys were in the back door?'

'Did you ask Grandpa? Maybe he wandered over here with the keys in the middle of the night.'

'Why on earth would he do that?'

'I dunno. Looking for you or something. Seriously though, Mum, you need to get him to the doctors. I swear he's getting Alzheimer's.'

'He's nearly ninety. He's a bit forgetful, that's all.' Kate came to a decision. 'There's something I want to show you.'

She strode over to the storeroom with Chloe on her heels. Shutting the door behind them, she retrieved the black sack and pulled out the defaced tablecloth. 'Take an end,' she instructed.

Chloe's eyes widened as she read the message. 'Bloody hell. Who did that?'

'Whoever let themselves in with my keys, I guess,' Kate said.

'Well, it wasn't me if that's what you're thinking,' Chloe said. 'Although it's true, he is a bloody pervert.'

'Chloe!'

'Come on, he's a grade one sleazebag. In my humble

opinion,' she added. 'Any one of the girls here could have done it.'

'But what if he or one of the guests had seen it?'

'Did they?'

Kate shook her head. 'No, thank God.'

Chloe shrugged. 'So what are you worried about? And on the plus side, at least they can spell.'

CHAPTER THIRTY-NINE

CHLOE

C hloe didn't know what all the fuss was about. It was probably just one of the girls playing a prank, and totally justified in her opinion. OK, so Patrick had never actually felt her up, but he'd come close a few times, like that day he'd straightened her tie in the hallway. The memory of him leaning towards her, his minty breath on her face, still made her shudder. She'd seen the way his eyes lingered over her when he thought she wasn't looking. She'd had a lucky escape. It was only because she made sure she was never alone with him that he hadn't properly tried it on.

There were so many rumours among the waitresses about him and his wandering hands. One girl had stormed out in tears after he pinched her bum while she was on her own with him in the storeroom, and another had almost reported him to the police after he forced himself on her as they closed up the bar for the night, according to the stories.

Chloe's mum had given her a funny look. 'He may be

demanding and difficult and downright unpleasant at times, but he's not a sexual predator, Chlo.'

'You think those girls were lying?'

'I'm saying I've worked here since I was seventeen. In all those years, I have never once witnessed Patrick behaving inappropriately with anyone, teenage girl or otherwise.'

But her mum always saw the best in people. And in Chloe's view, that was a weakness, not a strength.

No, there were too many rumours about Patrick for it not to be true. He was a dirty paedophile. And he deserved everything he got.

By half-past ten, the tables had been laid, and Chloe was helping her mum set out the table decorations. Each table was named after a brand of drink: Smirnoff, Baileys, Glenfiddich, Bombay Sapphire, Courvoisier and so on. In the centrepiece of each was a corresponding bottle with a string of LED fairy lights twinkling inside. It looked pretty cool.

Chloe's mum, usually an oasis of calm in the frenetic few hours leading up to a wedding, was flustered and jittery. Her eyes constantly roamed the room as she checked and rechecked everything.

'I can't help thinking I've missed something vital,' she said, picking up a champagne glass from the top table and holding it up to the light to inspect it for smears. 'Oh my God, is that the helicopter?'

They both cocked their heads to listen as the whirr of

rotor blades grew louder. Patrick ushered the staff into the hall and clapped his hands, the sound reverberating off the walls like a gunshot.

'Before the first of our guests arrive I wanted to remind you how important this wedding is for The Willows. There may only be two hundred guests here today, but we'll be on show to the rest of the world. So, I want nothing short of perfection. Congratulate our happy couple and remember to smile. Hands behind backs when not holding food and absolute discretion at all times. That means nobody trying to take photos or posting anything on social media *at all*. Do I make myself clear?'

They all nodded.

'You're all professionals. You know what you're doing. Go and do what you do best. Kate, can I have a quick word?'

Chloe's mum gave the waiting team a strained smile. 'Run through in five minutes, OK guys?'

Chloe pulled out the nearest chair and sat down, half-listening to the others as they second-guessed who was on the wedding list.

'I heard George and Amal are coming,' Shannon said, her eyes wide.

A haughty girl called Tanisha snorted. 'In your dreams. Edison's from Hackney, not Hollywood. We'll have a room full of wannabe C-listers, if we're lucky.'

Chloe scanned the room, taking in the hop garlands and fairy lights twisted around the oak beams and the opulent display of claret-red roses and peonies on the top table. Everywhere, polished glasses sparkled in the weak early spring sunshine. The Great Hall had never looked more beautiful. The bride and groom had thought of everything, from the personalised packets of love-in-a-mist seeds on every table to the goody bags stuffed with colouring pads, crayons and sweets for the children.

Her eyes drifted upwards to the bunting behind the top table that she'd hooked up with her mum the night before. It was definitely on the saccharine side of cutesy with its vintage-style hessian flags, white lettering and love hearts. Chloe could already picture the artfully-curated photos on Pippa's Instagram feed.

But something wasn't right. Caught up in her daydream, it took her a second or two to realise. Then her eyes widened, and she gasped.

Someone had ripped off some of the flags. What was left was a single word, with no mistake about its meaning. Five letters. One ugly word.

Paedo.

Chloe flushed hot, then cold, as she realised the gravity of the situation. In a few moments, the groom would be arriving with his best man and ushers, not to mention the photographer from the magazine. They could walk in at any second. Her eyes darted to the open doors. She couldn't risk anyone seeing the banner, but she couldn't reach it without a stepladder. She jumped to her feet, not bothering to push her chair back in, and scurried out in search of her mum.

She eventually found her in the kitchen with Pete, going over the list of guests with food allergies.

'Mum,' Chloe said.

Her mum held up a hand. 'Not now, Chloe. I'm busy.'

'It's important.'

Her mum sighed, apologised to Pete and ran an agitated hand through her hair. 'It had better be good.'

Chloe tugged her sleeve. 'You need to follow me. *Now*.'

'I don't have time for games.'

'This isn't a game,' Chloe muttered, dragging her mum out of the kitchen and along the hallway into the banqueting hall. 'Look at the bunting,' she hissed.

'Yes, it's still there,' her mum said impatiently.

'Look at it properly. What does it say?'

'Pippa and… oh *shit*. How the hell did I miss that?'

'I only just noticed it. We need to get it down before they arrive.'

Her mum closed her eyes for a second. 'Go and tell the others that Pete's briefing them on the menu in the prep room today. On your way back grab the stepladder. I'll tell Patrick there's a call for him in his office, then I'll meet you in a couple of minutes.'

Chloe nodded. She ran back into the hall, shepherded the others out towards the prep room and went in search of the stepladder. She arrived back at the hall at the same time as her mum. They worked together in silence, Kate holding the ladder while Chloe climbed to the top rung and reached up to unhook the bunting from the wall.

She wound it up roughly and stuffed it in the front pocket of her apron. 'What do we do if they ask where it's gone?'

'Don't worry, I'll think of something,' her mum said.

'And well done for spotting it. It could have ruined everything.'

'Who do you think could have done it?'

Her mum shrugged. 'The same person who spoiled the tablecloth?'

'But why?'

'I wish I knew.'

There was a scrape of wood as the door opened inwards and two men in black dress suits sauntered in. Chloe's eyes popped out on stalks at the sight of Edison Cooper and one of his impossibly-tanned fellow Love Island contestants.

She let out a long breath. 'In the nick of time. Still, no harm done, eh?'

Her mum rested a hand on her arm. Chloe wasn't sure whether she was offering reassurance or seeking it. 'You're right,' she said. 'No harm done.'

CHAPTER FORTY

KATE

Kate poured herself a large glass of Sauvignon, pulled up a chair and propped her phone against the fruit bowl. The urge to talk to someone other than a monosyllabic teenager, an irascible pensioner or an adoring labrador was overwhelming. She took a slug of wine, picked up the phone and called Adam before she could change her mind.

He answered on the fifth ring with a tetchy, 'Hello?'

'Oh, erm, hi, it's me. Kate.'

'Is everything all right?'

'It's fine. Why?'

'It's a quarter to eleven on a Saturday night. Is it Chloe?'

'Oh shit, is it that late?' Kate rubbed her forehead. 'I'm sorry, Adam. I should never have called. Were you asleep?'

'No.' He sighed. 'I'm reading court papers in bed. Very rock n' roll.'

'Living the dream,' Kate said, the tension behind her eyes easing a fraction.

'Indeed. Have you been at work?'

'Just got in. We had a celebrity wedding. It's been a bit full-on. Edison Cooper from Love Island got hitched to Pippa Harrington-Jones. You know, the Instagram queen?'

'I'm afraid I don't.'

Kate was silent. Was she being over-sensitive, or was there an edge of disdain to his voice? Maybe she was imagining it. She was tired, that was all. It had been a long day.

'And did it go well? This celebrity wedding?'

'It was fine. Look, I'll leave you to your court papers. Sorry to bother you so late.'

'Are you working tomorrow?'

'I'm always working, me. No rest for the wicked.' Kate tried to inject lightness into her voice, but it just came out a bit whiny. 'Night, Adam.'

'Goodnight, Kate. Take care.'

Kate took another long draught of her wine and stared at her phone, feeling a little foolish. All she'd wanted was to talk about her day, but Adam clearly hadn't been in the mood for a chat. And who could blame him? It was late, and he was far too cultured to want to dissect Edison and Pippa's big day if he'd even heard of them in the first place.

Rory would know who they were. Kate tapped the FaceTime app on her phone, and within seconds, her brother was grinning at her from the other side of the world.

'Hello, Katie, how's it going?'

'We had Edison Cooper's wedding today, the guy from Love Island.'

'Oh my God,' Rory said. 'He's sooo buff. Such a waste he's into girls.' He arched an eyebrow and Kate stifled a snort of laughter, her mood instantly lifted. 'He's engaged to Pippa Harrington-Jones, isn't he?'

'Not any more. They're Mr and Mrs Triple-Barrelled-Edison-Harrington-Jones now.'

'God, I bloody love her. Did you know she has almost as many followers on Instagram as Doug the Pug? Why wasn't I told they were getting married at The Willows?' he pouted.

'It was all very hush-hush. If I'd told you I'd have had to kill you.'

'Fair enough. So, spill. How did it go?'

Kate sipped her wine and described the wedding, from the moment Pippa glided in wearing a Caroline Castigliano wedding dress and faux fur stole to the moment Kate had left with the disco in full swing and things getting decidedly messy.

'Christ knows what state the place will be in tomorrow, but all in all the day went pretty well, considering how it began.'

'What do you mean?'

She hadn't intended to tell him about the graffiti-stained tablecloth or the defiled bunting. The fewer people who knew about it the better. But she had to tell someone otherwise she might burst.

'Someone broke into The Willows and spray-painted "Patrick Twyman is a dirty paedophile" on the top table.'

Rory's jaw dropped. 'You're kidding me.'

'I wish I was. And they even cut off some of the letters on the Pippa and Edison bunting, so it just said paedo.'

Rory burst out laughing.

Kate tutted. 'Not helpful.'

'I'm sorry,' he said, wiping his eyes. 'But seriously? Who would do a thing like that?'

'I genuinely have no idea.'

'What did you do?'

'Chloe and I managed to clear it all away before they arrived, thank God.'

'What on earth did Patrick say?'

'I didn't tell him.'

Rory frowned. 'Why?'

'He had enough on his plate. And you know what he's like.'

'I hope you at least reported it to the police? That's criminal damage.'

'I know.' Kate pulled out her ponytail, ran her hands through her hair and re-tied it as tightly as she could, Croydon facelift-style.

'And what did they say?'

Kate hesitated. 'I didn't call them.'

'What? Why?'

Kate lowered her voice. 'Because I was worried it might have been Chloe.'

'*What?*'

'She's convinced Patrick has been coming on to her. I've told her he's harmless, but she thinks I'm protecting him. I know he's a bit of a flirt and he likes a pretty face, but he's not a paedophile.'

'Are you sure, Katie? It doesn't sound like something Chloe would do.'

'There's something else. Whoever it was used my keys to get into The Willows.'

'Bloody hell.'

'Exactly,' Kate said. 'Chloe was the last to lock up on Friday night. So if I report it to the police, they're bound to want to talk to her about it, even if she had nothing to do with it. I can't let that happen. She's got enough on her plate at the moment.'

Kate found herself telling Rory about Chloe's panic attack. 'She's really down on herself. I don't know if it's because her A-levels are looming or the problems with Ben, but she's as miserable as sin. She's even talking about finding Noah.'

'That's not like Chloe.'

'I know. And that's why I don't want Patrick or the police finding out what happened.'

'Could you try to find her dad? You know, on the QT?'

Kate sat back in her chair. 'I don't have anything to go on.'

'You have a name. The world is a lot smaller now than it was nineteen years ago. You could at least give it a shot.'

'Maybe,' Kate said, knowing full well she wouldn't. That would be opening up a whole other can of worms. And what was the point?

CHAPTER FORTY-ONE

CHLOE

Chloe yawned, closed her textbook and threw another couple of logs on the fire, watching the flames as they hissed and crackled in the grate. She plugged her earphones in and found the Game of Thrones soundtrack. Dragons and battles. Perfect for a pyjama day.

With her mum at work and her grandfather and Max fishing, she had the house to herself. It was a rare luxury and she planned to make the most of the solitude. She would finish her history revision before lunch and spend the afternoon chilling.

She was more relaxed than she'd been for a while. Ben hadn't texted and since Adam had been in contact with Snapchat, there had been no more photos, and he'd been right, her notoriety at school had been short-lived.

Even so, she pulled her curtains closed every night.

The only niggle was her grandfather. Only that morning he'd pulled on his wellies, frowned, and said, 'My boots feel strange.'

Chloe had crouched down, running her thumb across

his toes as if he was a child in a shoe shop trying on his first pair of lace-ups.

'That's because you've got them on the wrong feet,' she'd said. 'Sit down, and I'll swap them over.'

He'd sat with a bump, and she'd pulled off first one boot, then the other, sliding them back onto the right feet.

'That's the ticket,' he'd said, standing again. 'Now, where did I put my coffee?'

Chloe handed him his flask and he'd ruffled her hair. 'What would I do without you, eh?' he'd said, before lumbering out, Max by his side.

Was he going senile? According to her mum he was just a bit forgetful, but Chloe wasn't so sure. She vowed to keep a close eye on him.

It was grey and blustery outside, but it was warm in the snug, and her eyelids were heavy. A quick power nap wouldn't hurt. She'd once read that it was best to revise before you dropped off to allow your memories to consolidate while you slept. It was probably a load of crap but who cared? She lay on the sofa, pulled her dressing gown over her feet, and slipped a cushion under her head. Ten minutes to recharge the batteries, then she would tackle an old history paper. Her eyelids fluttered closed, and the hiss and crackle of the fire faded as she slipped into unconsciousness.

Somewhere outside the room a floorboard creaked.

'Grandpa, is that you?' she called out sleepily. But there was no reply. She turned onto her side and succumbed to her dreams.

Hiss and crackle. Crackle and hiss. The scent of woodsmoke in her nostrils.

Her lungs tightened as if she'd just run a 100-metre sprint, which was silly, because she hated running. It was suffocatingly hot, and she tugged at the neck of her dressing gown. Someone was coughing. Loud, wracking coughs that reverberated around the room.

And someone was calling her name. No, not calling. Shouting.

'Chloe! *Chloe!*'

A hand gripped her upper arm, pulling her up.

'Go away!' she mumbled.

'Chloe, you need to wake up. Now!'

A man's voice. Not Grandpa. She prised her eyes open. It was Adam.

She felt herself being lifted and looked down to see his hands on the lapels of her dressing gown as he pulled her up.

'There's a fire,' he cried hoarsely. 'I need to get you out.'

Chloe looked over his shoulder, and her eyes widened. Billows of smoke hung in the air like storm clouds and flames danced between the legs of the coffee table.

'I d-don't understand.'

'Come on, quickly!'

Chloe's gaze fell on the cheap synthetic rug in front of the hearth. It was smouldering red, embers as angry as lava. Her eyes snapped back to Adam as a wracking cough gripped her diaphragm.

'A log must have rolled out of the grate and set the rug on fire,' Adam panted. 'You've breathed in a lot of smoke. You need some fresh air. Come on.'

She nodded and forced her legs to move as Adam's hand snaked under her arms, and he pulled her close.

'OK?' he said into her hair.

She nodded again and sank against him. He half-lifted, half-dragged her out of the snug, along the hallway, through the kitchen and out of the back door. He led her over to a bench, and she sank onto it, sucking air into her burning lungs.

Adam wrapped his coat around her shoulders and gently tipped her chin up to him. 'You OK?'

'Yes,' she croaked.

He touched the end of her nose. 'Thank goodness for that. You stay here. I'm going back in to put the fire out.'

'Be careful!' she called. He turned briefly by the back door and raised a hand in a salute before disappearing into the house.

Time stretched like elastic as Chloe tried to slow her breathing. Her head was pounding and her eyes, trained on the back door, felt gritty and sore.

She ought to call the fire brigade. Maybe Adam had called them already, and they were on their way. What if he hadn't? Her phone was still in the house, but the thought of going back into the smoke-filled snug filled her with horror. Instead, she staggered to the back door and called Adam as loudly as her lungs would allow.

She cocked her head. All she could hear was a roaring noise, but whether it was the fire or the whooshing of her own heart, she couldn't be sure. There was a moment when he didn't answer, and she panicked. Making up her mind, she held the bottom of her dressing gown over her mouth and nose and stepped into the kitchen.

At that moment, Adam appeared from the hallway with the smoking rug rolled up under his arm and a triumphant look on his face.

'I thought I told you to stay where you were,' he said, throwing the rug onto the patio and stamping on it, sending a cloud of acrid smoke into the air.

Chloe dropped her makeshift mask and coughed. 'I was coming to look for you.'

Adam guided her back to the bench and sat beside her. 'No need. I had everything under control.'

'Is the fire out?'

He nodded. 'Luckily it's only damaged the rug and scorched the table. But any longer and the whole house could have gone up.'

'With me in it.' Chloe shivered. 'Thank goodness you were here.' She paused. 'What *are* you doing here anyway?'

'I popped over to see your mum, and when there was no answer at the door, I came around the back to check she wasn't in the garden.'

'She's at work.'

'But her car's in the driveway.'

'She walks unless it's raining.'

'And your grandfather?'

'He's gone fishing with Max. I was here on my own.'

'Just as well I did pop round then.'

Chloe frowned. 'But how did you get in? The back door was locked.'

'I'm afraid I had to smash a window.' Chloe followed his gaze to the back door. The small pane of glass closest to the handle was broken, leaving a jagged edge like shark's teeth. 'I'll call someone out to fix it.'

'Thanks,' she said as her eyes drifted down to the crazy paving by the doorstep. It was littered with fragments of broken glass. She was lucky not to have cut her feet to pieces.

CHAPTER FORTY-TWO

CHLOE

C hloe stood under the hot shower, letting the water rinse the smell of smoke from her hair. She still had a headache, and when she blew her nose, the tissue had been black, but her lungs felt clear, and her breathing was back to normal. She'd had a lucky escape.

Adam had wanted to take her to A&E to have her checked over as a precaution, but she'd convinced him she was fine. He'd offered to call her mum to ask her to leave work early. He'd even volunteered to fetch Grandpa from his fishing trip. But Chloe wasn't having any of it. She couldn't bear the fuss.

As the water ran down her body in comforting torrents, she wondered again how the fire could have started. She'd been lighting their open fires for years. Grandpa had taught her when she was about twelve. He'd said it was an essential life skill, like being able to gut a fish or skin a rabbit. Not that she'd ever seen him skin a rabbit, but apparently he had during the war.

She'd drawn the line at rabbits, though had been

happy to master the art of starting a fire. But she was super careful and always used the fireguard, especially if the logs were damp and likely to spit. She pictured the fireplace in her mind's eye. Had the guard been there when Adam had pulled her to safety? She couldn't remember.

Her mum had bought the rug at a knockdown price from a stall at the local market. It was probably acrylic or nylon or something equally flammable. Chloe turned off the shower, squeezed the water out of her hair and wrapped herself in a towel. She'd been lucky this time. Smoke inhalation caused more than half of all fire-related deaths, according to Google. She'd looked it up as Adam had swept up the broken glass and called an emergency glazier. What if he hadn't been there to drag her to safety? She pushed the thought from her mind.

Drying herself quickly, she padded onto the landing and found clean clothes in the airing cupboard. When she was dressed, she headed back down to the snug to investigate the damage.

The caustic smell of smoke still clung to the sofa and curtains even though Adam had thrown open every window in the room. It was arctic-cold. Chloe stood in the doorway and hugged herself warm. Her schoolbooks and laptop were exactly where she'd left them on the coffee table. The fireguard was folded into four at the side of the brick chimney breast. How could she have been so stupid not to have put it in place after she'd lit the fire?

Chloe went in search of Adam, who was pacing around the garden, his hands thrust in his pockets.

'Everything OK?' he asked.

Chloe nodded.

'The glazier's promised to be here in half an hour. I'll wait until he's finished then leave you in peace. Are you sure you don't want me to phone your mum?'

'She'll only make a fuss. Thanks anyway. I'll stick the kettle on.'

Adam followed her back into the kitchen and watched as she busied herself making a cafetière of coffee. Her hands were still trembling as she placed his cup and saucer on the table.

'I think you probably saved my life,' she said.

'I happened to be in the right place at the right time, that's all. How's the revision going?'

Chloe rolled her eyes. 'Slowly. I've found it hard to keep focussed, what with that photo business and waitressing and everything. I'm so going to bomb my exams.'

'I'm sure you're not. Remind me what you need for Kingsgate?'

She grimaced. 'Three As.'

'And one of your kidneys?' Adam joked.

Chloe grinned. 'Not one of my smoke-damaged lungs, anyway. Ben's so lucky to have had an unconditional offer.'

Adam tilted his head and regarded her intently. 'It doesn't seem fair, does it? But my offer to set up a meeting with Jan Steel still stands. If she met you, saw how keen you were to get into the law school, she'd make you an unconditional offer, I know she would. Say the word, and I'll fix it.'

There was a rap at the front door, and Adam drained his coffee. 'That'll be the glazier. I'll let him in.'

Chloe flashed him a grateful smile and curled her fingers around her cup as she considered his offer. She was so bloody tempted. After all, life hadn't exactly been good to her recently. Ben's infatuation, him almost totalling his dad's car, the party, creepy Patrick and his terrible job, the photo on Snapchat, her panic attack and now the fire. It was no wonder she was finding it impossible to revise. She was stressed to the max. The way she was going, it would be a bloody miracle if she came away with three Bs, which wouldn't even get her into her second choice. She'd end up in clearing, under pressure to choose a crap course at an even crapper university and her life would basically be over.

And yet Adam was offering her the one thing she coveted most for no other reason than the fact he wanted the best for her. Chloe was pretty sure privately-educated kids had little compunction when it came to using their parents' network of contacts to give them a leg-up. And could she blame them?

One thing was for sure. She didn't want to end up like her mum, bowing and scraping to a tosser like Patrick all her life.

Adam wanted to help her. Chloe needed his help.

What would be so wrong in accepting a little help for once in her life?

CHAPTER FORTY-THREE

KATE

K ate felt the colour drain from her cheeks as she stared at her daughter.

'A fire?'

Chloe flicked her hair off her face. 'Don't get your knickers in a twist. It's fine. Adam put it out.'

'What was he doing here?'

'He'd come to see you.'

'But I told him I was working today.'

'He said he was driving past and saw your car in the drive. Luckily, he came around the back to see if you were in the garden and saw smoke coming out of the window of the snug.'

Kate was finding it all rather hard to take in. 'But you're all right?'

'I told you, I'm fine. I had a bit of a headache, but it's gone now. So you can stop fussing.'

'And what about the house?' Kate said, pushing past her into the kitchen.

'Your hearth rug is toast, the coffee table is a bit

251

singed, and there's a burn on the floorboards, but no other damage. It's a good job Adam turned up when he did.'

'A very good job,' Kate said faintly. 'Where was Grandpa when all this was going on?'

'Fishing with Max.'

Kate glanced at the line of boots by the back door. There was a space where her father's boots should have been. 'He's not back?'

'How should I know? I've been revising upstairs.' For the first time since Kate had arrived home, a flicker of doubt crossed Chloe's features. 'Come to mention it, I haven't heard him.'

'But it's almost dark.' Kate gazed out of the window. A tired-looking woman with deep frown lines glared back at her. With a start, she realised she was staring at her reflection. Christ, she looked knackered. She sighed. 'I'd better go and fetch him.'

'I'll come with you. I could do with some fresh air.' Chloe pulled on her boots and coat and wound a scarf around her neck.

'I hope he's OK,' Kate said, as they marched across the garden into the woods behind the house.

'He'll be fine. He's got Max with him.'

For once it was Chloe who was struggling to keep up as Kate strode through the woods towards the river. It was that bleak time between dusk and full-on darkness when the birds had stopped singing and the trees cast unearthly shadows in their path. At least as they drew closer to the river, the sound of rushing water filled the silence.

'He's probably up by the footbridge,' Chloe said. 'That's where the trout are biting at the moment.'

'How do you know that?' Kate said, surprised.

'Because I take the time to talk to him?'

'And you're saying I don't?'

'You're too busy telling him off for leaving crumbs on the table and nagging him about his maggots. So yes, since you're asking, I am.'

Stung, Kate plunged her hands deep into her pockets and peered into the gloom. She could just about make out the ebony arch of the old wooden structure against the indigo sky.

'Pa?' she called. 'Are you there?'

At once, there was a loud bark as Max came crashing through the undergrowth, almost knocking Kate over. She grabbed his collar, and he licked her hand. 'Pa,' she shouted again, trying to suppress the sense of unease that was settling like heartburn deep inside her chest. 'It's almost six. Time to call it a night.'

Chloe switched on the torch app on her phone. They both stopped while she waved it in the direction of the river. 'There he is,' she said, as the beam jerked and twitched over a chair-shaped shadow. 'Grandpa!' There was no answer.

'Something's not right,' Kate said, quickening her pace until she was almost running. Max, clearly thinking it was a game, capered beside her, his tail quivering in excitement. As she stumbled over a tree root, he broke free of her grip and bounded over to his master, but the old man didn't bend down to pat his head or tweak his ear. He didn't move at all. Kate's sense of unease deepened.

She took out her own phone, turned on the torch and shone it in her father's face. He was sitting in his fishing chair, his shoulders rounded, his eyes closed and his head slumped forwards. Chloe gasped.

'Oh, Christ.' Kate dropped to her knees in front of the chair and took his hand. 'Pa? It's me, Katie.'

'Is he asleep?' Chloe said in a small voice.

Kate shook her head. 'I don't know.' She dropped his hand and gave his shoulder a gentle shake. 'Pa, wake up. You're scaring us.'

But her father didn't move.

'Oh my God, is he dead?'

'I don't know, Chlo,' Kate said again. 'Phone for an ambulance. Tell them he might have had a heart attack. Or a stroke. I'm going to see if I can find a pulse.'

Chloe let out a small sob and stepped away, her phone pressed to her ear. Kate turned back to her father and tried to remember her first aid training. 'ABC,' she muttered. 'Airway, breathing, circulation.' She tilted his head back and leant towards him to see if she could feel his breath on her cheek, watching his chest all the time to see if it moved.

At first, she dismissed the faint flutter of air as the wind blowing across from the river. But when she saw his old Barbour jacket rise and fall, she rocked back on her heels and shouted to Chloe, 'He's breathing!'

'He's breathing,' Chloe relayed to the call taker in a shaky voice. 'But it's still an emergency so please, please come as quickly as you can.'

The next thirty minutes were the longest of Kate's life. She and Chloe draped their coats over the old man's shoulders, and they sat at his feet trying to rub warmth into his hands. His breathing was so slow and so shallow that Kate had to keep checking it hadn't stopped altogether. When she lost all feeling in her feet, she stood up and began collecting his things. The Tupperware box of maggots, his rod and landing net. The little wooden tackle box he'd had since he was a boy. The coffee in his flask was stone cold, so she tipped it onto the grass and screwed the lid up tight. She found the cup below the right arm of the chair.

'D'you think he's had a stroke?' Chloe asked quietly.

Kate shook her head. 'I don't think so. His face hasn't dropped.'

'A heart attack, then?'

'Possibly.' Tears were streaming down Chloe's face. Kate squeezed her shoulder and smiled. 'He'll be all right, Chlo. You know Grandpa, he's as strong as an ox.' She cocked her head, picking up the faint wail of a siren. 'Thank God, they're here at last.'

Within minutes, the ambulance had pulled up in the small gravel car park on the other side of the river, and two cheerily efficient paramedics loped over the footbridge.

'It's my father,' Kate said. 'Anthony Kennedy. We found him about half an hour ago. He'd been fishing,' she added unnecessarily.

The elder of the two paramedics took her father's hand and felt for a pulse. He nodded to his colleague. 'Stretcher please, Keith. And we're going to need some oxygen.'

'Is he going to be all right?' Chloe asked, hopping from foot to foot.

'He's still breathing, but he's unconscious, and his heart rate is very low, so we're going to blue light him to hospital. Would one of you like to travel with him?'

'I will,' Chloe said at once.

Kate shook her head, ready to protest, but Chloe put up a hand to silence her. 'You take the car, Mum. We'll need it to bring Grandpa home. And he's going to need his pyjamas and toothbrush and stuff if they keep him in for the night. I'll phone you when we get there to let you know how he is.' Chloe took her grandfather's hand. 'I'll stay with him,' she said again, broking no argument.

Kate's shoulders drooped. 'OK,' she said wearily. 'If you're sure.'

The paramedics busied themselves lifting her father onto a stretcher, draping a blanket over him and fixing an oxygen mask to his face. Under the blanket, he looked smaller, diminished, as if the life force was already leaching out of him. Kate shook the thought away. He would be fine. He was as strong as an ox.

'Had you better phone Uncle Rory?' Chloe asked as she climbed into the ambulance.

'Yes, you're right. I'll phone him from the house then follow you in.'

The ambulance door clunked shut and Kate was left alone in the gloom. She waved as the vehicle accelerated away, even though she knew Chloe couldn't see her. When it reached the road, its sirens and blue lights burst into life, and Kate watched as it vanished into the distance. She rubbed her face and stared at the fishing paraphernalia scattered at her feet, wondering how the hell she was going to carry it all home. Then she looked skywards. Kate hadn't been to church since her mother's funeral. Truth was, she hadn't been able to face it. She called herself an agnostic if ever anyone asked. But suddenly she felt an overwhelming need to send a plea to the Almighty.

'Please God,' she said, her voice scratchy. 'Let him be all right.'

CHAPTER FORTY-FOUR

CHLOE

C hloe hated hospitals, detested everything about them. The squeaky floors and the sharp tang of disinfectant. The hushed voices and the despairing faces. And the sick people, everywhere you looked. The old, the frail and the ailing. People waiting for outpatients' appointments, for blood tests, for X-rays, for death. And weaving among them, with their clipboards and sympathetic expressions, the hospital staff. Smiley nurses, earnest-faced junior doctors and, at the top of the tree, the god-like consultants wielding, so it seemed to her, the power of life and death.

One stood in front of Chloe now. An impossibly handsome dark-haired man in his late thirties with pearly-white teeth, a dark pirate's beard and an accent she couldn't quite place. Italian or Spanish, probably.

'Chloe Kennedy?' he said, holding out a hand. 'I'm Dr Martinez, the A&E consultant.'

Spanish then.

'Are you Mr Kennedy's next of kin?'

'Well, no. I'm his granddaughter. But my mum, his daughter, will be here any minute. She's trying to find somewhere to park.' Chloe turned at the sound of her name. 'In fact, there she is.'

They watched her mum scurry into the waiting room, pale-faced and clutching the grip of Grandpa's shabby overnight bag in one hand.

'Is he going to be OK?' she said, dropping the bag to the floor.

'The good news is that Mr Kennedy has regained consciousness,' Dr Martinez said.

'Thank goodness,' her mum said, squeezing Chloe's hand. 'Was it a heart attack?'

The doctor paused. 'Not according to the ECG but we're still waiting on the results of the blood tests.'

'So what then?' Chloe asked.

'We've ruled out a stroke and a pulmonary embolism. A cardiac arrest is still a possibility, but personally, I'm not convinced. It's an odd one.' He pulled on his beard. 'We're giving him oxygen as his levels are lower than we'd like. He's sleepy and confused, but there's no mention of dementia in his records…' Dr Martinez cocked an eyebrow at them.

'Well…' Chloe began.

Her mum shook her head. 'No dementia,' she said firmly.

'So we can only assume that his confusion is related to today's episode.' There was a beep, and the doctor gave them an apologetic smile as he reached for his pager. He frowned as he read the message. 'I'm afraid I have to go. We may know more when the blood results come back.

Mr Kennedy is resting now, but you are welcome to go and see him.'

He made to leave, then stopped and turned to them. 'Is Mr Kennedy on any kind of anti-anxiety medication?'

Chloe's mum blinked. 'Pa? No. Why?'

'It's probably nothing. It's just that he's presenting like someone who's been given...' He shook his head as his pager beeped again. 'I'm sorry, I have to go. I'll let you know when the test results are in.' He gave a brief nod and strode off, leaving Chloe and her mum staring at his back.

'What was all that about?' Chloe said.

'I have absolutely no idea. Come on, let's find Grandpa shall we?'

They found him in a bay of six beds in the acute medical unit. His eyes were closed, and an oxygen tube was attached to his nose. Chloe ignored the butterflies in her stomach and took his liver-spotted hand. His eyes fluttered open.

'Katie, is that you?'

'It's me, Chloe,' she said, trying not to cry. 'But Mum's here, too.'

'Oh, Pa, what happened?' Her mum took his other hand and stroked his cheek.

Confusion clouded his eyes. 'I can't say that I know. One minute I was fishing, and the next I wake up in this poor excuse for a hotel. I shan't be returning. I can promise you that. The customer service leaves a lot to be desired.'

'Oh Grandpa,' Chloe said, and despite the seriousness of the situation, she felt an uncontrollable urge to giggle.

'It's a hospital, not a hotel. You had a funny turn while you were out. We had to call an ambulance. We thought you'd had a heart attack.'

'A heart attack? Did I? I don't remember.' He jerked his hand free and pulled on the oxygen tube at his nose.

Chloe's eyebrows shot up, and she snatched his hand away. 'Don't do that, Grandpa. It's only oxygen to help you feel better.'

'The doctor doesn't think it was a heart attack,' her mum said. 'They're doing some tests to see what happened. Hopefully, they'll let you out tomorrow.'

'That would be nice,' Grandpa said, closing his eyes again. 'As long as the old ticker's fine. You two should go. It must be getting late.'

'Mum, did you remember Grandpa's things?'

'Oh, yes. I've brought you a pair of pyjamas, your shaving things, your toothbrush and some toothpaste. And the crossword and a pen. There's a fleece in case you're cold, although it's like a bloody oven in here.' She rolled her eyes. 'The germs must love it. I've also brought a box of tissues and some bananas. They're a bit soft, but it's all we had in. I'll see if I can find you some water. Won't be a sec.'

'Bye-bye Grandpa,'' Chloe said, bending down to kiss her grandfather's cheek. His unshaven skin felt as prickly as a thistle, but he smelt reassuringly of his favourite cologne. He patted her back.

'Don't you worry about me, Chloe. I'll be grand. Although I wish I could remember who it was.'

She straightened her back. 'Who what was?'

'The young chap who came to see me.'

She frowned, then her face cleared. 'You mean Dr Martinez? Nice, isn't he?'

'You think he likes your mother?'

'I'm not sure he…'

'I think he does. But don't tell her I said so.' He pressed a finger to his lips and chuckled. 'Our little secret, eh?'

Chloe nodded as her mum appeared with a jug of water. She poured Grandpa a glass and handed it to him. 'Are you sure you don't want us to stay a little longer?'

He fixed her with his penetrating courtroom gaze. 'Don't fuss, Katherine. I'll be fine. I'll see you in the morning. Now go.'

Chloe trailed after her mother along the hospital corridors and out through the main entrance. They stopped by the parking machine.

'Three pounds eighty? Daylight bloody robbery,' her mum grumbled as she fished in her purse for some change.

'I think you're wrong about Grandpa,' Chloe blurted.

Her mum raised an eyebrow.

'You told Dr Martinez he hasn't got dementia. But that's only because he hasn't been diagnosed. You've point blank refused to take him to the GP.'

Chloe's mum glanced at the queue of people behind them, all listening avidly. 'Can we continue this discussion in the car?'

She shrugged. 'Whatever.'

The Mini was parked so close to a wall that her mum had to reverse out before Chloe could climb in. She fixed her seatbelt and stared out of the window before finally beginning to speak.

'Grandpa's always forgetting stuff and losing things. He thought I was you just now!' A sob caught at the back of her throat and she swallowed it back down.

'He's eighty-seven, and he's had a horrid shock. He knew who you were really.'

Chloe knew her mum was trying to placate her, but she wasn't in the mood. Couldn't she see what was right in front of her nose?

'I keep telling you something's wrong, but you won't listen. You're burying your head in the sand as per normal. Grandpa told me he thought Dr Martinez fancied you. He's lost the plot.'

'And that's so totally ridiculous, is it? That a man might actually find me attractive?'

'That's not what I meant. But think about all the weird stuff that's been happening. My photo disappearing. Your work keys turning up at The Willows. The back door being left wide open in the middle of the night. It has to be Grandpa. I know it's not his fault and he doesn't mean any harm by it. But he needs professional help.'

Her mum sighed. 'If it'll make you happy I'll book an appointment with the GP once he's home from hospital.'

Chloe leaned back on the headrest and closed her eyes. 'It would make me happy, yes. Thank you,' she said.

CHAPTER FORTY-FIVE

KATE

Kate smoothed down her skirt and fluffed up her hair. She'd forked out over a hundred quid for highlights and a cut and blow-dry, but she didn't begrudge a penny of it. Her mousy brown tresses were streaked with gold and caramel and felt as swishy as a model's hair in a shampoo advert. She'd teamed her new embroidered knee-length skirt - a steal in the Boden autumn sale - with brown leather boots and a fitted jacket she'd discovered buried deep at the back of her wardrobe. With the scarf Rory had bought her for Christmas tied in what she hoped was a stylish fashion around her neck she felt, if not chic exactly, certainly more polished than in her normal go-to attire of jeans and a sweater.

She paused outside the Victorian building that had once been a terraced house but now served as the offices of Sullivan and Son Solicitors. It was less than a hundred metres along the street from the wine bar she and Adam had met for supper all those weeks ago. She thought the night had been a success. The meal at the pub, too. He'd spent a small fortune on wine, presumably to impress her. He'd opened up about his marriage. He'd sent flowers. That all meant something, surely? But he'd gone cold on her recently. He answered texts, eventually, with polite but reserved replies. If she tried to phone, it went straight to voicemail, and he'd made no attempt to arrange a third date.

Yet three days ago he'd turned up at the house to see her and had saved Chloe from what could have been... Kate gave a small shake of her head. No, she wouldn't even go there. What ifs were a waste of time and emotional energy. Better to focus on life's certainties and things she could control. And, now her father was home from hospital with Chloe babysitting, it was time to turn her attention to her love life or lack thereof.

Kate checked in her bag for the bottle of Bordeaux she'd bought in an expensive-looking off-licence. The £30 price tag included a wrap of slate grey tissue paper which crackled extravagantly under her touch. It was a thank you to Adam for saving Chloe, although, if she was honest, it was an excuse to see him.

The visit had been Rory's idea. He was calling a couple of times a day from Sydney to check on their father, and the previous evening, after a condition check on the patient - improving but a little peevish - the talk had turned to Adam.

'Why don't you pop around to his office with a bottle of something classy and thank him for the Big Rescue?'

'I already sent him a text,' Kate had said, stalling.

'So follow it up with a visit. Don't write him off quite yet. You need to see the whites of his eyes. Time it just before one o'clock and offer to take him out for lunch. You'll soon know if he's still hot for you.'

'You're incorrigible. I'll think about it.' Kate had said. And she had. All night. And when she'd woken up, she'd decided she would take Rory's advice. Because it made sense. At the moment she was treading water, unsure whether she and Adam were an item or not. At least if she saw him face-to-face, she'd be able to tell whether he was still interested. And when she'd managed to book a last-minute appointment at her favourite hair salon it hadn't just been serendipitous, it had been an omen she couldn't ignore.

She was about to rap on the door when she realised it was already ajar, so she gave it a push and found herself in a wide hallway with a terracotta tiled floor, picture rails and a high ceiling. The door on her right was open, and a middle-aged woman with her steel-grey hair swept back in a bun said, 'Do you have an appointment?'

Kate smiled. 'I'm afraid not. But I was passing, and I thought I'd pop my head in and see if Adam was free.'

The secretary raised an eyebrow. 'Mr Sullivan has someone with him at present. But you can wait if you'd like.' She indicated a chair by the window.

'Thanks.' Kate perched on the edge of the seat, her knees and ankles together and her hands clasped in her lap.

'And who shall I say is here?'

'Kate Kennedy.'

'Very well. I'll buzz him and let him know you're here. Would you like a drink while you wait?'

'Thank you. I'll have a...'

'There's a water cooler behind the door.'

Kate felt a flush creep up her neck as she pulled a plastic cup from the water cooler and filled it. The secretary swivelled her chair around and picked up the phone. Kate sipped her water and stared out of the window at the shoppers walking by.

'Can you put me through to your service department? Thanks, yes I'll wait,' the secretary said. 'I'm phoning on behalf of Mr Adam Sullivan. He needs an engineer to look at his boiler. The pilot light keeps going out. Yes, next Monday afternoon would be fine. It's forty-six Chapel Street.' She gave the postcode. 'Yes, someone will be in. Thank you.'

A small carriage clock on the mantel above the fireplace chimed one o'clock. The door opposite the window opened, and a nervy-looking Asian woman trotted out, a leather bag clasped to her chest. Adam, suited and booted, appeared in the doorway.

'Thank you, Mrs Chen. I'll see you next week. In the meantime, if you have any further questions, please don't hesitate to be in touch.'

The woman nodded and scurried out. Kate scrunched her plastic glass into a ball and stood.

'Hello, Adam.'

He leaned against the door and crossed his arms. 'Kate. What can I do for you?'

Aware that his secretary was pretending not to listen as she shuffled a pile of papers on her desk, Kate reached into her bag for the wine. 'I brought you a thank you present. For saving Chloe.'

An expression flickered across his face she couldn't read.

'You'd better come in,' he said, standing back and holding the door open.

'Don't forget your conference call at half-past,' the secretary called as the door closed.

'Christ, which charm school did she go to?' Kate laughed as she handed Adam the bottle.

'Sylvia's been with me since the firm opened. She's virtually family,' he said tightly.

'Oops. My bad. I wondered if you had time to pop out for some lunch? It's been ages since we last saw each other.'

Adam moved to his side of the desk and sat down. Kate took a seat opposite, feeling more like a client than a girlfriend.

'I don't have time today,' he said. 'I have a conference call with a QC. We're discussing a tricky child custody case. I can't miss it.'

She felt immediately chastened. 'Of course. It was silly of me to rock up without any warning. It's just I -'

The phone on Adam's desk buzzed. He held out a hand to silence her and picked up the receiver. 'Thank you, Sylvia. Put her through.'

Kate took in her surroundings, trying not to eavesdrop as Adam discussed protective orders and care proceedings with the person on the other end of the line.

Adam's enormous mahogany desk dominated the bright and airy room, which was painted duck-egg blue. On the wall behind him was a series of pen and ink drawings of London landmarks. Behind her, two low chairs were arranged round a coffee table on which sat a box of tissues. Blue and white Delft tiles edged an impressive cast iron fireplace. The desk itself was freakishly tidy, not a pen out of place.

Adam ended the call and replaced the receiver.

'I'm sorry about that. How's Chloe?'

'She's OK, considering.'

He frowned. 'She told me she was feeling all right when I left on Sunday.'

'Physically she's fine, thanks to you.' His expression remained neutral. 'But she's worried about her grandfather. They're very close, you see.'

'What's happened to him?'

'He had a funny turn while he was fishing the afternoon of the fire. We had to call an ambulance. He spent two nights in hospital.'

Adam picked up a pen, then set it down again. 'Do they know what's wrong with him?'

'They've ruled out a heart attack or stroke. We're waiting for the results of the blood tests to come back. He's feeling much better, but Chloe's pretty cut up about it. She has study leave on a Wednesday morning so is at home with him now.'

'I'm sorry to hear that. Send Chloe my best.'

'Of course.'

Adam glanced at his watch and pushed his chair back. 'I'm sorry, I'm going to have to get on.'

'Oh, right.' Kate took a deep breath. 'Adam, before I go... are we OK? I mean, we got on well when we went to the wine bar and the pub, but since then you haven't seemed… I mean… what I'm trying to say is, have I done something to upset you?'

His gaze darted to the door. 'Not at all. I'm swamped with work at the moment.' He gestured to his immaculate desk. 'You understand, I'm sure. Now if you'll excuse me…?'

'Of course. So sorry.' Kate picked up her bag and hitched it onto her shoulder. 'I'll see you around, then? And thanks again for what you did the other day. I don't know what would have happened if you hadn't been there.'

CHAPTER FORTY-SIX

CHLOE

C hloe and her grandfather sat either side of the fireplace in the front room, a jigsaw half-completed on the coffee table between them. Max lay at her grandfather's feet, opening an eye every time his master so much as moved a muscle. It was fair to say Grandpa's stay in hospital had shaken them all.

Chloe picked up a piece of sky and looked sidelong at her grandfather. Colour had returned to his pallid cheeks, and he was almost looking himself again. But there was a faint tremor in his hands as he held the jigsaw pieces and he was still a little unsteady on his feet. Chloe knew she had to face the fact he was nearly ninety, and one day he would go into hospital and never come home.

She chased the thought away. There was enough to worry about without catastrophising about the future. 'Is that the top of the lamp-post?' she asked, dipping her head at the piece he was holding between thumb and forefinger.

'You tell me,' he said, peering at it myopically before

handing it to her. 'Where was your mother off to this morning, all dressed up? Job interview, was it?'

Chloe clicked the piece into place. 'She said she was getting her hair done, but I'm not sure that's the whole story.'

'You think she's seeing the chap from the hospital?'

'Dr Martinez? I don't think so. I reckon she's seeing Adam.'

'Adam?' Her grandfather leaned forwards in his chair, and Max lifted his head.

'You remember, Grandpa. Ben's dad. You know, the boy I met at Kingsgate Uni open day?'

'Can't say as I do.' He leaned back again, and Max rested his head on his paws. 'Wait a minute, the chap who was here the day I went into hospital?'

'That's the one. Mum's got a bit of a thing for him.' Chloe ferreted in the jigsaw box for another piece of sky. 'He's nice. Actually, he's offered to do something for me that I wanted to talk to you about.'

'Oh, yes?' Her grandfather raised an eyebrow. 'When a middle-aged man wants to do something for a teenage girl, it usually spells trouble.'

'Oh Grandpa, it's nothing like that. Adam's a perfect gentleman.'

'So, what's he offering to do for you?'

Chloe scratched her ear with the jigsaw piece. 'You know I need three As to get into Kingsgate?'

'You're more than capable of that, m'dear.'

'But am I?' A memory of the suffocating terror she'd felt in the exam hall on the morning of her economics mock forced its way into her head. 'What if I have a bad day? What if I don't get the grades?'

Her grandfather dropped his jigsaw piece and looked at her. 'I still don't understand what this Adam chap has to do with your exam results.'

'He's old friends with Professor Jan Steel, the head of the law school. They were undergraduates there together. He's offered to take me to meet her. To have a chat, you know, and to talk about the course and see if she likes me. Adam reckons she might make the offer unconditional if I impress her. I'd still work hard for my exams, but it would take some of the pressure off.'

'In other words you want to use a personal connection to further your career?'

Put like that it sounded grasping and wrong. 'Well -'

Her grandfather chuckled. 'No need to look quite so hangdog. The idea that some of the biggest business deals are made on the golf course is a cliché, but that doesn't mean it's not true. Successful businesspeople call it networking. Professor Steel isn't going to offer you a place if she doesn't think you're worthy of one. It simply means she'll see you as a person, and not yet another name on one of hundreds of admission forms. Like it or not, having contacts does matter.'

'It's not what you know, it's who you know,' Chloe said, looking to her grandfather for confirmation.

'Quite. You'll probably find she's impressed you've gone the extra mile to connect with her. I think you should take this fellow up on his offer. As long as you're sure he doesn't have an ulterior motive.'

'Oh no,' Chloe said, smiling. 'He wants the best for me.'

While her grandfather was napping after lunch, Chloe tapped out a message to Adam.

I've been thinking, and I would like to take you up on your offer to meet Prof Steel if it still stands?

A reply pinged back almost instantly.

Of course! Only too happy to help. I'll ring her now and see when she's available.

Happy with her decision to enlist Adam's help and glad to have her grandfather's blessing, Chloe grabbed Max's lead and they headed out for a walk in the woods. Adam called before they'd even left the garden.

'That was quick,' Chloe said.

'I've spoken to Jan and she'd love to meet you. Is Friday any good? She's suggesting afternoon tea at her office at three o'clock, but it's going to take us a couple of hours to get down there, so we'd need to leave by one at the latest.'

Chloe pictured her timetable. She had double history

on a Friday afternoon. They'd already finished the syllabus and were only going over old papers. It wouldn't matter if she skipped a lesson.

'Friday would be great,' she said. 'Are you sure you're all right to drive me? I can easily take the train.'

Adam's voice was full of warmth. 'Don't be silly. You'd have to go into London and back out again. Anyway, I told Jan I'd be there, too. I'll pick you up from school at noon, OK?'

Picking up a scent, Max ran to the bottom of an oak tree and started barking loudly. Chloe pressed the phone closer to her ear. 'You don't know how much this means to me.'

'The pleasure's all mine.'

Chloe ended the call and slipped the phone into her pocket, feeling happier than she had for a long time. Grandpa was home. Ben had finally stopped hounding her and Adam was going to help her secure a place at Kingsgate University. Picking up a stick, she threw it for Max, feeling as though things were going her way at long last.

CHAPTER FORTY-SEVEN

KATE

Kate stared into the bottom of her coffee cup and wondered if there was something inherently wrong with her. She felt bruised, her already fragile ego in tatters. Adam had been so offhand, so *brusque*, that she felt discombobulated. Whatever could she have done to cause a slight of such magnitude that he had turned from attentive to indifferent without a single warning sign?

She gazed out of the café window and thought back to the last time she'd seen him. Their second date, if you could call it that. Pie and mash at the pub. Adam had been courteous and chatty. Perhaps he was just being polite. She picked up a spoon and prodded at the coffee grinds in her cup. No, dammit. He had genuinely appeared to enjoy her company. He'd even volunteered to put in a good word for Chloe with the head of the Kingsgate law school. Why would he offer to go out of his way to help Chloe if not to score points with Kate?

'Penny for them,' said the plump woman who'd taken Kate's order at the counter.

Kate gave a hollow laugh. 'I'm not sure they're worth that.'

'Oh, dear. Want to talk about it?'

Not really, Kate had been about to say. But the woman had kind, crinkly eyes, a motherly bosom and smelt faintly of lavender. And suddenly Kate had a yearning for her own mother. A tear leaked out of her eye and dropped into her empty cup with a blatant plop that neither of them could ignore.

'Sorry,' Kate sniffed. 'Man trouble, you know?'

The woman smiled her understanding. 'Mind if I join you? Looks like you could use the company,' she said, pulling out a chair. 'I'm Maggie, by the way.'

'Kate.'

'So, Kate, you've been playing with your coffee for the last hour and you have a face like a wet weekend. What's up?'

Kate gave a rueful grin and set the spoon on the saucer. 'The man I've been dating has gone all cold on me, and I've been trying to work out what I've done wrong.'

Maggie stared at her. 'What makes you think it's your fault?'

Kate rubbed her face. 'I don't know. I've been out of the dating game so long I kind of assumed it must be me.'

Maggie shook her head. 'Not so. And even if you had done something to upset this man of yours, why wouldn't he tell you?'

An image of Adam's ordered, perfect desk popped into Kate's head and it struck her that it reflected his personality to a tee. He was the personification of cool and in control. Detached and even, dare she admit it, uptight.

277

The most animated she'd seen him was in the wine bar when he'd railed against his ex-wife, Daisy. Only then had she glimpsed a hint of passion beneath his closed-book exterior.

Not like Noah the beach bum, who'd radiated warmth and fun and who she'd felt closer to in one night than she had in the six months she'd known Adam. Perhaps it was easier when you were nineteen.

'Kate?'

'You're right. I haven't done anything wrong. And do you know something else? I don't want to spend the rest of my life tip-toeing around a man, worrying every day in case I say or do something he doesn't like. It's not worth the aggro. Thanks, Maggie. You've opened my eyes to what's been staring me in the face for weeks, only I was too proud to admit it. Adam isn't interested in me. Not really. And if that's the case, I'm not interested in him either.' She reached in her bag for her purse. 'How much do I owe you?'

Maggie's eyes twinkled. 'Nothing, my lovely. This one's on the house.'

Kate turned the radio up and sang loudly all the way home. A strange mixture of relief and freedom coursed through her veins, as intoxicating as neat gin on an empty stomach. She hadn't realised how much headspace and energy she'd devoted to Adam over the past weeks and months. It was liberating to put it all behind her. No more checking her phone every five minutes to see if he'd deigned to contact her, no agonising over the contents of a text like a lovesick schoolgirl. She may have been in lust, but she wasn't in love. He hadn't broken her heart, and although her ego was a little bruised, she'd soon get over it.

It may have taken a chance conversation with a friendly stranger, but the scales had finally fallen from her eyes. A man like Adam would never be right for her. He was too dry, too conventional. They were like chalk and cheese. Square peg, round hole. She would feel suffocated by him, and he would be driven crazy by her. If and when she ever did fall in love, she wanted someone who was passionate and fun-loving and not frightened to show their feelings. Someone like Noah.

She pulled into their drive and parked behind her father's old estate car. She sat for a while, her eyes closed, and her head against the headrest. She'd set too much store by her chance meeting with Adam, convincing herself that fate had brought them together for a reason. But it was just that, she saw now. A random meeting at a university open day that would never have happened if she'd had one, not two, cups of coffee. In a parallel universe, she and Chloe had never met Adam and Ben. And wouldn't life be so much simpler?

It didn't matter now. It was over. They would be fine on their own, as they always had been. And she would be OK when Chloe finally went to university, too. She had her father, and Rory, and her job. It was more than enough.

Kate took the keys out of the ignition, gathered her bag and gloves and jumped out of the car. She walked across the gravel to the front door, her eyes firmly on her future. Adam and Ben weren't important. They never had been. And with any luck, she'd never see either of them ever again.

CHAPTER FORTY-EIGHT

CHLOE

The gunmetal-grey Audi TT was parked, engine idling, on the yellow zigzag lines outside the school gates in the same spot Ben had parked all those weeks ago. Chloe ran over to the passenger door, threw her bag in the footwell and flopped onto the seat.

'Quick, drive!' she giggled, glancing over her shoulder, half expecting the head of the sixth form to appear waving a fist.

'You did tell them where we're going?' Adam said, pulling away with a roar.

'I was going to, but I knew they'd tell Mum, and I don't want anyone knowing I'm meeting Professor Steel.'

'Are you sure that's wise?'

'You know I don't want anyone thinking I've bribed my way onto the course. You promised it was our secret,' Chloe reminded him.

'I did.'

'And you'll look after me, won't you?'

His mouth curved into a smile. 'Always.'

'How long will it take to get there?'

'A couple of hours. We'll pick up something to eat at a service station on the way.'

'Cool. I can change in the loos.'

'Change?'

'I brought a dress. I didn't think jeans would cut it.' Chloe leaned against the headrest and yawned.

Adam arched an eyebrow. 'Late night?'

'I haven't been sleeping very well. And I'm a bit nervous, to tell the truth. People yawn when they're nervous, did you know that? I heard it on the radio. I can't remember why. Something to do with your body wanting to get the oxygen in and the nerves out.' Another gurgle of laughter. 'Nervous people talk too much, too.'

'There's no need to be nervous. Jan's going to love you.'

'You think so?'

'You're beautiful, clever, and sparky. What's not to love?'

'Aw, shucks. Thanks, Adam. You're pretty cool yourself.'

He nodded and placed his left arm along the back of her seat. A protective gesture, Chloe thought. The kind of thing a father would do. She kicked off her Converse, drew her legs underneath her and watched the outskirts of the town fly past.

What would it have been like to have grown up with the standard two parents? When she was little, she'd hardly noticed she didn't have a dad. She hadn't known any different. It wasn't as if she was the odd one out, either. Plenty of her friends had dads who weren't on the scene. But as she'd grown older, she'd become aware of an ache inside her. An emptiness. A *longing*. Grandpa and Rory did their best to fill the hole, but it wasn't the same.

She looked sidelong at Adam. His right hand rested lightly on the steering wheel as they cruised along in the fast lane. Strong jawbone, dark brown hair flecked with grey at the temples. Delicate, long-fingered hands and surprisingly narrow wrists for someone with such broad shoulders. He was still smiling to himself and Chloe was itching to ask him why. But a sudden shyness caught her tongue. Instead, she took her phone out of her bag and pretended to check for messages, though she kept her eyes on the motorway. Reading in the car made her sick, and there was no way she was going to risk puking all over the TT's beautiful leather interior.

Traffic was light, and in no time at all, Adam was turning into the motorway services on the M25. Chloe pulled on her shoes and picked up her rucksack. Squeezed in between the textbooks were a navy print dress, a plum-coloured cardigan, a pair of opaque tights and her navy ballet pumps. Plus her hairbrush and make-up bag.

Adam pulled up and turned off the engine. He jumped out and opened the passenger door before Chloe had a chance to tie her laces. As they ambled across the car park, he touched her arm.

'I'll grab us something to eat while you change. What d'you fancy?'

'A sandwich and a Diet Coke would be great, thanks.'

He gave a little bow. 'Your wish is my command.'

Chloe stared at her reflection above the sink in the disabled toilet. Mascara and a flick of eyeliner accentuated her blue eyes. Nude pink lipgloss and a touch of blusher completed the 'barely there' look she was aiming for. The kind of make-up that took a good ten minutes to apply but looked as if you weren't wearing any at all. She brushed her hair upside down, giving it a blast under the hand dryer, so it fell in shiny waves around her shoulders.

Adam was already in the car and handed her a smoked salmon and cream cheese panini, a paper napkin and a can of Diet Coke that he'd already opened for her. He was such a gentleman.

'Aren't you having anything?' she said.

'I'm saving myself for later,' he said with a mysterious smile.

Chloe took a long draught of the drink and wiped her chin with the napkin. 'Are you and Mum going out?' She couldn't remember her mum mentioning it, but she didn't always listen.

'I'm planning a special meal. It's going to be a big surprise. But I know you won't tell.'

''Course not. Anywhere I know?'

'I don't think so. It's off the beaten track and rather unprepossessing. Some might even venture to call it austere. But I would argue it has a charm of its own.'

'Sounds interesting,' Chloe said, biting into her panini. 'You'd better be careful. I might tag along.'

'You'd be very welcome. Do you want to finish your drink before we get going? I wouldn't want you to spill it down your lovely dress.'

'Good thinking, Batman.' Chloe took another slug of Coke, then another, and soon the can was empty.

'Let me take that,' Adam said, reaching for the can. He crushed it in his hand, wound down the window and lobbed it into a nearby bin.

'Hole in one,' Chloe said.

He winked at her. 'That's the aim.'

Soon they were back on the motorway, cruising at a steady 80mph. Adam tuned the radio into a station playing chill-out tracks and Chloe tipped her head back, closed her eyes and let the soporific music wash over her. She felt heavy. Torpid. As if she hadn't slept for weeks. And she hadn't, she thought drowsily. Not properly. She'd been so worried about Ben and his stalkerish behaviour. The photo on Snapchat and the endless texts and phone calls. The panic attack and the fire. But she was safe here, cocooned in the opulent luxury of Adam's sports car. He had promised to look after her and he would, she was sure of it.

As if on cue he said, 'That's right, angel. You have a nice sleep. I'll wake you up when we're there.'

'Thank you for everything,' she attempted to say. But her tongue felt thick and unmanageable, like the body of one of those giant African land snails she'd admired during a long-ago trip to Woburn Safari Park with her mum and Uncle Rory.

A little nap, that's what she needed. Forty winks. A bit of shuteye. To recharge her batteries before the important thing they were doing. What was it again? She tried to remember, but it was as though her brain had stopped working, all the synapses paralysed by the force of her exhaustion. They were definitely going somewhere to see someone, she knew that much. But the rest was one big blank.

She tried to turn her head towards Adam, but the muscles in her neck refused to work, and her eyelids stayed stubbornly shut. Another wave of lassitude hit her, and she teetered on the edge of consciousness. She didn't know where she was going and who she was seeing. And, suddenly, she didn't much care.

CHAPTER FORTY-NINE

KATE

K ate was up a ladder clearing a matted mess of wet leaves from the guttering outside the dining room when the phone in her back pocket began buzzing.

'Bugger,' she said, as a clump of fetid grot slid down the inside of her sleeve.

She jumped down, pulled off her rubber gloves and shook the leaves onto the ground. As she reached for the phone, it stopped ringing.

'Oh, for fuck's sake,' she muttered. She stared at the screen and felt a flutter in her stomach. A missed call from Chloe's school.

Please not another panic attack. But Chloe hadn't mentioned any tests. In fact, she'd looked happier than she had for a long time when she'd left to catch the bus that morning.

Kate sank onto the lichen-covered bench below the dining room window and called the school, her fingers drumming a beat on her thigh as she waited for one of the secretaries to answer.

'It's Kate Kennedy. Chloe's mum. You tried to call me. Is everything OK?'

'Mrs Kennedy, thanks for calling back. I'm going to put you through to Mrs Bentley.'

Before Kate had a chance to ask why, the head of the sixth form was on the line, asking her if there was any reason why Chloe might have walked out of school without signing out.

'Is there a dentist or doctor's appointment you have omitted to inform us about?'

'No,' Kate said.

'Any other reason why she might have left without permission?'

'Are you sure she's not in the library or something?'

'I've checked with her close friends, and they haven't seen her since morning break. It's not like Chloe, as I'm sure you're aware.'

'Of course I'm aware. I'm her bloody mother,' Kate snapped before she could stop herself. 'Sorry. That came out wrong.'

'That's all right, Mrs Kennedy. I'm sure there's a perfectly reasonable explanation. But you understand I had to let you know and that this will go down on her records as an unauthorised absence.'

Kate closed her eyes. 'Yes, of course. Thank you.'

'She probably wasn't feeling well and forgot to sign out.'

'I'm sure you're right.'

The teacher's voice softened. 'She's a lovely girl. I know we're not supposed to have favourites, but I've always had a soft spot for her. That's why I was concerned. It's so out of character.'

'I'll try her mobile now,' Kate said. 'I'll let you know when I hear from her.'

She ended the call and tried Chloe's number. It went straight to voicemail.

'Chlo, it's Mum. Can you phone me, please? Now.'

She sent a text, too, then called Annie, who picked up on the second ring.

'Annie, I've had a call from Mrs Bentley saying Chloe's gone AWOL. You don't know where she is, do you?'

Annie was quiet.

'She's not in any trouble. I need to check everything's OK after, you know, the panic attack and everything.'

Kate could hear Annie suck in a breath. 'I don't know where she's gone,' she said finally. 'But she was acting a bit weird this morning. A bit *wired*.'

'In what way?'

'Agitated, you know? Checking her phone every five minutes. I wondered if Ben had started texting her again.'

'Ben?' Kate said sharply.

''Cos I don't think there were any more photos doing the rounds. She would have told me.'

'What photos? What do you mean, doing the rounds?'

'On Snapchat, you know.' There was a pause. 'Oh, crap. You did know, didn't you?'

Kate tried to keep her voice even. 'I didn't, no. But I'd like you to tell me.'

'I can't believe she didn't tell you herself. It was like, weeks ago. Someone with a fake account sent a photo of her to half the sixth form.'

289

Kate's insides turned to ice. 'What kind of photo?'

Annie hesitated for a second before answering. 'A photo taken from your back garden while she was getting dressed.'

'Who took the picture, Annie?'

'Ben, of course. He's super-weird.'

'You've met him?'

'Only that time he picked Chloe up from school in his dad's car.'

It was Kate's turn to be silent.

'You didn't know about that, either?' Annie guessed. 'Chloe had no idea he even knew where our school was. It was totally awkward. She wanted me to go with her, but I'd told Mum I'd mind Nathan. She got home all right, though. I made her promise to text me she was OK.'

'What else has Ben done that I should know about?' Kate said.

'Um, well, in the beginning, he was always texting her. Then he started following a few of us on Instagram and stuff even though Chloe told him she wasn't, like, interested in him or anything. Then, after the Snapchat thing, it all went quiet. I assumed he'd got his revenge and lost interest.'

'And now? What do you think?'

'I don't know,' Annie said. 'But there's something else about today you should know. She had a dress and make-up in her bag. I think she was bunking off to meet someone. Maybe she changed her mind about Ben. Maybe she was meeting him.'

Kate stared at her phone for a long time after hanging up. She tried Chloe's number again, and again it went straight to voicemail. She didn't have a number for Ben, so she tried Adam. His phone rang and rang until his familiar voice informed her he couldn't get to the phone right now, and if she left a message he would return her call as soon as he was able.

'Strange question I know, but you don't know if Ben and Chloe were meeting up today? Only she's not at school, and her friend Annie thinks she and Ben might have hooked up.' Kate screwed up her face. Hooking up sounded suspiciously like a euphemism for sex. 'Anyway, perhaps you could give me a call when you get a minute?'

Kate slouched forwards with her hands between her knees. So what if Chloe had skipped a couple of lessons? Playing hooky was hardly the crime of the century. Kate had sneaked out a handful of times during her last year at school. It was normal teenage behaviour. So why did she have an unshakeable sense that something was very wrong?

CHAPTER FIFTY

CHLOE

C hloe's head was thumping and her mouth was dry. Not just dry. *Desiccated*. And her eyes felt puffy, like the time she'd had conjunctivitis when she was six and had woken up screaming, thinking someone had superglued her eyes together while she slept.

She prised them open. Dark shapes swam in and out of focus. She blinked. Once. Twice. But when she opened her eyes again, her vision was still blurry.

She tried to rub them, but her hands seemed stuck to her sides. More superglue. That didn't make sense. If only she could marshal her thoughts. But her head was as foggy as her surroundings.

'Hello, Chloe.' Hot breath in her ear and a voice as smooth as honey. Chloe moved her head sideways. It felt as loose as a puppet's. A face appeared, centimetres from her own.

'Adam?'

He reached out and smoothed away a strand of hair

plastered to her forehead. 'My darling. I thought you'd never wake up.'

'Wha-what's happening? Did we have an accident?'

He chuckled. 'You fell asleep in the car, do you remember?'

Chloe extracted a memory. 'We were going to see Professor Steel. Are we there?'

'We are, my love.'

'Where is she? What happened to my head? And I can't move my arms. Adam, what's happening?' Chloe's voice rose several octaves until it was little more than a high-pitched squeak.

'Hey, there's nothing to worry about, little one. You're with me, that's all that matters. And I promised I'd look after you, didn't I?'

'But where are we?' Chloe's eyes darted from side to side. Slowly their surroundings were gaining form. They were in a cavernous room, lit by the flickering glow of candles. Breeze-blocked walls, a couple of desks and office chairs. Boarded-up holes where the windows should have been and stained grey carpet tiles on the floor. The whole place reeked of damp, the musty odour filling her nostrils.

'Kingsgate University,' Adam said. 'My old alma mater.'

'But this isn't the law school.'

'It's the old law school,' Adam corrected her. 'It's where I studied for my degree. It was condemned by the university a few years ago. Concrete cancer. That's why they built the new one. This place is due to be demolished later this year.'

'I don't understand. Why are we here?'

'Because I wanted you all to myself, Chloe. I don't want to share you with Jan Steel. Your mum. Ben. Anyone. We're going to have a romantic dinner and talk about our future. It's all planned.'

He moved to one side and waved his arm at a table laid with a claret-red tablecloth, crystal wine glasses and a pair of wrought-iron candlesticks.

Chloe felt as if she'd been shaken awake in the middle of a dream. Scratch that. A nightmare. Adam was her mum's boyfriend. He was a father figure to her. The dad she'd always wanted. And yet he was staring at her with a hunger in his eyes that made her dizzy with fear.

'Adam -'

'You are so beautiful, Chloe darling. I can hardly bear to take my eyes off you.' He ran a finger along her cheek and tilted her chin up. 'May I kiss you?'

Chloe's eyes widened in alarm, and she flung her head back, hitting it against the wall. Adam's grip on her chin tightened until he was squeezing it like a vice. He leaned forwards. She clamped her mouth shut, fearing his teeth were about to come crashing down on hers. But the kiss, when it came, was as light as a caress, which made it infinitely more terrifying.

Adam rocked back on his heels and strode over to a wicker picnic basket at the side of the room, from which he produced a bottle and two flutes.

'I think our first proper date is a cause for celebration, don't you?' he said, twisting the wire off the bottle and easing the cork out with a muted pop. 'Champagne, darling?'

Chloe shook her head. The last thing she needed was

to feel muzzier. She needed to collect her wits, work out how the hell she was going to extricate herself from this nightmare.

Adam's face had taken on a faraway look. 'It's a 2009 Dom Perignon. An excellent vintage, vibrant and silky. The harvest began on the twelfth of September after idyllic growing conditions.' He waved a glass under his nose. 'The perfect marriage of Pinot Noir and Chardonnay. A match made in heaven. A bit like us, one might say.' He took a sip and swirled it round his mouth. 'Apricots and nectarines, followed by a zing of citrus. What do you think?'

He held the glass to her lips and, before she had a chance to swallow, tipped some in her mouth. The bubbles fizzed down her airway and she choked, sending a spray of champagne into his face. His features darkened and Chloe shrank back. Her eyes watered as she struggled to gain control of her breathing. Adam placed the glass on the floor, took out a white silk handkerchief and dabbed fastidiously at his cheek.

Memories forced their way into her head. A handkerchief pressed into her hand. The feel of the satin-smooth silk between her thumb and forefinger. A scrap of white silk caught on the thorns of a rose bush. She forced herself to look at him.

'Did you... did you follow me out into the garden the night of the party?' she said in a ragged voice.

'You followed me, actually.'

'What do you mean?'

'I'd gone outside to make a call. You came to find me.'

'I went outside because I felt unwell.'

He smirked. 'If you say so.'

'I was sick on the patio. And then you…' Another memory hit her like a slap in the face. A hand slipping into her jeans, fingering the lace trim of her thong. Her flesh crawled. 'What did you do to me?'

His eyes narrowed. 'What did I do to you? It takes two to tango, Chloe. You wanted it as much as I did.'

Shit. Did that mean they…?

He shook his head as if reading her mind. 'We only kissed, if that's what you're worried about, Little Miss Modest.'

Chloe let out a long breath. *Thank God.*

'But we can put that right tonight, can't we?' He reached out to stroke her cheek again, and Chloe lowered her eyes. There was a bulge in his crotch. Panic swept through her body and, before she could stop herself, a tear slid down her cheek.

'Why the tears, little one? It was obvious you wanted me the moment we met. Flirting with me. Befriending Ben so you could be close to me. Coming to me when you needed help.'

'I'm sorry if I've given you the wrong idea,' she gabbled. 'I didn't mean to.' A sob rose in her throat as his fingers traced a lazy path down the front of her dress. 'You and my mum, you're perfect together. You're the dad I never had.'

His hand stopped, and he fixed her with a menacing gaze. 'What did you say?'

'You've been like a father to me these last few weeks. That's why I asked you for help. Not because I…I… was into you.'

'A *father*?' He spat the word out, and Chloe flinched.

'If you let me go home, I promise I won't tell a soul. Not Mum, not anyone. We can forget this ever happened.'

Adam gave her a sad smile. 'I'm afraid that's not an option.'

'But why?'

'Because I always get what I want. And what I want right now, Chloe darling, is you.'

CHAPTER FIFTY-ONE

KATE

Kate stood on the pavement and stared up at Adam's house, looking for signs of life. The red-bricked semi was late Victorian, judging by its high-pitched roof, ornate gable trim and bay windows on both the ground and first floors. Glossy-leaved standard bay trees in terracotta pots flanked the front door, which was painted a smart navy blue with stained glass panels.

She should have seen the warning signs when Adam had never once asked her back to his place. But the fact that he'd never really been serious about her was of no consequence to Kate now. All she cared about was Chloe.

A movement in the first-floor window caught her eye. When she stepped back to get a better look, a pale face stared down at her. Ben, watching her, half-hidden behind the curtain.

'Where's my daughter?' she shouted.

Ben cupped a hand to his ear and mouthed, 'I can't hear you.'

'Then open the fucking window!' she yelled, hardly

registering the shocked look on the face of an elderly man shambling past with a miniature poodle.

She growled in frustration as Ben disappeared. 'Where's Chloe? I know she's in there. Let me in!' she yelled, rushing up the front path and pounding on the door.

Several minutes passed, and Kate was about to give up hope, when there was a click, and the door opened an inch. Ben's long fingers curled around the door jamb, but he stood behind it so she couldn't see his face.

'She's not here,' he muttered.

'I don't believe you.'

'It's true, I promise.'

'So where is she?'

'It's not me you should be asking.'

'What the hell's that supposed to mean?'

His fingers fluttered. 'Nothing.'

Kate slipped a foot in the gap between the door and its frame. She kept her voice measured. 'If she's not here, what's the problem? Let me in, and I can see for myself. If you're telling the truth, I'll apologise and go home quietly. But I'm warning you, *Ben*,' she spat out his name, 'I'm not going anywhere until I know for sure. So let…me…in!'

There was a pause. 'I can't,' he whispered.

'Why not?'

'Because I'll be dead if I do.'

Ben tried to push the door closed, but Kate was a step ahead of him. White heat was surging through her body, and she welcomed it with open arms. Anger was good. Anger made her strong.

'Just let me in!' she yelled, barging the door open with

her shoulder. Ben stepped back, his eyes wide. 'You've tricked her into coming here, haven't you? Where's my daughter?'

'She isn't here,' he said again.

Shaking her head, Kate pushed past him to the stairs. 'Chloe, where are you? It's Mum,' she called. 'I'm coming up.'

'You can't!' Ben cried.

'Don't tell me what I can and can't do, you little shit. I know you've been pestering Chloe to go out with you and I know you've been spying on her. I know about the Snapchat photo. I've more than enough evidence to go to the police and get you arrested for stalking so cut the crap and TELL ME WHERE SHE IS!'

Ben wrapped his arms around his head and he rocked on his heels, back and forth. Ignoring him, Kate ran up the stairs to the bedroom with the bay window at the front of the house and flung open the door. Expecting to find herself in a teenage boy's room, with posters on the walls and dirty clothes on the floor, she was perplexed to find herself in an immaculate, tasteful and unashamedly masculine room that could only have been Adam's.

Her gaze took in the cool grey walls, the dark wood fitted wardrobes and huge double bed with a dark grey bedspread. An antique chaise longue fitted perfectly in the window, and the room's deep pile carpet was the colour of clotted cream. Otherwise, it was empty.

'Which one's your room?' she demanded, as Ben appeared at her shoulder.

A slight incline of his head told Kate it was at the back

of the house. Ben stumbled after her as she marched along the hallway. She stopped by a closed door. 'This one?'

He nodded silently. Kate pushed the door open with the tips of her fingers.

In stark contrast to Adam's impeccably neat room, this one looked as if a particularly thorough gang of burglars had recently ransacked it. The bed was unmade, and clothes and textbooks littered the floor. Empty crisp and biscuit packets, crushed cans of Pepsi and dirty plates surrounded a gaming chair. A female urban warrior with a camouflage bandana and Marilyn Monroe curves was busy loading an assault rifle on a huge flatscreen TV. There was a fuggy tinge to the air that hinted at sweaty socks and rotting food. Kate itched to throw the window open. Instead, she called her daughter's name and listened. But there was no answering tap on a closed closet door, no muffled cry for help from under the bed.

'See? I told you she wasn't here.'

'What have you done with her?'

'Nothing. I've said it enough times, haven't I?' he said sulkily.

'I know she bunked off school to meet a boy. It was you, wasn't it? And please don't insult my intelligence by denying it.'

'Not a boy.'

'What?'

'Chloe wasn't meeting a boy.'

Kate's eyes bored into his. 'Then who was she meeting?'

'I can't tell you.' The petulant scowl faded and, head

hanging, he walked to the window and stared out at the garden. 'I'm sorry,' he mumbled. 'I just can't.'

Kate sank onto the end of the bed and considered her next move. Her bad cop routine had got her precisely nowhere. She needed to tone it down a bit. She cleared her throat. 'I'm sorry, too. I shouldn't have accused you. But I'm so worried about her, Ben. I need to know she's OK.'

He gave an almost imperceptible nod of the head. Kate pressed on. 'I know she's not here. But I think you know where she might be.'

Silence.

'I also know you care about her and wouldn't want her to come to any harm. We're both looking out for her. We're on the same side.'

He turned to her with anguished eyes. 'But he'll kill me.'

'Who will? Please, Ben, you have to tell me where she is. I'll make sure you don't get into any trouble, I promise.' She placed a hand on her heart for emphasis. 'Is it one of your friends from school who saw the Snapchat photo?'

He shook his head.

'Then who, Ben? Who?'

'She's with Dad.'

'Adam?' Kate said incredulously. 'Why would Chloe be with *Adam*?'

'Because... because she thinks she's meeting Professor Steel.'

The vice-like grip squeezing Kate's chest eased a little. Professor Steel, head of the law school at Kingsgate

University. Of course. Adam knew her. They'd studied for their degrees at the same time. He'd offered to put in a good word for Chloe a while back, hadn't he? Perhaps she'd decided she needed a helping hand after all. But why hadn't she told Kate? She wouldn't have minded Chloe skipping school for something so important. Why the big secret?

While the thoughts were racing around Kate's head, something about Ben's choice of words made her look at him sharply. 'What do you mean she *thinks* she's meeting her?'

'That's what Dad told Chloe so she'd agree to go with him.'

'And they're not?'

Ben's face sagged. 'I don't think so, no.'

Kate shook her head. It didn't make sense. Why would Adam lie to Chloe? Ben was the one who was infatuated with her. He was the one they couldn't trust.

'What makes you say that?' she said.

He gave one of his trademark shrugs. 'He's done it before.'

'Done what before?'

He pulled at the neck of his teeshirt. 'Become fixated on someone. A girl.'

Kate reeled. This couldn't be true. Not Adam. 'Ben?' she said softly. 'What girl?'

He turned back to the window. 'My friend Lucy. She used to live next door.' He jerked a thumb towards the far wall of the bedroom. 'She was always around ours, and he became, well, he became obsessed with her.'

'How old was she?'

'Fifteen. He's not a paedo. He just has a thing for teenage girls.'

There was a ringing in Kate's ears. She shook her head, chasing the noise away. Ben must be lying because Adam wasn't some degenerate pervert. He was a normal guy. They'd been on two dates, if you could call them that. She'd know if anything was off-kilter. She wasn't stupid. She'd be able to tell.

'You don't believe me do you?' he said.

'I… I don't know what to believe.'

Ben crossed the room to a built-in cupboard next to the chimney breast. Rummaging through the contents, he grunted with satisfaction as he pulled out a shoebox from under a pile of scruffy trainers and football boots. He sat on the bed next to Kate with the box balanced on his lap. 'There's something you should probably see,' he said, lifting off the lid to reveal a stack of old birthday cards and two framed photos. 'That's my mum,' he said, passing Kate the top one. 'With me, when I was a baby.'

A petite blonde woman with a tousled blonde bob and a dewy complexion was smiling hesitantly at the camera. On her lap, a black-haired baby wearing a blue romper suit slept soundly. His tiny fingers curled round her right index finger.

'Daisy,' Kate said.

Ben nodded. 'She fucked off about two months after this was taken.'

'She looks so young.'

'She was nineteen when she had me.'

The same age Kate had been when she'd had Chloe, she thought with a pang. But there was no way she'd have ever walked out on her baby. The thought of her daughter dragged Kate back to the present.

'Why are you showing me this? What's it got to do with Chloe?'

'It's this one I wanted to show you,' Ben said, handing Kate the second frame.

She stared, blinked, then stared again. Ben and a slim girl in a vest top and frayed denim shorts were sitting on a bench in a park eating ice creams. Kate's grip on the frame tightened as she took in the girl's ash-blonde hair, piercing blue eyes and heart-shaped face.

She tried to speak, but the words caught in her throat.

'This is Lucy,' Ben said, prising the picture out of Kate's hands. 'My dad has a type, you see. Young, blonde and pretty. You can see the resemblance, can't you?'

Kate nodded, finally forcing the words out.

'She looks like Chloe.'

CHAPTER FIFTY-TWO

CHLOE

C hloe stared at Adam in disbelief.

'But I'm... I'm young enough to be your daughter.'

'Age is a number, my love. You're old enough to marry, aren't you? I almost forgot. I've bought you a little something.'

Adam crossed the room and picked up a white designer bag with La Perla written in silver capital letters on the side. Chloe watched from the corner of her eye as he pulled out a package wrapped in tissue paper. He kneeled in front of her and pulled the paper open. Two scraps of powder-pink silk slithered onto the floor. He picked one up and held it by its delicate straps. It was, Chloe realised with horror, a camisole top and matching French knickers.

'It's Italian silk with ivory frastaglio. Do you know what that is?' he asked.

Chloe neither knew nor cared. All she could think

about was having to undress in front of him. The thought made her faint with fear.

'It's an antique Florentine embroidery technique made famous by La Perla.' He fingered the fretwork. 'It's attached to the silk by hand, so it sits perfectly against the skin. See?' He held the camisole against her cheek and stroked it up and down. Chloe slumped forwards and tried to swallow the lump at the back of her throat, but her mouth was too dry. She ran her tongue over her lips. Adam smiled.

'I can see you're getting turned on already,' he said softly.

'No,' she said, shaking her head. 'You've got it all wrong. I'm not. I'm sorry if I led you on. I didn't mean to, I really didn't.'

He dropped the camisole and grabbed a handful of her hair, forcing her head backwards. 'You'd rather screw my pathetic excuse for a son, is that it?'

'No!' The word leapt out of Chloe's mouth, followed by a rush of hot tears.

'Then what do you want, you little prick-tease?'

'Home,' Chloe sobbed. 'I want to go home.'

CHAPTER FIFTY-THREE

KATE

K ate sat on Ben's bed with her head in her hands.
'You think she's with him?'

Ben nodded.

'They arranged to meet outside her school at noon. I saw the text he sent her.'

Kate's heart lurched. 'Where would he have taken her?'

'I don't know, but I can find out.' Ben reached into the pocket of his jeans and pulled out his phone.

'What are you doing?'

'Checking Find My Friends. I like to keep tabs on him.' He tapped away at the screen, his lips pursed in concentration. He raised an eyebrow. 'They're at Kingsgate.'

A tiny flicker of hope. Maybe Adam was introducing Chloe to Professor Steel after all. Ben might have the wrong end of the stick. How did she know she could trust him anyway? He could be lying, laying a false trail, taking the heat off himself.

'But they're not at the law school,' Ben continued,

thrusting the phone under Kate's nose. 'They're on the other side of the campus. Look.'

Kate stared at the map, trying to orientate herself. There was the main sports hall and theatre, the library and, not too far away, the students' union.

'Where's the law school?' Kate said, trying to remember.

Ben zoomed in. 'There.'

'Where's his phone showing?'

He zoomed out again. 'Over there.'

'But that's near the accommodation block Chloe liked. Springett Court, where your dad lived. You don't think they could be there?'

Ben switched off his phone and slipped it back into his pocket. 'We're not going to find out sitting here, are we?'

———

Kate was in no mood for small talk, so was glad when Ben plugged in his headphones. According to the satnav, there was some slow-moving traffic on the M25, otherwise, the route was clear. They should be there by seven.

As they sped along the motorway, Kate wondered if she should have phoned the police to report Chloe missing. She tried to picture how the conversation might go.

'So when exactly was Chloe last seen?'

'When she left school before lunch.'

'You don't think she might have bunked off?'

How could Kate explain that she was worried the man she'd been dating had a predilection for teenage girls and had abducted Chloe? What were they going to do? Send a patrol car to Kingsgate on the off-chance? What if Adam and Chloe were sitting with Professor Steel right now, talking about Chloe's future? She would look ridiculous. She only had Ben's word for it, after all.

She glanced at him. His eyes were closed, and his mouth had fallen open. Kate's adrenalin levels had rocketed, yet he was able to nap. She clenched her jaw then shook his shoulder, pulling him from sleep.

'What did he do to her?' she said.

Ben pulled his earbuds out and rubbed his eyes. 'What?' he said blearily.

'Lucy, the girl next door. What did your dad do to her?'

'I don't want to get him into any trouble.'

'If what you say is true, he's already in a whole heap of trouble.'

'Exactly! What will happen to me if he goes to prison? I don't have anyone else.'

If Adam had abducted Chloe, Kate would happily lock him up for life and throw away the key, but that wasn't going to help her winkle information out of Ben. She had to keep him on side.

'If we find them before he does anything to her, the police need never know. I won't tell them. But I need you to tell me what he did to Lucy.'

Ben sighed. 'Nothing, at first. Her family moved next door when I was eight, and she was nine. She went to my primary school, and we used to lift share. Her mum would look after me after school some nights till Dad was home from work. We were round each other's houses all the time, you know? It was nice.' Ben was fiddling with his headphones, twisting them round and round his fingers like a complicated game of cat's cradle. 'Everything changed when she went to secondary school. She was in the year above me. We still used to hang out a bit, but she had her own friends then.'

He paused. 'You have to understand, she was beautiful. And popular. She always had a string of boys mooning after her.' He swallowed. 'Including me. I was always badgering Dad to invite them around like we used to, but he was always so busy at work. Then we bumped into Lucy and her mum in Sainsbury's one Saturday morning. Lucy had finished her GCSEs and looked amazing. Like some kind of model. Dad miraculously found the time to invite them over for a barbecue that afternoon. That's when it happened.'

'What happened?'

'When they arrived he turned the charm on full blast,' Ben said. 'Like he does with you and Chloe,' he added, looking sidelong at her. 'Because he's not like that with me. He's a miserable bastard most of the time. Anyway, Lucy was flattered, I could tell. He cracked open one of his precious bottles of Dom Perignon, the pretentious wanker, and insisted she had a glass to celebrate the end of her exams. And he kept topping up her glass when her parents weren't watching.'

'He got her drunk?'

'Just merry. Eventually, Lucy's parents went home, but she stayed. The new Avengers film was out, and we were going to watch it together, her and me. Like old times. I went inside to download it and sort out snacks and stuff, and when I came back out, I couldn't find her or Dad.'

Kate gripped the steering wheel tighter.

'After a bit, Dad appeared from the end of the garden, saying Lucy didn't want to watch the film after all and had decided to go home. I was a bit pissed off because I'd got everything ready and she hadn't even bothered to say goodbye. Dad was back in miserable bastard mode, ordering me to help him clear up. I was loading the dishwasher when I noticed a scratch on his neck, and I started wondering what had happened in the garden.'

Kate's stomach clenched. There were too many parallels between Ben's story and the night of the party to doubt his account.

'When Dad finally went up to bed, I went out and texted Lucy to check she was OK,' he continued. 'When I heard her phone ping I realised she was still outside. I found her hiding behind her old Wendy house, crying her eyes out.'

'Did she tell you what had happened?'

'Not at first.' Ben had wound the lead of his headphones so tightly around his fingers that the tips had turned white. 'But I prised it out of her eventually. It was a clear night, and he'd been pointing out the stars to her. Always keen to share his superior intellect, my father. Fucking prick,' Ben added viciously. 'She was cold, so he put his arm around her, and the next minute he'd ripped off her top and was forcing her down onto the grass.'

'Oh, my God. Did he…?'

'Rape her? No. He didn't get a chance. She managed to wriggle away and ran home. But she didn't want her parents to see her in a state, so she hid in the garden until they went to bed. That's when I found her.'

'Poor Lucy.'

'She kept saying it was her fault. That she must have given him the wrong idea.'

Kate let out a long breath and tried to ignore the rising panic inside her. *Breathe*. She realised Ben was still talking.

'But grown men should know the difference between a flirty sixteen-year-old who's had a drink too many and a proper come-on from a woman their age, shouldn't they?'

She glanced at him. The fear in his eyes mirrored hers, but there was nothing she could say to make this better.

'They should,' she agreed.

'Do you think Chloe is all right?'

'I'll try calling her again.'

They listened in silence as the phone rang and rang. Voicemail eventually kicked in. Kate's voice was strangled as she left yet another message. 'Chloe, it's Mum again. I know what's happened and why you can't call. You probably won't even be able to listen to this message. But if you can, I want you to know that I know where you are and I'm coming to get you. Stay safe, sweetheart. I'll be with you very soon.'

Kate stamped her foot on the accelerator. Chloe was in danger. There was no time to lose.

CHAPTER FIFTY-FOUR

CHLOE

Chloe's iPhone burst into life on the other side of the room. Adam sprang to his feet and rootled through a cardboard box by the door. His handsome features remained emotionless as he pulled the phone out, checked the screen, and tossed it back into the box. Chloe felt a stab of despair as it fell silent.

'Was it my mum?'

He gave a curt nod and pulled out something else. A red satin dress, the folds of fabric as silken as water. Holding the dress in his outstretched arms, he crossed the floor and knelt in front of her again.

'Ralph Lauren,' he said. 'Only the best for my girl.'

Chloe took a deep breath. 'You should have let me answer my phone. She'll be frantic.'

Adam shot her a quizzical look. 'Who will?'

'My mum.' Chloe could only hazard a guess at the time, but it must have been at least seven. 'I should have been home from school hours ago.'

He shrugged. 'So?'

'You don't understand. Mum's such a worrier she'll have probably reported me missing.' Chloe bit the side of her cheek and looked Adam squarely in the eye. 'I don't want you to get into trouble with the police.'

He laughed without humour. 'I'll take my chance.' He draped the dress over the back of a chair and began untying Chloe's laces.

'What are you doing?' she cried in alarm.

'Helping you change for dinner.'

'I can do it myself!'

His eyes narrowed. 'How do I know you won't try to run away?'

Chloe swallowed hard and gazed at him with pleading eyes. 'I won't, I promise.'

'Because there's nowhere to go, darling girl. This place has been derelict for years. We're surrounded by wooden hoardings and the only building within half a mile is Springett Court, and no-one there'll give a toss what's happening down here. So it's pointless you even trying to escape, do you understand?'

Chloe nodded.

He sat back on his heels and assessed her. Chloe kept her expression as neutral as possible. After what seemed like minutes, he gave a quick nod. 'OK. You change while I prepare supper.'

He reached into a Waitrose carrier bag for a knife and sliced through the tape binding Chloe's wrists together. She bit back a whimper as she rotated her aching shoulders and massaged her wrists. Climbing stiffly to her feet, she scooped up the underwear and took the dress from the back of the chair.

She held it against her body and gave a half-hearted attempt at a twirl. 'It's beautiful. Thank you.'

'The pleasure will be all mine,' Adam said, a smile playing on his lips.

Chloe jerked her head towards a stack of tables near the back of the room. 'I'll change behind them. So it's a surprise.'

Adam leaned forwards and brushed a strand of hair away from her face. Chloe stood her ground, aware that if she flinched, he would know she was bluffing. But it seemed his arrogance knew no bounds. 'Missing you already,' he said to her retreating back.

Chloe squeezed herself between the stack of tables and the wall. She rested her burning forehead against the dank plaster, breathing deeply to chase away the terror. She couldn't afford to lose her nerve. She needed to stay focussed. Clear-minded. She had to give the performance of her life.

She pulled off her Converse, one by one, dragged her dress over her head and peeled off her tights and pants. She slipped on the camisole and French knickers, hating the feel of the cold silk against her skin. Her hands were shaking so much the dress slithered out of her grasp, spooling like a pool of blood on the carpet tiles. She picked it up and yanked it over her head, not caring if it ripped. It fitted her like a second skin, and for a second Chloe wondered how much it had cost. Hundreds of pounds, probably. But the thought gave her no pleasure, it merely added to her growing sense of dread. What pound of flesh would Adam expect in return?

'Well?' Adam said loudly, making Chloe jump. 'How does it look?'

Chloe closed her eyes, ran her hands through her hair, and forced herself to smile. 'I'm not sure I do it justice,' she said, stepping out from behind the tables.

Adam's gaze was proprietary as he looked her up and down, his eyes lingering on her breasts. He sighed with pleasure. 'Oh you do, Chloe, my love. You do.' He clapped his hands together. 'Come, sit down. It's almost ready.'

He was by her side in an instant, taking her elbow and escorting her to the table. Chloe scanned the array of dishes. Smoked salmon blinis. Figs and parma ham sprinkled with Stilton. Goats' cheese tartlets. A plate of gnarly oysters.

'Food for lovers,' Adam said, pulling out her chair. 'I've chosen a cheeky Grand Cru for supper. Tell me what you think.'

Chloe took a tiny sip and forced herself to smile. 'Mmm. Lovely.'

Adam busied himself laying a starched white napkin on her lap, letting his hand graze her thigh, before taking a seat on the opposite side of the table.

'You've gone to so much trouble,' she said.

'Don't sit there staring at it. Tuck in,' he ordered.

Chloe's stomach was knotted with anxiety and eating was the last thing she felt like doing, but she reached for a blini and popped it in her mouth anyway.

Adam nodded his approval. 'What about an oyster?'

'No, thanks.' The creamy flesh inside the pearlescent shells and the faint smell of the sea was enough to turn her stomach upside down.

'Nonsense,' Adam said. He grabbed her wrist roughly and placed an oyster shell in her left palm. 'They're native oysters, fresh this morning. They're a delicacy.'

'But I don't like them.'

'Have you ever tried one?'

'No,' she admitted.

Adam cocked his head to one side. 'So tell me, Chloe, how do you know you don't like oysters when you've never even tried one?'

Because they're slimy and yucky and gross and revolting and they're just *wrong*, she wanted to say. Instead, she lowered her eyes and said nothing.

Perhaps Adam took her silence for acquiescence because he picked up a second oyster and smiled encouragingly at her.

'Take the shucking knife and make sure the oyster is detached from the shell, like so.' He picked up a small knife with a two-inch blade and a sturdy wooden riveted handle and eased it around the shell. 'Hold the shell with the wide end towards your mouth and take a sip of the liquor.' He demonstrated, wiping a trickle of the clear juice from his chin with the back of his hand. He grinned at her. 'It reminds me of...' he broke off and stared at Chloe with undisguised lust. 'Let's just say there's a reason it's considered an aphrodisiac. Go on, take a sip.'

Chloe stared at the oyster with trepidation, Adam's gaze on her like the harsh beam of a spotlight.

'Take the knife,' he repeated, pressing the little knife into her right hand.

Chloe closed her fingers around the short, stubby handle and felt a flicker of something. Hope? Courage?

With the knife, she could… But she mustn't get ahead of herself. She couldn't let him know what she was thinking. He was a narcissist, that was clear. He needed to believe she was under his spell.

'Like this?' she said, running the knife around the oyster's shell.

'Good girl,' he said approvingly. He swiped the knife out of her hand, and Chloe's heart plummeted. 'And now take a sip.'

Chloe held the shell to her lips and drank. The liquor tasted briny, almost metallic, like she'd accidentally swallowed a mouthful of seawater. It wasn't pleasant, but it wasn't totally disgusting.

'And now the oyster itself. It's a myth that you should swallow it without chewing. Think of an oyster as a grape. If you don't chew the grape, you don't get the full flavour. Here, have a squeeze of lemon juice.'

Chloe took a slug of wine and watched Adam eat his oyster. She eyed the rest of the plate. There were at least a dozen more arranged fastidiously around a quartered lemon. At least six more times with the knife in her hand. Six opportunities to escape. She pressed the shell to her lips, tipped her head back and swallowed.

CHAPTER FIFTY-FIVE

KATE

They reached the outskirts of the city just before half-past seven. One eye on the satnav, Kate navigated through the streets towards the university. Ben stared out of the window, his phone clasped loosely in his hand, his headphones in a tangle on his lap. For once, he wasn't playing with the hem of his teeshirt or worrying at the neck of his jumper. Kate had never seen him so still.

'My mum was only seventeen when she met Dad. Did you know that?' he said suddenly. 'She was eighteen when they married and nineteen when she had me.'

'Still a girl,' Kate said, half to herself.

'I found their wedding certificate with her birth certificate and passport.'

Kate frowned. 'She didn't take them with her?'

'They're at the back of the filing cabinet in Dad's study.'

'Where was it she went again?' Kate said, feigning indifference.

'The note she left said she was going to Israel to work on a kibbutz.' Ben scratched a spot on his chin. 'But she can't have because she didn't take her passport with her, did she? Dad reckoned she'd been having an affair and moved away with her new bloke and the kibbutz was a red herring to keep him off the scent.'

'And he didn't report her missing?'

'Why would he? She obviously didn't want to be found.'

'What about her parents? Weren't they worried?'

'They hadn't spoken to her since she married Dad.'

'And you never heard from her again? No birthday cards? Phone calls?'

Ben shook his head. 'She forgot all about me.'

Before Kate had time to digest this unsettling revelation and what it meant, she saw a sign for Kingsgate University. She flicked the indicator and turned left onto the campus. Pulling up outside the new law school building, she faced Ben.

'I want you to go to Jan Steel's office to check Chloe and your dad aren't with her. I'll go to the old law school to see if I can find them there.'

'But -'

Kate held up a hand. 'No arguments. Give me your number. If I don't phone you in...' she checked the time on her phone, 'fifteen minutes, I want you to alert campus security and tell them what's happened. Have you got that?'

Ben nodded, his eyes fearful.

'Good. Now *go*.'

He jumped out of the car and sprinted across the wide pavement to the entrance of the law school. Kate breathed a sigh of relief as he let himself in and disappeared up the stairs. She slammed the car into first gear and sped off towards the accommodation blocks and the old law school building, her heart thudding in her chest.

CHAPTER FIFTY-SIX

CHLOE

Chloe picked up her fifth oyster, took a deep breath and tipped its slimy mass down her throat, not bothering to chew. She had swiftly changed her mind about them. The first might have been just about palatable, but the second made her gag, and by the fourth, she'd have rather eaten a bowl of her own sick.

Adam reached across the table, grabbed her hand and began rubbing his thumb in a circular motion on the inside of her wrist. She fought the urge to snatch it back. She had to keep up the pretence. It was her only hope.

'This is nice, isn't it?' he said, increasing the pressure. 'I know it's not the most romantic of settings for our first date, but needs must.'

'You've thought of everything,' Chloe said, her eyes sliding to the shucking knife, tantalisingly close on the plate of half-eaten oysters on the table between them.

Outside, the wind had picked up, blowing a chill draught through the boarded-up windows. She shivered.

'You're cold,' Adam said, his voice full of concern. 'My poor baby. Let me warm you up.'

He made to stand, but Chloe shook her head. 'I'm fine. I'm still hungry. Can I have the last oyster?'

'You don't need to ask, my love.' He passed her the knife, watching tenderly as she ran it around the shell. At that moment there was a loud tapping noise on the nearest window. Chloe froze.

'What was that?'

'Stay here,' Adam ordered. He crossed the room in a couple of strides and pressed his ear to the plywood board. While his back was turned Chloe slipped the knife under her thigh.

The wind soughed, and the tapping began again. Adam shook his head and laughed. 'No need to panic. It's only a branch.' He returned to the table, dragged his chair close to Chloe and slung his arm over her shoulder. 'Now, where were we?'

'Eating your delicious supper. I've decided you should have the last oyster. You've gone to so much trouble.' Their eyes locked, and Chloe parted her lips. 'Let me feed you.'

He pulled away, his pupils dilating, turning his brown eyes as black as coal. 'If you insist.'

Chloe picked up the last shell. 'I understand why you chose oysters. They are a very sensual food,' she said softly, leaning forwards to give him an eyeful of her cleavage.

Adam nodded eagerly.

She reached out a hand to stroke his cheek. A half-moan escaped his lips.

'Close your eyes and concentrate on the taste and texture.' She traced his lips with her finger and then gently closed his eyelids. 'I want you to tell me what it reminds you of,' she said huskily.

Her eyes never leaving his face, Chloe's fingers reached for the knife. Her hand was by her side, and she'd eased her thigh off the plastic seat when his eyes flickered open. Ignoring the flutter of anxiety in her chest, Chloe whipped her hand away, waggled a finger at him and gave him a stern look. 'No cheating.'

Instantly contrite, he closed his eyes again, resting his hands on the table. 'Sorry, my love.'

'That's better. Now,' she said, picking the oyster shell up in her left hand while taking the knife in her right. 'Open wide.'

Adam did as he was told. Chloe waited for a beat, raised her right hand and, as she tipped the oyster into his mouth with her left, swung the knife down in an arc, impaling his hand on the table.

Adam's eyes flew open, and for a second, they stared at each other in shocked silence. Then he gave a howl of rage, grabbed the handle of the knife with his good hand and pulled it out. Quick as a flash, Chloe curled her foot around the leg of his chair and whipped it from under him, sending him crashing to the ground. She ran for the door, praying that by some miracle he'd left it unlocked.

'You bitch!' he cried, lunging for her leg as she raced past. But she danced out of his way, her eyes on the door. She heard him struggle to his feet behind her, his breathing laboured. *Please be open, please be open*, she intoned, reaching for the handle. When it turned in her grip, she could have wept with relief. Until a muscular forearm wrapped itself around her neck and pulled her backwards.

She squealed in pain as her arm was twisted behind her back, almost wrenching her shoulder joint out of its socket. Adam was panting in her ear. Warm, briny breath that made her recoil.

'You stupid little cock-tease,' he whispered, his voice heavy with menace. 'That's how you want to play it, is it? Have it your own way. But I'm getting what I want, Chloe. I always do. Don't tell me I didn't warn you.'

Suddenly, the fight seeped out of her, and she went limp. Perhaps suspecting a feint, Adam tightened his grip until she feared he was about to snap her arm in two. He twisted her around to face him. His usually immaculate hair was dishevelled, and his eyes were crazed.

'I know you want me, you little whore,' he hissed. His mouth came crashing down on hers. Terror raced through Chloe's veins like a shot of pure adrenalin, but she was rooted to the spot. It was no use. She would never be able to escape. He was too clever, too strong. There was nothing she could do.

Blood dripped from his hand as he forced her onto the carpet tiles. One knee on her sternum and his left hand pinning her arms above her head, he yanked her dress up.

'Please, Adam, don't. You're hurting me,' she sobbed. One last attempt to bring him to his senses. But her plea fell on deaf ears.

Chloe whimpered as he reached for his flies. Then she turned her head to the side and closed her eyes.

CHAPTER FIFTY-SEVEN

KATE

K ate's Mini screeched to a halt outside the entrance to Springett Court. She turned off the engine and looked around wildly. According to Ben, the old law school was close by, but all she could see in the inky blackness behind the accommodation block was the framework of trees lit by a couple of street lights.

The orange-tipped glow of a cigarette caught her eye. A boy not much older than Chloe was lounging against the wall of the accommodation block, smoking. Kate strode over.

'Where's the old law school?' she demanded.

The cloying smell of cannabis filled her nostrils. The boy turned bloodshot eyes to her. 'The wha'?'

'The old law school. Where is it?'

The boy took a long drag and blew smoke into Kate's face. 'I don't know what you're talking about, lady. The only building down there is the one they're about to knock down.'

'Where?'

'Follow the yellow brick road,' he said, pointing to a narrow track leading through the trees that Kate hadn't noticed. He gave a bark of laughter, which turned into a cough, then tapped his heels together. 'There's no place like home.'

'For fuck's sake,' Kate muttered, pushing past him. She turned on the torch on her phone to light the pitted and overgrown asphalt path. She jogged steadily along, following the wavering beam of light, and after a couple of hundred metres, the trees gave way to reveal a clearing, in the centre of which stood a shadowy building surrounded by wooden hoardings.

Kate slowed to a walk, careful to point her torch to the ground. She gazed at the crumbling concrete edifice. No doubt an architect had once considered it to be cutting edge. But the three storey building reminded her of the ubiquitous slab-like structures from 1960s Soviet Russia.

She spotted a gap in the hoardings and slipped through, her pulse quickening. The building was in darkness and, as she stood outside the double doors, she paused. What if she was wrong? What if this derelict building was as empty as it looked? What if Chloe and Adam were sitting in Professor Steel's office right now, sipping tea from porcelain cups and discussing the law?

Her hand tightened around her phone. She could call Ben, to see if he'd found them. It would save her having to go inside what, after all, was a condemned building that could be in danger of collapse.

But what if she was right? What if Adam was in there somewhere, holding Chloe against her will? Kate was kidding herself that she had a choice. There was nothing else she could do.

She tried the rusted door handle and pushed with her shoulder. With a sigh, the door swung open, and she stepped into a large entrance area with signs still on the walls pointing to different lecture rooms and offices. Kate hesitated again. Three storeys, each with a dozen different rooms. Where the hell should she start?

Then she heard it. A faint scream that made the hairs on the back of her neck stand up. Chloe. She'd know her daughter's voice anywhere. It was coming from above her. Kate bounded up the stairs two at a time.

At the top of the first flight, she stopped and listened. At first, all she could hear was the blood rushing in her ears. But then there was a crash, followed by a thud. She craned her neck, all her senses on high alert, as she tried to work out where the noise was coming from. There were three corridors leading left, right and straight on. Another muffled cry came from the right. Kate pressed a couple of buttons on her phone, slipped it into her back pocket and hurtled towards the noise.

She would never be able to forget the sight that greeted her when she pitched into the room at the end of the corridor. It was etched in her memory, as impossible to erase as indelible ink. Chloe on her back on the floor, a red satin dress rucked up around her waist, her head turned towards the door and a look of pure terror on her face. Adam's bulky form looming over her, one hand pinning her arms down, the other reaching for his flies…

'NO!' Kate roared.

His head shot up, and he pulled back, his eyes wide.

Kate charged towards him with her arms outstretched, ramming into him with as much force as she could muster. Taken by surprise, he toppled onto the floor, banging the side of his head on the corner of the table as he fell. She grabbed the nearest chair and held it above his motionless body like a shield.

'Run!' she yelled to Chloe, who tugged her dress down and scrambled to her feet. 'Ben's on his way with help.'

Chloe's eyes darted from Kate to Adam and back again. 'What about you?'

Kate smiled briefly at her daughter. 'I'll be fine, Chlo, I promise. Please go.'

She nodded mutely, turned and fled from the room, her bare feet hardly making a sound as she scurried along the corridor to safety.

Kate exhaled slowly, relief making her light-headed. At her feet, Adam hadn't moved. She prodded his back with her toe. Nothing. That's when she saw a trickle of blood dripping from a small gash behind his right ear.

She looked around the room, taking in the tablecloth and linen napkins, the plates of half-eaten food and the crystal glasses. The empty champagne bottle and the La Perla bag. It was a scene set for seduction. But Chloe was still a child.

Without thinking, Kate set the chair down and aimed a vicious kick at Adam's kidneys. 'You dirty, dirty bastard,' she spat. 'How dare you touch my daughter.' He groaned but didn't move. Her gaze fell on a roll of duct tape on the floor by Adam's head. He must have used it on Chloe. How fitting she could now return the favour.

As she tiptoed towards the tape, a hand shot out and

grabbed her ankle. She shrieked and tried to kick him again, but his grip was so strong it was as though she was caught in a trap.

'You think I wanted you, you silly bitch?' he said thickly. 'I used you to get to Chloe. She's all I wanted, from the moment I saw her. Golden and innocent. *Luminous*. Women like you, you're dried up and past it. Sullied goods. You disgust me.'

Kate's voice rang with incredulous laughter. '*I* disgust *you*? You're unreal. You prey on young girls, and you think *I'm* disgusting? Face facts. You're a paedophile, Adam Sullivan, and you're about to get your comeuppance.'

'A paedophile?' Adam said, his voice crackling with indignation. 'Of course I'm not a paedophile.'

'I know what you did to Lucy. Don't try to deny it. Ben told me. You're lucky her family didn't call the police. And what about Daisy?'

Adam's grip on Kate's ankle loosened a fraction. 'What about her?'

'Where exactly did she go, Adam? Did she really fly to Israel *with no passport*, or is she buried in a shallow grave somewhere after she grew too old for you?'

It had been a complete shot in the dark, but Adam's reaction was unequivocal. He released her ankle, pulled himself to a sitting position and stole a glance behind him as if to check no-one was in earshot.

'What did you say?' he said in a low voice.

Kate stepped backwards, so she was out of his reach. 'Oh my God, I was right. You killed her, didn't you?'

CHAPTER FIFTY-EIGHT

KATE

As Adam's demeanour switched from alarm to outrage, Kate shrank back against the table, her heart crashing in her chest.

'She was better off dead,' he said.

Kate couldn't believe what she was hearing. 'Are you mad?'

'She'd lost her mind. Didn't wash, didn't cook, didn't care if I was alive or dead. She had no time for me, just the baby. Ben this, Ben that, it's all I heard. She used to worship the ground I walked on, but when the baby was born, it was as though I ceased to exist. And her body...' His mouth curled in disgust. 'Stretch marks, flabby thighs and saggy tits. She sickened me.'

'So you killed her.'

'She was going to leave me. I found a letter she'd written to her parents admitting she'd been wrong about me and begging for forgiveness. She was planning to go and live with them. Claiming *I* was selfish and irrational!' His voice rose in indignation.

'She was going to leave Ben with you?'

Adam shook his head. 'She wouldn't have left him. He was all she cared about. But there was no fucking way that crazy bitch was taking him away from me.'

'What did you do?'

'You think you've got it all worked out, don't you?' he sneered. 'You think I killed Daisy.'

'Didn't you?'

'Sorry to disappoint you, Miss Marple, but no. She did that all herself. The GP had prescribed Rohypnol for her anxiety, even though she was breastfeeding. He was a useless fucker, too. The night before she was planning to leave, she overdosed. She was cold when I found her on the floor of the nursery.'

'Did you call an ambulance? The police?'

'Of course not. They ask too many questions, Katherine. And with my reputation to uphold, I couldn't risk the scandal. People would have suspected I had something to do with her death. No smoke without fire, and all that.'

'What did you do with her body?'

'What does it matter? No-one cared.'

Apart from Ben, Kate thought bleakly. He'd grown up wrongly believing his mum had abandoned him. No wonder he was so needy.

'Where is she?'

'It's of no consequence. She could be on a kibbutz in Israel, living with her parents or - if your overactive imagination is to be believed - buried in a shallow grave. It doesn't matter.'

Kate leaned back against the table. Adam's arrogance took her breath away. He was the most egotistical, vain man she had ever met. Her neck grew hot as she remembered how she'd once, not so long ago, harboured feelings for him. How blind she'd been. How naive. He was a monster masquerading as the perfect catch. And Kate had fallen for his charms.

As she digested his words, parts of another puzzle rearranged themselves in her head.

'You gave Chloe Rohypnol the night of our party.' It was a statement, not a question.

He shrugged. 'Sometimes, people don't know what they want until you make it obvious. Your dear, sweet, innocent Chloe was gagging for it that night. I could have had her there and then, but the thrill of the chase can be more fun than the conquest itself.'

'You're sick.'

'And you're entitled to your own opinion.'

Something else clicked into place. 'You turned up at our house the day of the fire, even though you knew I was working. Why?'

Adam smirked.

'Did you -'

'- start the fire?' He held up his hands. 'Guilty as charged, m'lud.'

'But *why*?' Kate cried.

'So I could rescue Chloe. Come to her aid in her hour of need. Who could have imagined it would have been that easy to win her trust?' He was animated now, gesturing wildly with his bloodied hand as he spoke. 'She didn't even notice the glass from the broken pane in the door was outside, not inside. But that's teenagers for you. Completely self-absorbed.'

Kate's head was spinning so frantically that it took a while for his words to sink in.

'You let yourself into the house? But Chloe said the back door was locked.'

A manic laugh. 'You made it all so *easy*. Didn't you wonder what happened to your keys? Making sure your dear old papa didn't come home in the middle of it was the trickiest part. Thank Christ for Rohypnol.'

Kate remembered the flask next to her father's chair, the coffee dregs she'd poured away. 'You drugged him, too? And I blamed Ben for everything,' she said, shame seeping through her like ink on blotting paper. 'But he's as much of a victim in all this as Chloe. Your own *son*. How could you?'

Adam touched the back of his neck with his uninjured hand and inspected his fingers. They looked as though they'd been dipped in cochineal. 'You're wrong. He's obsessed with her.'

She shook her head. 'It's a schoolboy crush.'

Adam gave a derisive snort. 'He has a framed photo of her under his bed that he takes into the bathroom every morning while he has his shower. Whose face do you think he's looking at while he's tugging away, eh?'

Kate recoiled as if Adam had slapped her. He laughed again. 'Too much information?'

She slowed her breathing and attempted to regain her composure. 'And The Willows,' she said finally. 'That was you?'

'You can't go around preying on innocent girls. Your boss had it coming.'

She stared at him in morbid fascination. His capacity

335

for self-justification was mind-blowing. 'Right now, Ben is telling security what's happened. They'll be here any moment. Aren't you worried?'

Adam smoothed down his hair. 'God, no. Who are they going to believe - two hysterical women and a spotty teenager or me?'

'And this?' She half-turned and motioned to the table and its detritus of food and drink. 'How are you going to explain all this?'

He shrugged. 'It'll be Chloe's word against mine. And it doesn't look good for her. She skipped school to spend the afternoon with me, remember. She could have run away at the service station, but she didn't. She could have called you. She didn't. She's not underage. Everyone will believe me. They always do.'

Anger surged through Kate. She rushed at him, clawing at his face. 'You bastard, you won't get away with this!'

He grasped her wrists and held her at arm's length, watching with contempt as she wriggled and writhed like a trout on the end of her father's fishing line. She kicked out at his shin, but he dodged out of her way.

'That's enough,' he said coldly.

Suddenly the rage evaporated as quickly as it had bubbled up, and Kate stopped struggling. As she did, the door flew open, and a brawny security guard strode in, followed closely by Ben and Chloe.

'We've had a report of a disturbance,' the security guard said, his gaze sweeping the room before resting on Adam. 'I've called 999.'

Adam stepped away from Kate and dusted down his

shirt and trousers. 'Just a silly misunderstanding, my friend,' he said. 'No need to involve the police.'

'It's too late, Dad,' Ben said. 'They're on their way.'

Adam waved an impatient hand and strode towards the door but the security guard blocked his path and placed a hand on his shoulder.

'Get your hands off me,' Adam snapped.

'I'm sorry, sir, but I need you to stay where you are until the police arrive.'

'And what exactly am I being accused of?'

The guard's eyes narrowed. 'Breaking and entering, for a start. Now please step away from the door, or I'll have to call for reinforcements.'

'This is ridiculous,' Adam blustered, tutting loudly as he pulled up a chair and sat with one leg crossed over the other, a picture of studied indifference. It was a shame a twitch in his jaw gave him away.

'I'm sure the police will sort everything out, sir,' the guard said.

'They will when I've spoken to the ACC,' Adam snapped.

Kate had no doubt Adam was on first name terms with the Assistant Chief Constable. But it wasn't going to be easy for him to talk himself out of trouble this time. She reached for her phone and stopped the recording she'd started in the moments before she'd burst into the room. Eighteen minutes and forty-three seconds of incriminating material. He had as good as admitted he'd drugged Chloe and her father, and disposed of Daisy's body. Kate had been around lawyers long enough to know that there was enough evidence to open a missing persons case into

Daisy's disappearance and to charge Adam with sexually assaulting Chloe, maybe even attempted rape. He'd also confessed to breaking into their house and arson. He was banged to rights. Serve him bloody well right.

'Mum?' said a small voice by her side. Chloe's face was wan, and she was shivering uncontrollably. Kate shrugged out of her coat, wrapped it around her daughter's shoulders and led her to a corner of the room.

'You OK, sweetheart?'

'I've been so stupid,' Chloe whispered. 'It was Adam all along. Ben told me everything.'

Kate let out a weary sigh. 'If only Ben had told you everything before, none of this would have happened.'

'Don't blame him. It's not his fault.' Chloe pulled Kate's coat more tightly around her slim body. She looked impossibly young. 'I thought Adam wanted to help me like, you know… like a dad might want to help his daughter.'

'Chlo, I'm so sorry.' Kate stroked a tear from Chloe's waxen cheek.

'What for?' Chloe sniffed. 'It's not your fault either.'

'I'm sorry you don't have a dad. I'm sorry it's just me.'

'Don't be,' Chloe said fiercely, squeezing her so tight Kate thought her ribs would crack. 'You're all I need.'

CHAPTER FIFTY-NINE

CHLOE

Six months later

The air hostess shimmied up the aisle of club class and stopped by Chloe's seat. The upgrade was Uncle Rory's early Christmas present to them both. Chloe had vowed never to travel economy again.

'Can I offer you a drink, madam?' the air hostess asked, all ruby-red lips and false lashes. Her name badge revealed she was called Taylor. So deliciously American. Chloe wiggled her toes with pleasure and glanced at her mum. She had tipped her seat back and pulled on an eye mask, but Chloe could tell by her breathing that she wasn't asleep. They were as full of nervy excitement as each other.

'Mum, do you want some wine?' Chloe said, elbowing her gently in the ribs.

Kate sat up and pulled off the eye mask. 'Is the Pope Catholic?'

Chloe giggled. 'I think that's a yes,' she said to the air hostess.

'We have a rather lovely 2016 Cabernet Sauvignon,' Taylor said, taking a little plastic bottle from her trolley and showing it to them in the palm of her hand. 'It's from the Napa Valley. It was a good year, I believe. My mom's a bit of a connoisseur.'

Chloe's mum grimaced. 'God no, nothing fancy. Just your bog-standard dry white for me, please.'

'I'll have the same,' Chloe said. 'Seeing as we're celebrating.'

'Oh, yes?'

Chloe nodded, her cheeks turning pink. 'We're going to meet my dad.'

'He lives in California?'

'San José,' Chloe confirmed. 'He's a software developer for Google.'

It was a cliché, but who cared? Certainly not Chloe. It had been remarkably easy to track him down in the end. She wished with all her heart that they'd tried sooner. But it wasn't until Adam came into their lives that she'd realised how much she missed having a dad. And why she'd been so desperate for Adam to step into the role.

She'd been making toast one morning about a month after Adam's arrest when her mum had bowled in, still in her dressing gown and her hair all mussed.

'I've remembered something else about Noah,' she'd announced breathlessly.

'Our Noah?'

'Our Noah. He told me he was tone-deaf.'

Chloe pulled a face. 'And that's going to help us track him down how exactly?'

'Stick with it, kiddo. I told you about the guy at the beach party playing the guitar? We were all singing along except Noah. When I teased him about it, he said he was tone-deaf, even though his dad was a professional violinist.'

'And you've only just remembered this?'

'It was a long time ago, Chloe. But there can't have been too many professional violinists in San José in 2000, can there?'

Chloe felt a rush of excitement as she'd started typing furiously into her phone. 'He would have played with an orchestra, right?' Her face fell. 'San José Symphony Orchestra folded in 2001.'

Her mum grabbed the phone. 'But the musical director is mentioned by name. I wonder if he's on Facebook.'

After half a dozen false starts, they tracked him down. And as they scrolled through his list of friends, her mum had stopped at a photograph of a distinguished-looking man with silver hair wearing a dinner jacket, a violin tucked under his chin.

'Why have you gone quiet?' Chloe had demanded.

'Because it's him,' her mum said, her voice all emotional. 'Well, him but older.'

Chloe's fingers had trembled as she'd clicked first on Marcus Robinson's profile, then on his friends list. And, towards the end, there he was. Marcus's son. A man with broad shoulders and hair even blonder than hers, laughter lines fanning out from his denim blue eyes and a smattering of freckles across his nose. Chloe hadn't needed to ask her mum if it was their Noah. It was like looking at a picture of herself.

Her toast had burnt to a crisp, but she couldn't have cared less.

Her mum had insisted on checking out Noah's profile before making contact.

'We have to remember he might have a wife, children,' she'd reasoned. But Noah, it turned out, lived with a fluffy tabby cat called Oscar in an apartment with a small garden in a suburb of San José and worked in Silicon Valley. According to his Facebook status, he was single.

Her mum had sent him a message there and then.

Hey Noah, I don't know if you remember me? English Kate? We met in Phuket in the summer of 2001. I hope you don't mind me contacting you out of the blue like this, but I wanted to introduce you to Chloe. My daughter. She's just turned eighteen, in case you were wondering. Love Kate.

She included a photo of them both that Uncle Rory had taken during a flying visit that spring. Arms around each other's shoulders and laughing at one of his wisecracks.

It was rash, maybe. Audacious, certainly. But it had worked. Seven hours later - at six in the morning in San José - Noah had messaged back.

English Kate! I'm sure you won't believe me if I said I think about you a lot. But, godammit, it's true! I wish I had never let you slip through my fingers, and now you've found me. And you have a daughter. She looks a lot like you. But she also looks a lot like me. Is there something I should know?

Her mum had taken a long time composing her next message.

She is yours, Noah. I feel terrible I didn't let you know at the time, but I didn't find out I was pregnant until I'd left Thailand. And I didn't know how to contact you. I'm so sorry to drop this bombshell, but Chloe's had a tough time recently. She could use a dad right now. Kate x

Noah had taken even longer to reply. When a whole day had passed, and he still hadn't been in touch, Chloe had resigned herself to the fact that he didn't want to know.

And then, finally, a message.

Wow, I can't pretend your news hasn't thrown me for a loop. I've thought about nothing else all day. I have a daughter! Can we stop with the messaging and talk properly?! I would love to meet her. Noah x

And that evening - Noah's morning - Chloe had Face-Timed her dad. It had been amazing, no other word for it.

343

Discovering they had the same sense of humour, the same mannerisms. They both licked their lips when they were nervous and rested their head on their chins when they were listening to the other. Their words tumbled over themselves as they caught up on the last eighteen years. Chloe's mum had diplomatically left them to it, pretending she had something urgent to do upstairs, but when their conversation eventually began to dry up, Noah had casually asked if she was around.

'She's upstairs. D'you want me to get her?'

'Seems rude not to say hello after all this time,' Noah had said with a grin.

Her mum had been horrified. 'Oh my God, he can't see me looking like this! I need to change, wash my hair. Tell him I've gone out.'

'Too late. He knows you're here. And you look fine.'

Chloe had watched in amusement as her mum had sat in front of the computer, self-consciously playing with a strand of her hair. She and Noah had chatted about inconsequential stuff, from their jobs to their mutual love of *Billions*. But it was blatantly apparent to Chloe there was still a spark between them.

She was in contact with her dad every day after that, even if it was a quick text chat or an exchange of photos of things that had made them smile. And Chloe slowly began to heal, the horrors of the last few months fading like a scar. Still visible, but no longer an open wound.

It helped that Ben's wounds were healing, too. After finding out the truth about his mum, he'd decided to track down his maternal grandparents. With Chloe's help, he discovered they'd retired to Hove and, contrary to the lies

Adam had spun, they were elated to meet their only grandson. He moved in with them while Adam was still on remand, and he and Chloe had stayed in touch. As proper friends this time.

After a couple of months, Noah invited Chloe and her mum to California. 'It's beautiful this time of year,' he'd said. 'You'd love it.'

'We have to wait until after the trial,' Chloe had said.

His face had grown serious. Her mum had told him what had happened. Adam had been charged with attempted rape, sexual assault, false imprisonment, voyeurism and sending indecent images of a person under eighteen. In fact, they'd thrown the book at him. It turned out he wasn't as well-connected as he'd liked to think. He'd denied everything, of course, which meant both Chloe and her mum would have to give evidence. The two-week trial was fixed for the end of June, after Chloe's last A-level. She was dreading it. But if there was a trip to California to look forward to afterwards, she knew she could get through it.

Adam was found guilty of all charges, and the judge sentenced him to seven years' imprisonment. He would probably be out in four. Chloe tried not to think about that. She wasn't prepared to let him ruin any more of her life.

'San José is beautiful this time of year,' Taylor said, bringing her back to the present.

'That's what my dad said.'

Taylor handed her two plastic glasses and two bottles. 'Well, you guys have yourselves a great trip.'

'Don't worry, we intend to.'

Chloe's mum poured them each a glass of bog-standard dry white wine. 'Cheers,' she said, clinking glasses. 'We should think of a toast.'

Chloe's heart felt as light as air as she clinked back. 'To us,' she said. 'And to new beginnings.'

THE END

AFTERWORD

I hope you enjoyed *Should Have Known Better*. It would be great if you could spare a couple of minutes to write a quick review on Amazon or Goodreads. I'd love your feedback!

ABOUT THE AUTHOR

A J McDine lives deep in the Kent countryside with her husband and two teenage sons.

She worked as a journalist and police press officer before becoming a full-time author in 2019.

Endlessly fascinated by people and their fears and foibles, she loves to discover what makes them tick.

She writes dark, domestic thrillers about ordinary people in extraordinary situations.

When she's not writing, playing tennis or attempting to run a 5K, she can usually be found people-watching in her favourite café.

A J McDine is the author of two psychological thrillers: *When She Finds You* and *Should Have Known Better*.

ALSO BY A J MCDINE

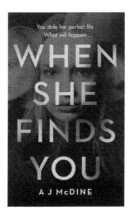

When She Finds You

Sophie Saunders has the perfect life.

Happily married to handsome Matt and expecting her first baby, she is the envy of her childhood friend, Lou.

Lou's family has splintered. Her husband is dead and her son has left home. She would give anything to turn back the clock.

But there's a secret buried deep in their past that the two friends can never forget.

And when Sophie's world starts spiralling out of control, it's her new friend Roz to whom she turns.

Trouble is, secrets have a habit of unravelling. And when they do, you can kiss your perfect life goodbye.

Sometimes, it's better when the truth stays hidden.

When She Finds You **is the gripping debut psychological thriller by A J McDine.**

AVAILABLE IN THE AMAZON STORE

Made in the USA
Columbia, SC
02 December 2020

26137945R00214